Murder on LAKE GARDA

TOM HINDLE

Murder on LAKE GARDA

C

CENTURY

1 3 5 7 9 10 8 6 4 2

Century
20 Vauxhall Bridge Road
London SW1V 2SA

Century is part of the Penguin Random House group of companies whose
addresses can be found at global.penguinrandomhouse.com.

Penguin
Random House
UK

Copyright © Tom Hindle 2024

Tom Hindle has asserted his right to be identified as the author of this
Work in accordance with the Copyright, Designs and Patents Act 1988.

First published by Century in 2024

www.penguin.co.uk

A CIP catalogue record for this book is available from the British Library.

ISBN: 9781529902198 (hardback)
ISBN: 9781529902204 (trade paperback)

Typeset in 13.5/17 pt Fournier MT Std by Jouve (UK), Milton Keynes
Printed and bound in Great Britain by Clays Ltd, Elcograf S.p.A.

The authorised representative in the EEA is Penguin Random House Ireland,
Morrison Chambers, 32 Nassau Street, Dublin D02 YH68

www.greenpenguin.co.uk

For Lynn

Laurence Heywood and Eva Bianchi request the company of . . .

The bride's side
Vito and Paola Bianchi
Dina Bianchi
Giulia Russo
Beatrice Marino

The groom's side
Margot Heywood
Jeremy Lambourne
Stephen and Abigail Dalton
Chadwick Grant
Miles Allen
Toby Heywood and Robyn Whitford

Also in attendance
Sofia Greco
Harper Bale
Cam Nolan

By the time the scream reached Stephen Dalton, he and the groom had been standing for several minutes at the end of the aisle, awaiting the arrival of the bride.

Laurence didn't seem remotely fazed by the delay, passing the time by making cheerful small talk with the celebrant. How could he be so calm? Stephen was only the best man, and yet this deviation from the schedule was making him even more restless than he'd been in the minutes before his own wedding.

That was just Laurence, though. Nothing had frightened him in all the years they had known one another. With a glimmer of resentment, Stephen imagined how that must just be what came of a life spent walking above a safety net spun from pure gold.

The sun was beating down. Castello Fiore was already slightly raised, a short path having sloped upwards from the jetty to the gates. But once inside, a steep flight of ancient steps had also needed to be climbed in order to reach the terrace on which the ceremony would be performed. The resulting view was breathtaking. Just shy of a mile away, on the nearest shore, Stephen could make out terracotta-tiled roofs and pastel-coloured buildings. Behind them, mountains reached for the sky, giving the impression of a basin, and as for the water . . . On the flight to Verona, he had read that Lake Garda was thirty-four miles from top to bottom. Seeing it in person, it seemed to stretch for ever, the most brilliant shade of blue, until, somewhere on the horizon, the water and the sky simply blurred into one.

At the front of the terrace, a small canopy had been set up, shading a table with a crisp white cloth, along with seats for the bride, groom and celebrant. It was under this canopy that Stephen and Laurence now stood. The guests hadn't been so lucky, their own seats exposed to the midday heat. Some on the English side were turning a troubling shade of red, while even the Italians across the aisle were beginning to struggle. Light glinted from the rims of designer sunglasses, sweat beading at hairlines.

Stephen looked around, taking in the small congregation behind them, and locked eyes with Abigail. He gave his wife a small smile, which she didn't return. He couldn't blame her. He was just glad he'd managed to talk her out of flying home.

Turning back towards the front, he looked out across the lake. The string quartet played, but there was no chance of the music distracting the guests from the increasingly unbearable heat. Laurence flashed him a grin, and Stephen realised that for a good minute or two he hadn't been listening. He forced a smile, then checked his watch.

Ten minutes late.

What the hell was Eva doing? It wasn't as though she could get lost on her way to the venue; she and the bridal party had been on the island all morning. Had she changed her mind? Got cold feet?

More likely she was with the photographer. She was going to be on a magazine cover, after all. She wouldn't think for a second about making them all wait in this heat if it meant getting the perfect shot before she walked up the aisle.

He felt a sudden flush of bitterness, wishing more fervently than ever that Laurence and Eva had never met. Even as schoolboys, it had always felt as if they'd had more of a partnership than a friendship. Stephen did the work while Laurence took the credit. It wasn't perfect, but for Stephen, who had only attended Rushworth on a bursary designed to make the school appear slightly less elitist, it had always worked. Having Laurence take such a shine to him in those early days had felt like a godsend. Doubly so when, after university, Laurence had ushered him straight into the Heywoods' hedge fund management business.

It hadn't been until Eva arrived on the scene that everything had started to go wrong. When Laurence, in an effort to please her, had begun indulging some of his darkest impulses.

Again, Stephen looked around. As he did, he spotted the photographer. She was standing at the top of the steps leading up to the terrace. Waiting.

Stephen frowned. That meant she wasn't with Eva. And if she wasn't with Eva . . .

His nerves became impossible to ignore. Something was off. He couldn't tell what, but he was certain something wasn't right.

A breeze strayed across the terrace, prompting audible sighs from several of the guests. It was then that the sound reached them. It was distant. But without doubt, it had come from the island. Somewhere inside the castle.

Harper Bale was sitting alone at the back of the congregation when she heard the scream.

She should have been accompanying the photographer, making sure she had everything she needed. That was, after all, the reason she had come. Not as a guest. Eva would never think to extend such an invitation to her lowly agent. As ever, she was there as little more than an assistant.

She looked across the terrace, taking in the aisle strewn with rose petals, the groomsmen in their linen suits, the view across the lake. Harper should have been delighted. The photos, undoubtedly, were going to be stunning. But in that moment, she had bigger things to worry about than a magazine feature.

After everything she'd poured into Eva Bianchi . . . All the work. All the stress. All the time. When the agency had wanted to let Eva go, it was Harper who had argued to keep her. When there hadn't been a single brand that would touch her, it was Harper who had worked night and day to salvage her reputation. When Eva, with one devastating stroke of naivety, had driven her own career to the edge of ruin, it was Harper who had single-handedly steered her back from the brink.

6

She wished she'd never bothered. Because now she knew exactly how grateful Eva was for her efforts.

Harper had always understood that Eva didn't appreciate everything she did. She'd even suspected, once or twice, that Eva wasn't fully aware of it. But never, at any point, had she thought Eva was so oblivious that she was at risk of being fired.

She took a breath, trying hard to keep herself from panicking.

She had made a mistake. Lashed out in anger. The best she could do now was play dumb. Wait for someone else to spot what had happened and then do her very best to appear oblivious. And if, somehow, the blame was laid at her feet – if she was discovered – she would have to plead for mercy. Eva had betrayed her. Underappreciated and disrespected her for so, so long. How could anyone blame her for a momentary lapse of judgement?

Harper fanned herself with an order of service, completely unprepared for the sheer relentlessness of the mid-July heat. She looked enviously towards the front, where Laurence stood beneath the canopy with his best man, cheerfully chatting to the celebrant. She was even jealous for a moment of his mother's wide-brimmed hat. She might as well have been sitting with a parasol on her head.

Squinting at the lake, Harper looked for the boats that had ferried them to the island. She knew it was futile. It was just short of a mile back to the mainland, no more than fifteen minutes. The boats would have made it back to the harbour at least half an hour ago. She wouldn't see them again until midnight, when the reception ended and they came to carry everyone back.

She swore under her breath. There was no way around it. She was stuck there.

Taking out her phone, she checked the time. Eva was nearly ten minutes late. Harper sniffed. Hardly a surprise; Eva would one day be late for her own funeral. But it was someone else's problem now. She would make sure the photographer was happy, and that was it. Her days of chasing after Eva Bianchi were done.

But as the scream rang out, skirting across the terrace on a sudden breath of cool air, her eyes snapped up. The musicians stopped playing, and all thoughts of the photo shoot immediately slipped from Harper's mind. Even the heat was forgotten, her blood turning to ice.

Vito Bianchi had already been panicking for several minutes.

'Have they found her?' he demanded. 'Where is she?'

'Any moment now, *signore*,' had been the response from the wedding planner. 'The island is small. There are only so many places your daughter could go, and all three of the bridesmaids are looking for her. I'm sure we'll be getting under way in just a few minutes.'

'Relax, *amore*,' Paola said to him. 'You know how important this magazine is to her. She must just be having another photograph taken.'

He forced a smile. It was easy for his wife to be calm. She had no idea about the argument he and Eva had had that morning. Just as she had no idea two criminals had sneaked onto the island with the rest of their guests.

At least it was over now. He'd done exactly as they'd asked; the worst thing, perhaps, that he had ever done. But if they kept their word, they would finally leave him alone. The constant harassment. The threats against his family. It was all finally going to stop.

He went to the window and threw open the shutters. Music drifted down from the terrace, filling the courtyard below.

'*Fottuto inferno*,' he whispered. 'Where is she?'

'Vito . . .' Paola put a hand on his shoulder. 'She's a few minutes late. That's all.'

He looked her in the eye, but he couldn't speak. For an entire year, he'd done so well at making sure she knew nothing of the trouble they were in. He'd clawed and begged, doing everything – anything – he could to keep his debtors from their door.

'You're right,' he said. 'Of course.'

Paola took his hands and began to sway to the distant sound of the string quartet. 'It's Eva's wedding day,' she said, smiling at him. 'Our eldest. Years from now, we'll remember this day as one of the happiest of our lives.'

He swayed with her, letting her guide him. One of the happiest days of their lives . . . He wondered if Eva still felt that way, having learned the truth that morning. Learned what he'd done.

He took a deep breath. There was no need for this. The ordeal was over. Any minute now, Eva would arrive and he would walk her up the aisle. Then, after the wedding, they would talk. He would explain it all – how much danger he had saved them from – and she would forgive him. She would understand.

He pulled Paola a little closer, taking the lead as the quartet continued to play. 'Eva's wedding day,' he repeated. 'One of the happiest of our lives.'

It was then that another sound rang out, pouring through the open shutters and drowning out the music in an instant.

His panic returning, Vito ran to the window, but there was nothing to be seen in the courtyard; it must have come from somewhere else on the island. Not that he needed to see. He knew exactly what he had heard.

It was a scream. An unmistakable sound of terror.

Two days before the wedding

1

In the week since she'd received it, Robyn had lost count of how many times she must have read Jess's message. Enough that she could easily have recited it word for word. But that didn't stop her, as they drove down yet another nondescript Italian road, from absent-mindedly taking out her phone and reading it again.

> Hey Rob, how's things? Long time no speak! My editor announced this morning that she's recruiting for a new Junior Reporter ... Interested?? If so, I'll put in a good word. She's looking to interview in a few weeks. Drinks soon? Xx

Just as with every other time she'd read it, Robyn's thumb hovered over the keyboard, a reply seemingly just out of reach.

She was well aware of how fierce the competition for a permanent role at *Cosmopolitan* would be. Most of her old course mates would happily walk through fire to be in with a shot. And yet, she couldn't bring herself to do it. Not when a small, infuriating voice, too deeply ingrained in her subconscious to be silenced, whispered over and over that there was no point.

That even if — somehow — she could win this job, it just wouldn't be for her.

She put the phone away and looked out of the window.

For the most part, the transfer from Verona Villafranca Airport had consisted of busy motorways flanked by vast fields of olive trees and grape vines, before they turned off and rolled through a smattering of anonymous-looking towns. They passed supermarkets, petrol stations, weathered roadside hotels at which it was impossible to believe anyone might actually stay. But now, after nearly an hour's drive, they must finally be beside the lake. The road wove through thick woodland, the trees beside them sloping steeply downwards, and through the passing foliage Robyn caught glimpses of light glinting on water.

She felt a knot begin to twist in the pit of her stomach.

The last time she had met a boyfriend's family had been during university, when she was still clinging to wide-eyed teenage ambitions of becoming an investigative journalist. His parents had come to London for the weekend and she had joined them one evening for dinner. It had been a nerve-wracking experience, but a compact one. This time, the meeting ahead of her was infinitely more daunting. Of course, there was the small matter of the wedding. But even without that particular challenge, they were abroad, in a country she had never visited, and about to spend three nights together in a luxury villa.

Turning away from the window, Robyn looked at Toby, sitting beside her in the back of the people carrier.

He'd barely said a word since they left the tarmac at Gatwick. That wasn't necessarily strange in itself. He could often be thoughtful. Pensive, even. But in the year they'd been together she'd never seen him so still. He was always tapping his foot or drumming on his knees, nodding his head in time to some silent tune. Right now he was completely frozen, eyes wide as he stared out of the window.

Robyn reached for his hand. 'You OK?'

He nodded and gave her an unconvincing smile.

'Do you really think they'll try something?' she asked. 'I know how badly your brother wants you to go and work with him, but it's his wedding. Isn't that a bit . . . much?'

Toby gave a hollow laugh. 'Last year alone they tried on my birthday, on Christmas Day and at Uncle Graham's funeral. I don't think Laurence is going to be put off by his own wedding.'

Robyn winced. 'I really think you should just tell them you've applied for the loan. I get that they don't approve of the bar, but won't it show them how serious you are? Maybe get them to back off a little?'

Toby shook his head. 'The loan hasn't even been accepted, Rob. Probably won't be. There's no point aggravating them more than I need to.'

'But what if it is? Won't that just be more of a bombshell for you to have to drop?'

He didn't reply.

'If you did tell them . . .' Robyn tried, 'wouldn't they at least be a little proud of you? For wanting to do it under your own steam?'

He gave another smile, even less convincing than the last, and rubbed the back of her hand with his thumb.

They drove in silence for another minute or two, climbing

gently through the woodland. Outside, villas began to roll past, each adorned with tiled terraces and brightly painted shutters.

'What about you?' Toby asked suddenly. 'Here I am being broody when you're the one about to face the Cambridge Inquisition. You feeling OK?'

Robyn chewed her bottom lip. She was now so nervous it was beginning to make her feel nauseous. But she didn't want to admit it. Toby seemed to be dreading these three days with his family even more than she was. She didn't want him to have to worry about her too.

As if saving her from answering, the car slowed, rumbling off the road towards a pair of wrought-iron gates built into a low, white-brick wall. Behind them resided a squat, two-storey building of grey concrete and tinted glass, with an AstroTurf lawn, gravel drive and potted palm trees occupying the front garden. The place was certainly impressive, but it looked as if it should be in Beverley Hills, rather than on the shores of an Italian lake. It didn't help that Robyn couldn't actually *see* the lake. She was sure that on the other side of the villa must be the most incredible view. But right now the building filled her entire field of vision, an angry stone barrier that seemed intent on keeping its vistas to itself.

The only thing that didn't look out of place was a bright red sports car. Robyn had never taken much interest in cars but this was unquestionably a Ferrari, with a silver stallion prancing in the centre of the front grille. More than that, it was quite clearly a vintage model. It boasted sweeping scarlet bodywork, with a bonnet stretching several feet and a roof that sloped down towards the back bumper like the crest of a wave. Even to her untrained eye, it wasn't just a vehicle. It was a work of art.

Switching off the engine, their driver climbed from the people carrier to open Robyn's door for her. It was four in the afternoon, well past the hottest hour of the day. Still, the heat enveloped her immediately, drawing the breath from her lungs. While she'd never been to Italy before, she had known that in the middle of July it would of course be hot. But she hadn't expected it to be quite so intense. Within seconds her skin was prickling, the air so thick it seemed almost to press down on her shoulders like a heavy overcoat.

As the driver fetched their suitcases from the trunk, the front door to the villa swung open and a bold voice called out to them.

'As I live and breathe. It seems all I had to do to lure my baby brother out of hiding was get married.'

Robyn had spent a considerable amount of time studying Laurence Heywood's Instagram account, and it was evident from his online persona alone that he and Toby were like night and day. But seeing the two brothers together, in the flesh . . . Laurence looked as if he'd dressed for the Henley Regatta, wearing a pink shirt, slim-fitting shorts and flip-flops. Toby, meanwhile, had arrived in a dark T-shirt, jeans and an old pair of Reeboks. Still, looking at their faces, there was no denying the familial resemblance; the sandy hair, the chiselled cheekbones and the pointed chins. Toby might be four years Laurence's junior, but if they were to swap clothes they could be mistaken for twins.

Laurence pulled the reluctant Toby into a hug, before

turning his attention to Robyn. 'Nice to finally meet you,' he told her. 'We were starting to wonder if we ever would.'

With the people carrier trundling back onto the road, Laurence ushered them inside. There must have been air conditioning, and it must have been working double time, as the villa was so immediately cool that Robyn gave an involuntary sigh of relief.

Finding herself in an entrance hall so spacious it contained a couple of sofas and a coffee table, she cast a look around, taking in the glass staircase and the enormous piece of brightly coloured abstract art that hung upon the wall. The sound of music drifted from another room. Nina Simone.

'You're the first to arrive,' Laurence called over his shoulder. 'Stephen's flight was delayed. Chadders and Miles are en route, apparently.'

'What about Jeremy?' Toby asked.

'He'll be here soon enough.'

Robyn frowned at Toby. 'Chadders?' she mouthed.

Toby rolled his eyes.

Trailing behind them, Robyn followed the brothers into an open-plan area that could comfortably have covered the same floor space as her entire Greenwich flat twice over. A suite of snow-white sofas and a TV screen that wouldn't have looked out of place in a small cinema adorned the living space, while a varnished table large enough for ten high-backed chairs occupied the dining area. Following the sound of the music, Robyn saw that speakers had been mounted in each corner of the room.

The decor, however, didn't hold her attention for long. Instead, with floor-length windows occupying an entire wall, it was here that she was finally treated to her first breathtaking view of Lake Garda.

While she had done some reading on the place, and of course had seen plenty of pictures, Robyn was entirely unprepared for the real thing. The lake stretched for miles, sheer faces of pale rock and vibrant foliage reaching towards the sky on either shore, like walls that had been raised solely to contain the vast body of glittering water. Approaching the glass, Robyn saw the town of Malcesine laid out beneath them, a patchwork of terracotta rooftops that sloped down towards the lake.

And there, suspended almost perfectly between the eastern shore and the west, was Castello Fiore.

The island was only small, with the castle clinging so closely to its edges that the sand-coloured walls seemed almost to have climbed from the lake itself. Entranced, Robyn saw how it rose gradually out of the water, a short path sloping upwards from a small jetty while half a dozen different buildings and walled-off courtyards all congregated like a set of Russian nesting dolls waiting to be stacked. There were pinpricks of green; trees, presumably, that were growing inside. And looming over them all, smaller from this distance than a matchstick, a watchtower reached towards the sky.

'How very *you*,' said Toby.

'Eva chose it, actually,' Laurence replied. 'She's wanted to get married there since she was a child. The day after I proposed, she was on the phone to them, thrashing out dates. Small ceremony, immediate family and close friends only. Of course, you'd know this already if you bothered to follow her on Instagram. She's been posting about the place incessantly.'

'And where's Eva now?'

'Joining us tomorrow. She's gone home to Bologna for a couple of days so that she can travel up with her parents.'

Behind them, the sound of footsteps echoed in the hallway, rattling off the stone walls. Turning to face the new arrival, Robyn saw a woman in her fifties step into the lounge.

She felt her nerves begin to strain. She hadn't yet met this woman, but she had seen her in photos. And even if she hadn't, it was immediately clear from her resemblance to the two brothers that this was their mother, Margot Heywood.

'Toby,' she said flatly. 'You could have worn something with a collar.'

Toby stepped forward and she presented her cheek for him to kiss. 'Mum,' he said. 'This is Robyn.'

An unreadable expression on her face, Margot Heywood's eyes flicked up and down as she sized Robyn up. Barely more than five feet tall, she had to tilt her head slightly to do so. Still, Robyn found herself feeling painfully self-conscious. Every item of Margot's clothing was subtly but undeniably designer, from the glistening earrings to the high-heeled shoes. Robyn wished she'd had a minute to tidy up, although she didn't suppose it would have helped. Seeing Toby's mum looking as if she could quite comfortably have modelled for Harrods, she knew that nothing she'd cobbled together would have been up to scratch.

'Thank you for having me, Margot,' she said. 'It's so nice to meet you.'

Margot was silent for a moment, her lips twitching into the smallest of smiles. 'Would you like a drink?' she asked. 'You've had a long journey. I'm sure Laurence can pour you some wine.'

'They're the bartenders,' Laurence chided. 'Shouldn't she be pouring it for me?'

Robyn saw Toby scowl, but breathed a silent sigh of relief when he didn't rise to his brother's taunt. Instead, he chatted a little with Margot about their flight as Laurence disappeared into another room. Robyn heard the sound of a fridge opening and glassware being fetched from a cupboard. Returning a moment later, he pressed a glass of white wine into her hand and slumped onto a sofa.

'Tell us about yourself, then, Robyn. I gather you and Toby don't work in the same bar.'

'I actually work in a restaurant.'

'Would I know it?'

'Possibly. It's the Willows, in Soho.'

He nodded. 'Nice place. I've been once with a client.'

Robyn tensed slightly. Perhaps Toby had been right. They really might be planning to talk shop.

'I was only wondering,' he continued, 'how the two of you might have met. You've been together a year and yet Toby's barely told us a thing about you.'

'You were picturing a bartenders-only speed-dating night?'

Toby stifled a laugh, although Laurence looked less than amused. As, for that matter, did Margot.

'We met through friends,' Robyn explained. 'Although I've been a few times to Toby's bar. I'd say he makes some of the best cocktails I've ever had.'

'Is that right? Perhaps I should have had him serve the drinks at the wedding.'

Toby grimaced, this particular tease apparently too much to

let slide. 'Are you still going to have paps crawling all over the place?'

'No one's going to be crawling over anything. It'll be one photographer. Chances are, you won't even know she's there.'

'I still can't understand why a magazine would want to cover your wedding.'

'I'm sorry.' Laurence motioned towards the window. 'Did you *miss* the Italian castle? The editor follows Eva on Instagram. Apparently she wants to do a glossy feature on a glittering influencer wedding.'

'That sounds exciting,' Robyn volunteered.

'See.' Laurence gestured in her direction. 'Robyn gets it. The photographer will take plenty of pictures and when we go back to London a reporter will interview us about how it all went. *London Living* will get a shedload of sales from Eva's followers, while Eva gets to tell the world that a national magazine wants to cover her wedding. It's a win-win.'

'It's cheap.' Margot's voice was like steel, landing so heavily that for a few seconds Laurence looked completely disarmed. He swirled the wine gingerly around his glass, a painful silence hanging in the air.

'Where's our room?' asked Toby.

'Left at the top of the stairs,' said Laurence, any enthusiasm having drained from his voice. 'Second door on the right.'

Toby nodded, taking Robyn's hand and leading her back towards the hallway.

'There's an envelope on your bed,' Laurence called after him. 'A role we should talk about while we're here.'

Immediately Toby tensed. 'How many times, Laurence?'

'As many times as you need to hear it. Dad set this firm up

for *us*. Not just to inherit but to build on. To expand. You have a responsibility. We both do.'

'You've got HCM running perfectly well without me.'

'And what are you going to do instead?'

Toby didn't reply, his eyes dropping to the floor.

'You aren't still sour about that bloody bar?' said Laurence. 'Toby, come on. Mum was never going to release your inheritance early so that you could waste it on—'

'Waste it? It wasn't going to be some back-street dive. If you'd so much as looked at the plans I drew up, seen the place I'd found, you'd know how upmarket it was going to—'

'Enough.' Margot didn't need to raise her voice. Her tone, alone, was enough to silence the two brothers. 'We aren't dredging this back up.'

Robyn looked at Toby. In the year they'd been together she'd never seen him so utterly deflated.

'Margot . . .' she said carefully. 'It might not be my place, but I really think it would be worth you looking over the business plan Toby put together. He's put a ton of work into it and I think it would really lay some of your concerns to—'

'Leave it, Robyn,' Laurence spat.

'I'm only saying that—'

'And I'm telling you to leave it. This is a family discussion.'

Toby took a step forward, his face twisting into a scowl. Still holding his hand, Robyn squeezed his fingers, holding him in place.

It was Margot who broke the ensuing silence, lifting her glass so casually to her lips that Robyn couldn't help but wonder if she'd actually noticed just how close her sons seemed to have come to exchanging blows.

'I'm sorry, Toby,' she said. 'But I won't change my mind.'

He didn't answer, instead turning and leading Robyn towards the hallway. Neither Laurence nor Margot attempted to call them back, but she could feel their eyes burning into her with each step.

2

As promised, when they found their room an envelope emblazoned with the words *Heywood Capital Management* was
waiting on the bed. Without even opening it, Toby tossed it
straight into the bin.

Robyn fixed him with a pleading look. 'I'm sorry. I should
have left it alone. I didn't mean to make things worse.'

'It's not your fault. It's them.' He gave a thin smile. 'You see
now why I don't want to tell them about the loan. I could run the
most successful, most upmarket cocktail bar in the world, but as
long as I'm pouring people drinks for a living, they're going to
tell me I'm wasting my life. It isn't about proving to them that I
can do it. And it certainly isn't about making them proud.'

'So what is it about?'

Toby hesitated, taking a moment to collect his thoughts.

'Laurence is never going to understand,' he said slowly. 'The
way he sees it, if I'm not working for HCM I might as well be
spitting on Dad's grave. And you know what? Maybe Dad
would have agreed. But I was so young when he died . . . It's
different for Laurence. They had a relationship. But I can't live
my life trying to please someone I barely remember.'

'Is that why you hated Rushworth, too?'

Toby's frown intensified. 'I guess. Again, it was different for Laurence. Every day in that school you're told you deserve to be there because of who your family is. Who your parents are. Laurence bought into all of that. But I didn't know who my dad was. For a long time after he died Mum wouldn't even talk about him. All I knew was that I was spending every day with three hundred kids in tailcoats who all believed they were born to be Prime Minister. By the time I left I just wanted to do something different. Something that was mine.'

Robyn nodded. 'Did they really not read the plans you'd drawn up for the bar?'

'They didn't even look at them. I put together a PowerPoint presentation, Robyn. For my own family. A fucking *Power-Point*. But Mum wouldn't hear about it.'

Robyn paused, carefully choosing each word. 'Couldn't you just put the bar on hold until you're thirty? That's when your dad's inheritance comes to you, right? It wouldn't matter any more what your mum thinks; she couldn't keep it from you any longer even if she tried.'

'That's three years away. I don't want to wait that long. And even if I did, there's a part of me that doesn't *want* their money now. I know how ungrateful that probably sounds. I really do. But maybe *that's* what it's about. It isn't about proving to them that I can do it. It's about proving it to myself.'

Nearly two hours passed before they went back downstairs. Only once they had heard the groomsmen arrive, and Toby was satisfied the sound of music and laughter echoing up the stairs was raucous enough that Laurence would be too distracted to ask him about HCM, did he concede that they should join them.

In the lounge, Nina Simone had been silenced in favour of Calvin Harris, synthesisers blaring from each corner of the room. Through the panoramic window, Robyn saw Laurence on the patio with two other young men. They were laughing beside the pool, each sipping bottled lager.

'Chadwick and Miles,' Toby explained. 'Rushworth through and through, those two. Chadwick studied global business management at LSE. Now he works in tech, whatever that means. Miles is heir to a jewellery empire. He deals with branding at the moment, choosing their models, influencers. That sort of thing. But he'll run the entire company one day.'

'I'm surprised he hasn't done any work with Eva.'

'He has. How do you suppose she and Laurence met?'

Robyn's gaze strayed from the three laughing men, settling on a fourth. He stood a little way apart, a phone in his hand. He was typing something, his eyes glued to the screen.

'What about him?'

'That's Stephen. Laurence's best man.'

'Isn't he Rushworth, too?'

'He's a special case. They let in a few kids every year on a bursary. It's their way of trying to show the world that they aren't quite as exclusive as everyone believes.'

Before Robyn could question Toby further, an older man approached them. This new arrival she did recognise. With Toby reluctant during their first few months together to share much about his family, she had gone to the HCM website to see what little she could learn there instead. The man approaching them now was Laurence's godfather, Jeremy Lambourne.

Looking him in the eye, she couldn't help but be startled. He was perhaps the only person she had ever met who looked exactly like his photograph, from the pair of thick-rimmed glasses adorning his slender nose down to the quietly unimpressed facial expression. Easily into his sixties, with slate-grey hair brushed in a neat comb-over and dressed for the heat in a pale linen blazer, he gave her the impression of a carefully manicured scarecrow. He held a glass of wine, although it looked as if he hadn't yet touched it.

'Toby,' he said in a curt tone, putting out a hand for him to shake. 'It's nice to see you. And you must be Robyn.' He shook her hand too, although he didn't pause for a reply. 'I trust you had a good journey.'

'Fine, thank you, Jeremy. And yours?'

Jeremy hummed. 'Before you join the others, I just wanted to say that I'm aware Laurence has told you about a role we need to discuss. I understand you haven't felt ready, but there are exciting things happening at HCM and your father would have wanted you to be involved. I hope we can at least have a conversation.'

The smile Toby had forced into place waned slightly. 'After the wedding, perhaps. Tonight doesn't feel like the right time.'

Jeremy said nothing, his expression unreadable. After a moment of uncomfortable silence, he shook Toby's hand again, repeated how good it was to see him and went outside, where he joined Margot at a table on the patio.

'He's intense,' said Robyn.

'He's always been that way. Makes me wonder what my dad must have been like for someone like Jeremy to be his best friend.'

'Is he your godfather too?'

Toby shook his head. 'Just Laurence's. Mine was a Rush-worth boy as well, but he moved to Hong Kong when I was just a kid. I've no idea what happened to him after that. I don't remember what he even looks like, if I'm honest.'

'And Jeremy's the chairman, right? Of HCM?'

'On paper, yes. In reality, he's running the place. Laurence might be the face of HCM, but believe me, Jeremy's the brains.'

'Does Laurence see it that way?'

Toby snorted. 'He bloody well should. He'd be a shambles without Jeremy. But then, that's always how it's been. When-ever Laurence makes a mess — no matter how serious — it's Jeremy who steps in, pulls the right strings and makes every-thing go away.'

Robyn might have imagined it, but a hint of bitterness seemed to creep into Toby's voice.

'Fancy a drink?' she asked, forcing some levity into her own.

'God, yes. I'll get them.'

'*I'll* get them. You go and join Laurence.' Seeing that he was about to protest, she raised her voice slightly. 'It's his wedding, Toby. And he's your brother. If you don't actually spend some time with him this weekend you'll never hear the end of it. Now go on. You don't have to like it but you'll be glad of it later.'

With Toby reluctantly agreeing, Robyn moved from the lounge into an equally impressive kitchen. All of the surfaces were black marble, the cupboards smart pinewood. For a moment, she stood thinking of the rickety self-catering cot-tages she and her parents would stay in on their own family holidays. This was a different world. One in which she was quickly beginning to feel she didn't belong.

Fetching a bottle of rosé out of an enormous fridge, she began searching the cupboards for wine glasses.

'Above the coffee machine.'

Turning to face the unfamiliar voice, she saw a young woman in a loose-fitting floral dress standing in the archway. She looked a few years older than Robyn – thirty, perhaps – with freckled cheeks and sandy hair held back in a clip.

'I saw Margot fetch some a few minutes ago,' she explained with a warm smile. 'You must be Toby's girlfriend. I'm Abigail.'

'Robyn.' She cocked an eyebrow. 'And you're with . . .'

'I'm Stephen's wife.'

Robyn crossed the kitchen to a coffee machine that looked as if it might cost an entire month of her bartender's salary. As promised, she opened an overhead cupboard to find a dozen neatly arranged wine glasses.

'Pour you some wine?'

'I wish.' Abigail put a hand to her stomach. 'I'm four months in. Don't suppose there was any lemonade in that fridge? I'm craving it like mad.'

Robyn shook her head. 'I saw some sparkling water, if that would be any good? I could always add a drop of orange juice to it?'

'That would be amazing.'

Ducking back into the fridge, Robyn set about making the drink.

'Are the boys being nice to you?' Abigail asked. 'These Rushworth guys can be a lot. First time I met Chadwick and Miles I thought they were speaking a different language.'

'I haven't actually met them yet.'

'We can go together, then. I hate being the only woman when those two are together. It's like they're thirteen years old again, back in their dorm rooms.'

'Stephen isn't like that too?'

'God, no. I don't think I could have married him if he was.' With her sparkling water in hand, she smiled again and motioned toward the archway. 'Shall we go? I'll introduce you.'

Crossing the lounge, they stepped out onto the patio. With the evening drawing in, and the sun dipping just low enough to graze the tops of the mountains on the opposite side of the lake, the temperature was now a good deal more comfortable than it had been during the afternoon. Robyn heard birds chattering in the surrounding woodland, and the distant hubbub of the town below them.

Noticing that Toby and Laurence weren't with the rest of the boys, she swept a glance around, spotting them at the far end of the patio.

'Back in a sec,' she told Abigail, raising the wine glasses. 'I'll just give one of these to Toby.'

Crossing the patio, she felt her nerves begin to ease a little. She didn't suppose she would ever manage to feel at home here, but she was fairly confident she could at least make a friend in Abigail. And with Laurence's groomsmen around to keep his own spirits high, perhaps she could even try again to make a good impression.

As she stepped closer to the two brothers, however, and gradually began to hear what was being said, her growing optimism was quickly snuffed out.

'Look,' Laurence was saying. 'I don't want her leading you on with this. She seems like a nice girl, but if she's encouraging you to keep going with this crazy idea of opening some bar, she's clearly a bad influence . . .'

'A bad influence?' Toby protested. 'That's pretty rich, considering what Eva had you—'

Catching sight of Robyn, Toby stopped mid-sentence. Laurence frowned, following his gaze as he searched for whatever had distracted his brother. At the sight of Robyn, he scowled. He chewed his lip for a moment, before apparently recognising that the conversation was over and marching back to Chadwick and Miles.

'Sorry,' Robyn said once he was out of earshot. 'I only wanted to give you this.'

Taking one of the glasses, Toby threaded his fingers through hers and planted a kiss on her head.

'Nothing to apologise for,' he said. 'That was just Laurence being Laurence. You want to go back inside?'

Robyn shook her head. 'We should join the others. I'm hardly going to win over your family by hiding in our room.'

She smelled the aftershave from several feet away. As they grew closer, she saw a gold watch hanging from Chadwick's wrist and a pearl necklace from Miles's neck. Both were dressed in floral shirts and loose-fitting shorts. Chadwick sported a carefully styled beard and a pair of designer glasses; Miles, meanwhile, was clean-shaven, with a deep tan and gleaming teeth. Neither was unattractive. But the way they carried themselves – very much, as Abigail had said, like two thirteen-year-olds in a dorm room – was more than a little off-putting. On the edge of the group, Stephen lingered, shoulder to shoulder with Abigail. He tried to smile at a joke Chadwick had just made, although it seemed to Robyn like more of a grimace.

'Right.' Miles slipped a phone into his pocket as they approached. 'Taxi's on its way.'

'You're leaving?' Toby asked.

'Heading into town – find some drinks and grub. You game?'

Toby looked to Robyn. She hadn't eaten since Gatwick, and the thought of a restaurant was sorely tempting. Eager, however, to appear laid-back in front of Laurence's friends, she gave what she hoped was an easy, nonchalant shrug.

'Sure. Probably wouldn't hurt to get our bearings. Might even get a closer look at the castle.'

'Whoa!' Upon hearing Robyn's pronunciation of 'castle', Chadwick took a sudden step back, breaking out into a broad grin. 'Bloody hell, Toby. You didn't say she was Northern. I haven't had my shots.'

Toby glowered, but Robyn held up a hand, forcing a laugh. 'Guilty as charged. No need to panic, though, guys. I've lived in London since I was eighteen. No shots required.'

'Is that a Yorkshire twang?' Miles asked her.

'Lancashire.'

'That's a pity. I quite like Yorkshire. And what do you do?'

Before Robyn could answer, Laurence leapt in. 'She works in wine.'

'Really?' Miles raised an eyebrow, curious. 'Who do you work for? Anyone we'd have heard of?'

Feeling Toby tense beside her, Robyn gripped his hand. 'I work at the Willows. In Soho.'

'And you're a manager?'

'A bartender.'

She said it as brightly as she could manage. Even so, Miles rolled his eyes. 'For Christ's sake, Laurence.'

'All right, all right,' said Laurence. 'I'm being cruel. Yes, Robyn's a bartender. But she's going to be a journalist.'

'Writing for the *Grimsby Times*, presumably?' said Miles.

'Or the *Big Issue*,' said Chadwick.

Another chorus of laughter rippled around the boys. Robyn had no answer this time, though. She looked to Toby, knocked completely off guard by their knowledge of her journalistic studies.

'That's enough,' said Toby, a hard edge to his voice. Although if the groomsmen noticed, they didn't show it. 'I said that's enough. Laurence, make them stop.'

Laurence gave a little shrug, smirking as he took a swig from a bottle of lager. 'Stop what? I'd have thought Robyn would fit right in at the *Grimsby Times*.'

Toby growled, teeth showing as his lips drew back into a snarl. 'Come on,' he said, tugging Robyn's hand.

'All right, wait,' said Laurence sharply. 'Just wait. It's a joke, Toby. There's no need to be so defensive.'

Frowning, he withdrew a phone from his pocket. It vibrated in his hand, the screen lighting up.

'Eva?' asked Chadwick.

'Client. He's persistent, this one.'

'Can't you get rid of him?'

'Of course.' Laurence turned to his best man. 'Stephen. Give him a buzz, will you? He's only going to keep calling me until someone speaks to him.'

Stephen hesitated, quelling what looked to Robyn like a spark of frustration. But if it was defiance she'd seen, it didn't surface. He nodded and took out his own phone, giving Abigail a weak smile as he left. Robyn noticed she didn't return it.

'In all seriousness, though, Robyn,' said Laurence. 'I am curious. Why *aren't* you a journalist?'

'I'm sorry?'

'You can't want to work behind a bar for the rest of your life. Why would you? Toby says you studied journalism. So why aren't you a journalist?'

'It . . .' She hesitated, acutely aware that all eyes were now on her. From across the patio, she even thought Margot and Jeremy might now be listening. 'I did plan on being a journalist. At one point, I really wanted to. But it just wasn't for me.'

'Why?'

'Sorry?'

'Well, it just seems a waste of time, doesn't it? To go to the trouble of studying for something only to not do it.'

'I . . .' Robyn looked at Toby. He was bristling.

'Tell us about this magazine feature, Laurence,' said Abigail. 'Will the photographer be with us for the whole day?'

'Hold on a moment,' said Laurence. 'Let's not change the subject. I want to know what Robyn's planning to do with her life. You studied to be a journalist. And yet you aren't a journalist. So what's your plan? Are you holding out to work in Toby's bar?'

'I really don't know.'

For several seconds, Toby and Laurence glared at each other, the tension so palpable that even Chadwick and Miles looked momentarily uncomfortable. It wasn't until the sound of an engine, and of tyres crunching on gravel, drifted round from the front of the villa that the two brothers seemed to break away.

'Taxi,' Miles announced cheerfully. 'Drink up, chaps.'

The little group began quickly to disperse, downing drinks and putting on flip-flops.

'Are we going with them?' Robyn asked.

Toby didn't reply. He simply stood, glaring at the back of Laurence's head as his older brother stalked away.

Beginning to despair, Robyn locked eyes with Margot across the patio. Realising that she had indeed been watching them, Robyn offered a small smile. If she'd hoped Margot would return it, though, she was to be disappointed. Instead, with a look of barely veiled disdain, she turned back to Jeremy, leaving Robyn's heart to sink at the thought of just how badly this first evening was going.

3

When, at almost midnight, Laurence finally allowed them to return to the villa, Stephen was so relieved to close the bedroom door – to have a physical barrier between himself and the others – that he couldn't help but breathe a sigh of relief.

When they first met, he had been desperately grateful for Laurence Heywood's attention. Even now, he could still vividly recall his first day at Rushworth. He remembered saying goodbye to his parents, the pride on their faces that their son was clever enough to win a place in this ancient institution. He remembered the other boys barging past him in the corridors in their tailcoats. They laughed and called out to each other as they went, relationships already firmly formed during their years in prep school. He remembered the tennis courts, the miles of surrounding countryside and the looming clock tower that chimed on the hour. The houses into which they were all sorted, the school song and the plaques on the wall dedicated to students and masters who had fallen during the two World Wars.

But more than anything else, he remembered the sense of being completely out of place. Dropped into an alien landscape, he'd never felt so alone. And in all the years since, nor had he ever understood why Laurence Heywood, of all people, had first taken a shine to him.

It didn't require a genius, however, to recognise what had held Laurence's interest.

Before long, Stephen had been helping with Laurence's homework. Rewriting his essays. Coaching him for exams. Not that he had complained. He'd clung on for dear life, his friends at home having long forgotten him while the other boys at Rushworth saw him as nothing more than a curiosity. An out-of-place object that drew the eye. And Laurence, likewise, had clung to him like a lucky coin.

They were an odd pair, Stephen ensuring Laurence's grades remained healthy, while Laurence, in return, would invite him to visit the Heywood family home during the summer. Those summers . . . Even after a year at Rushworth, the first time he saw Laurence's home Stephen had barely believed his eyes. He remembered driving through a leafy Cambridgeshire suburb, surveying the passing houses. Although 'houses' was perhaps the wrong word. 'Mansions' might have been more appropriate. He remembered the gates swinging gently open, the driveway curving round in an arch, enclosing a perfectly mown half-moon lawn with a gently trickling water feature. A Jaguar had been parked in front of the house, with a Porsche tucked closely behind it. He remembered pristine stone, gleaming windows and a vast porch complete with spotless white railings.

On his first visit, he had stood completely still in the hallway, terrified that if he moved he might accidentally break something. It was at that point that Laurence had followed him inside, kicking off his trainers onto the polished floorboards and calling him through to the living room. They were going to play Xbox games, apparently, and maybe take a dip in the pool after lunch.

There was no denying how much he had relied on Laurence during their Rushworth days. Were they friends, though?

He had never quite been sure. It had always felt more like a partnership than a friendship. When the time came for university, with Stephen going to study economics at St Andrews, he'd wondered if he and Laurence might have seen the last of each other. If the arrangement he'd made to survive Rushworth might simply have run its course.

It wouldn't have been the end of the world. Far from it. He enjoyed university a great deal more than he'd enjoyed school. Being careful not to divulge the details of his Rushworth days, he made a group of friends who hadn't gone to school in tailcoats, he earned himself a good degree, and of course, he met Abigail.

Rushworth being a boys' school, for Stephen's entire teenage life speaking to a girl his own age had been a rare occurrence. More than that, he had spent his Rushworth career training himself to be invisible. To quietly get by but never stand out. To minimise, as much as possible, the risk of anyone discovering that he didn't belong.

So when a friend had introduced them at a party in their student halls, and Stephen realised Abigail might be the most beautiful girl he'd ever met, he'd completely fallen apart. He stumbled over his words. When she told him she studied English Literature, the names of virtually every book he'd ever read seemed to fall from his head.

In reality, Abigail had since told him that his nervous efforts to ask about her life had been endearing. And while he might momentarily have wished he could be more like Laurence, there was little that would have more quickly persuaded her to put down her drink and walk away. But it wasn't until the end of the evening, when he'd offered to walk her back to her own flat, and with a grin she had teasingly asked at the door if he wasn't going to take her number, that he'd realised he might not have ruined his chances as badly as he'd thought.

For the first time since his parents left him at Rushworth, he was genuinely content. So much so that, by the time his three years at university were over, it was becoming increasingly rare for him to think about Laurence at all.

And yet, shortly after graduation, the phone had rung. It had been Laurence, more or less handing him a job at Heywood Capital Management.

'It'd be good to bring in a Rushworth chap, and there's no one I'd trust more. Think about it. Just not for too long.'

A Rushworth chap.

Stephen hadn't felt like one when he was there, and he certainly didn't feel it with a few years' distance from the place. Nor, for that matter, had he ever considered a life as a hedge fund manager. But the salary Laurence offered had made his eyes water, and when Abigail agreed that he couldn't pass it up, he'd called back the same day to accept.

Once again, it didn't take long to see why Laurence had been so eager to have him around. While he signed contracts, lunched with clients and played endless rounds of golf, Stephen laboured behind the scenes. Twelve-hour days became the norm. Weekends were few and far between. But he hadn't complained. Over the years, his HCM salary had paid for his and Abigail's four-bedroom house in Surrey. The Audi parked on their driveway. The holiday they had just taken to Mauritius. In short, the kind of lifestyle that, growing up, he could only have dreamed of.

He was all too aware of just how different his life might have been if he hadn't met Laurence. And yet, there he was. Wishing for exactly that.

He knew what the turning point had been. He might not have recognised it at the time, but he knew now when being in Laurence's orbit had ceased to be a good thing. It was the day he'd met *her*.

It was Miles who had introduced them, when Eva was modelling for his family's jewellery empire. Laurence and Stephen had been due to meet him after work one evening for drinks. With her shoot overrunning, they'd sat in for the last few minutes, watching as Eva posed for picture after picture in diamonds worth more than a semi-detached house. Laurence hadn't stood a chance. Completely smitten, he'd invited Eva to join them and the rest had been history.

At first, they had all got along. They'd gone for dinner, even talked about going on holiday together. But these days, Abigail had made it clear she was determined to keep Eva at arm's length. Stephen could hardly blame her. After all, it was Eva's fault things had changed. Eva's fault Stephen no longer lived in Laurence's debt, but at his mercy. Abigail had wanted them to miss the wedding altogether, but that had become impossible when Laurence asked Stephen to be his best man.

Best man . . . So they *were* friends. Or at least, Laurence seemed to think so. But his best man? Really? What about Toby? Or someone else from Rushworth?

'Has to be you,' Laurence had insisted. 'Chadders and Miles will be groomsmen. But you're the only one I'd trust enough to be my best man.'

Chadwick and Miles . . . Rushworth alumni through and through; the resentment Stephen carried for those two would never burn out. If they hadn't done what Laurence had asked . . . What *Eva* had asked . . .

It wasn't fair. He shouldn't even have been involved. He'd been trying to stop them. To talk them out of it. No one would believe that, though. A man had died and Stephen had been there. If the truth ever came out, that was all anyone would care about. He would be one of them, plain and simple.

He remembered how Laurence had come into his office the day after it had happened. How convinced Stephen had been – terrified, even – that at any moment the police would surely arrive and take them away.

'Don't worry, mate,' Laurence had said. 'It's all taken care of. You, Chadders and Miles . . . Nobody will ever know.'

And that was exactly how it had been. The police hadn't come. Nobody had asked any questions. It had bubbled away under the surface, but had always remained unspoken.

Inside their room at the villa, Abigail began getting ready for bed, carefully removing her earrings. She'd put on a good show downstairs. He was grateful for that. But now they were alone, it seemed she felt no need to keep up the pretence.

Going to the window, he looked out across the lake. On the opposite shore, pinpricks of light twinkled like fireflies, their reflections shimmering on the black surface of the water.

'Amazing place,' he said, forcing some cheer into his voice.

She didn't reply, fetching her sponge bag from the suitcase and going straight into the en-suite bathroom.

'Robyn seems nice,' Stephen tried. 'Looked like you two were getting along earlier.'

Still Abigail said nothing, standing in front of the mirror as she dabbed away at her make-up.

'Abi, come on. It's only a few days. We just need to get this wedding out of the way and we'll be home again before you—'

'You know full fucking well that it isn't just a few days.'

There was such venom in her voice that Stephen was stunned into silence. He stood in the doorway, watching as tears began to well in the corners of her eyes.

'Things are different now, Stephen. It isn't just us any more. What if everything comes out when the baby arrives? What if you're arrested?'

'But I didn't do anything. It wasn't me.'

'You were there! It doesn't matter what you did or didn't do. You were involved!'

Silence hung between them.

'What do you want me to do?' he asked, his voice thin.

'You know what I want. I want you to leave HCM. I want you to get Laurence and Eva out of our lives. I want not to be afraid that at any moment I might find myself bringing up a baby on my own, because you've been carted off to prison.'

He sighed. She knew it wasn't that simple. They'd had this conversation so many times . . . He remembered the last time he'd tried to leave HCM, before Laurence and Eva had even met. He'd been offered an amazing job at another firm. A job he'd realised he actually wanted.

'Come on, mate,' Laurence had said cheerfully, upon hearing the news. 'You know I can't let you leave.'

Within an hour, he'd been offered a pay rise so substantial he'd had no choice but to stay at HCM. But Laurence's words held an altogether different meaning now. And Stephen was quite certain they wouldn't come with a pay rise.

'You know he'll never let me go,' he said. 'I'm practically doing his job for him. He won't just let me leave when he's the one making sure no one ever . . .'

He tailed off, and for a second it looked as if Abigail might let the tears come. But before they could fall, she forced them back.

'I don't know how you're going to do it,' she said. 'And frankly I don't care. But we can't have this hanging over us. Not any more. Before the baby comes, you need to make it go away.'

She took a step closer, and for a second he thought she might be about to hug him. Remind him that they were a team. Instead, she reached for the door handle, and with his guilt suddenly threatening to overpower him, closed the bathroom door.

One day before the wedding

4

Robyn woke early, sunlight pouring into their room through the gossamer-light curtains. With Toby still snoring gently beside her, she checked the time on her phone. It was barely seven o'clock.

Usually she would enjoy being the first up. More often than not, they would stay at her flat – a poky two-bedroom place she shared in Greenwich with a friend from the Willows – and while Toby snoozed she would take the opportunity to read under a blanket in the open-plan living area. When he eventually emerged, bleary-eyed, he would kiss her sleepily before fixing some coffee and breakfast. From there, they would head out into the city.

Given how many evenings they each worked, dates often involved daytime visits to galleries and exhibitions, although there would also be the occasional matinee performance of a show or even a bookshop talk by a writer Robyn admired.

Most of the time, Toby was happy for her to choose, but on the odd occasion she insisted he take the lead, he would usually be excited by the prospect of trying a new restaurant. Within just a few weeks of seeing each other, Robyn quickly learned that his interest in cocktails might only be matched by his passion for food. As such, he would often take them to independent places, off the beaten track and so small they would sometimes only have five or six little tables.

Sometimes they would stay in and just watch TV. For the most part, this would work in Robyn's favour. She had a carefully curated list of dramas and documentaries that she wanted to see, meaning that if it was her turn to choose, they would land on something pretty quickly. Toby, on the other hand, would scroll aimlessly through the endless offerings on Netflix, before eventually giving up and letting her choose anyway.

But on that particular morning, in Lake Garda, being the only one awake didn't have its usual shine.

It was safe to say her first evening with the Heywoods hadn't gone as she would have liked. After Laurence and the groomsmen disappeared into town, Toby had rummaged around in the kitchen for some dinner. There hadn't been much to choose from – the Heywoods clearly weren't planning on cooking – but he had just about managed to fix them each a sandwich. Toby had then fetched his laptop and Robyn a book, and they spent the remainder of the evening in the cavernous lounge. Sitting on the snow-white sofa, silently working their way through a bottle of wine, the crowning jewel had been when Toby broke the news of how they would be spending the following day.

'Laurence has chartered a yacht for the day,' he said. 'It's going to take us all the way around the lake. Chadwick and Miles are apparently calling it the "shag do".' He had paused at that point to roll his eyes. 'Laurence has had his stag. And Eva's had her hen. Now they're having one together.'

At the time, Robyn had tried to feign excitement. And she

knew that she *should* be excited. A yacht, on Lake Garda . . . If someone had told her upon first meeting Toby that in a year's time, this was where she would be, she would probably have laughed at them.

But now, with Toby sleeping beside her, she stared at the ceiling, trying to suppress a rising sense of anxiety.

There weren't many people who knew that she was afraid of deep water. In part, this was because spending her entire life living in two places as landlocked as Lancashire and London meant keeping it under wraps had been pretty easy. But mostly it was because she did all she could to keep it to herself.

It wasn't the sight of water that put her on edge. She loved to be on the beach. She would have loved to sit with Toby on the side of Lake Garda. But there was no amount of money in the world that could tempt her in. Even the thought made her palms sweat.

She knew exactly where this fear originated. When she'd been small, she went for swimming lessons on Saturday mornings. Her dad was a maths teacher at a nearby college and would sit by the side of the pool, marking assignments, while she splashed around in a feeble attempt at front crawl.

She remembered loving it. Until the morning she didn't.

She had ventured into the deep end of the pool and somehow managed to lose her coordination. Sinking beneath the water, she could remember the exact moment she realised nobody had seen her disappear. The teacher leading the lesson was trying to get two other unruly kids under control. The lifeguard, so fresh-faced one of his parents had probably dropped him off for his shift, was distracted by someone else. Even her dad was absorbed in his classwork.

51

She couldn't have been under the water for more than a few seconds before her swimming teacher realised what had happened and hurried over to lift her back above the surface. Still, it was enough that she steadfastly refused to go in a swimming pool again for the best part of ten years.

Priding herself on being a deeply logical person, this fear irritated Robyn immensely. She was so worried he might just laugh at her that she hadn't even told Toby about it.

Dread settling in the pit of her stomach, she wondered if there was any way of getting out of the day on the yacht. She had known that on the morning of the wedding they would need to take a short boat ride in order to reach the castle. That alone had put her on edge. But the thought of spending several hours drifting on the lake . . .

She would have to go through with it. Claiming she was sick either wouldn't be believed or would draw even more disapproval from Margot and Laurence. And, of course, there was the small matter of the yacht being where she would first meet Eva. Robyn was painfully aware that her arrival at the villa hadn't gone well. Making some feeble excuse to avoid her first meeting with the bride would hardly help her case.

Eager for a coffee, she lay in bed for a few more minutes, listening for movement downstairs. Hearing nothing, she crept as softly as she could down to the hall, where she was relieved to find the kitchen empty.

Popping a silver pod into the coffee machine, she thought as it hummed about what Laurence had said the previous evening.

Toby must have told him that she'd studied to be a journalist. Quite why he would have done that, she couldn't say. But that wasn't what had bothered her.

You studied to be a journalist. And yet you aren't a journalist. So what's your plan?

Why *wasn't* she a journalist? It had been a while since she'd asked herself that question. At one point, she had wanted it. Spurred on by teenage ambitions of chasing down leads and exposing injustices, she really had chosen her degree with the specific goal of one day becoming an investigative reporter.

So what had happened?

It had taken some time to accept, but the truth was that her dreams hadn't survived her studies. By the time her three years were up, she'd become so jaded by the reality of modern journalism – the bias, the misinformation, the endless drive for clicks and ad revenue – that she simply didn't want it any more. Even if she had, most publications had been forced in recent years to slash their staff numbers so severely that the prospect of landing a job as a reporter felt near impossible. Some of her old course mates were trying to make their way as freelancers, although they seemed to spend more time chasing overdue invoices than doing any actual reporting. Plenty of others had gone on to work in PR instead. Jess was by far the most successful, with her full-time position at *Cosmopolitan*. Robyn was well aware of just how enviously their old peers must now look at her.

In the end, it had been too much. Too disheartening. After she graduated, Robyn had felt adrift, spending six months half-heartedly applying for junior roles at tiny news sites she'd never heard of before giving up entirely.

She felt a twinge of sadness for her teenage self. She could almost hear her, like a disembodied voice, proudly telling her parents about how she wanted to make a difference. To work on investigations that would change the world.

The sadness quickly gave way to a sudden rush of resentment. Of all the ways Laurence and his friends had tried to degrade her – laughing at her accent and her job at the Willows – this was perhaps the worst. They'd reminded her of how much her eager teenage self would disapprove of the twenty-six-year-old she'd grown in to. They'd reminded her that she was a failure.

She went into the lounge, walking straight to the panoramic windows. As her eyes settled on the castle, resting like a seabird on a rock, her unease began to grow.

If she absolutely had to, she could call a taxi to the villa and go back to the airport. But once the boats dropped them off for the wedding, she would be stuck. Cut off, with a group of people who made her feel as if she was some kind of cuckoo, intruding on a family she had no right to.

She swallowed back a lump that had formed in her throat. In a little over twenty-four hours, they would all be on that island, with no escape, should she need it, until the boats came to fetch them at midnight.

In short, she would be trapped.

'Good morning.'

She jumped so violently that her coffee sloshed over the sides of the mug and onto the tiled floor. Turning to see who had crept up on her, she found Jeremy Lambourne sitting on the sofa. He hadn't crept up on her at all. The lounge was simply so large she'd walked past him without even realising he was there. A book rested in his lap, and despite the earliness of the hour, he was already fully dressed.

'Apologies.' He rose to his feet, fetching a handkerchief from his pocket. 'I didn't mean to startle you.'

She forced a smile, taking the handkerchief and mopping up the spilt coffee.

'You're up early, Mr Lambourne,' she said as brightly as she could manage.

'A long-standing habit, I'm afraid. Looking after HCM has rarely afforded the luxury of a full night's sleep and I've never had the patience to spend the morning in bed.' He looked out at the lake. 'I imagine you'll be going out today on the yacht.'

She tried not to wince. 'Are you joining us?'

'I shouldn't think so. What Laurence has planned sounds like more of a young man's game. Margot would like to go into town instead, so I expect I'll join her. There's a church with some supposedly magnificent architecture that I'd very much like to see.' Standing beside her, he nodded towards the castle. 'Really a rather interesting place. It dates back to the first millennium, controlled for quite a few centuries by the Lord of Verona, before being eventually claimed by the Republic of Venice. Very well preserved, as I understand it. There's even a museum.'

'A museum?'

'Only a small one. It contains a few artefacts from the castle's history. But there are certainly some interesting pieces.'

He held out the book he'd been reading, a glossy guidebook full of photos of antique weaponry and embroidered gowns. He flicked through the pages, settling on a large picture of a dagger. It was beautiful, with a short blade of immaculate steel and an ornate bronze hilt that twisted around itself like the cords of a rope. By far its most distinctive feature, however, was a bright green jewel. Robyn had never seen a gem quite like it. It was difficult to tell from the photograph alone, but in person she imagined it must be the size of a small fruit.

As Jeremy lingered on it for a moment, she gave a shiver, which she chose to blame on the air conditioning.

'How did Eva manage to book it for the wedding?' she asked.

Jeremy gave a small smile, closing the book. 'I gather weddings are how the place makes most of its income these days. It isn't open to the public, although it seems there's the odd exhibition as well.'

Robyn was sure they were both wondering the same thing; whether or not Eva had mentioned how popular a wedding venue Castello Fiore was to *London Living*. Somehow, she doubted it.

She looked at the book, a sticker from the shop in which he'd bought it still in place on the back cover. He must have picked it up specifically for the trip.

'Do you take quite an interest in history, Mr Lambourne?'

'I studied it at Oxford.'

'And is that where you met Toby's dad?'

Robyn had no idea why she said it. Eager to avoid an uncomfortable silence, she had just let it pour out, the first thing she could think of.

Jeremy's eyes narrowed slightly. 'Toby's told you about his father?'

'Only a little.'

'I'm surprised he's told you anything at all. My understanding is that Toby didn't care a jot for Alastair.' He sighed. 'We shared a dorm at Rushworth. Inseparable, very much like Laurence and Stephen. When he set up HCM, he asked if I'd join him. And of course, when Laurence was born he did me the honour of naming me godfather.'

Jeremy shook his head. 'It was a tragedy that he died while the boys were still so young. And, of course, while he was still young himself. Barely into his forties. They say five people die on Everest every year. But you never think . . .'

'They've been lucky to have you,' said Robyn.

'I hope so. I've certainly tried to be there over the years. I suppose I feel a sense of . . . responsibility. Not just for HCM. But for all of them. Laurence. Margot. Even Toby. I know he doesn't see it this way, but I only want what's best for him. What his father would have wanted.'

Another silence settled. Realising Jeremy hadn't yet seen her take a sip from the coffee, Robyn saw her escape.

'I should take this up for him,' she said, raising the mug. 'Before it goes cold.'

'Of course,' Jeremy agreed. 'Don't let me keep you. I suppose I'll see you this evening. At dinner.'

'Dinner?' Robyn repeated.

Jeremy frowned at her again. 'Has Laurence not said? We're dining this evening with Eva's family. A chance for Margot to meet her parents before the wedding.'

Laurence hadn't told her. Although Robyn did her best to sound unfazed. 'I'm sure that will be lovely.'

Jeremy gave a small smile. 'Yes,' he said. 'Yes, I'm sure it will.'

Glad to be away, Robyn hurried from the lounge. In the hallway, she stopped for a moment, looking back towards Jeremy. He was still standing by the window, staring at the castle.

5

As determined as she was not to let it show, by the time the others had emerged from their rooms and had breakfast on the patio, Robyn's nerves were growing by the minute.

Laurence's plan was to travel to Riva, a larger town at the top of the lake where the yacht would be moored. Once at the marina, they would be met by the bridesmaids, as well as Eva's agent, Harper, and the photographer from *London Living*.

Robyn was surprised to hear that Harper and the photographer would be attending, prompting Toby to explain that Eva wanted shots of the groomsmen and the bridal party living it up on the lake. Harper's role would be to see that the shoot went smoothly, and make sure the photographer had everything she needed.

At eleven o'clock, the group gathered outside the villa, where a couple of large taxis were waiting. They were smart, a Mercedes and an Audi. But Laurence, it seemed, had no intention of riding in them. Instead, he strode straight towards the Ferrari Robyn had seen the previous afternoon.

'I'm going to drive,' he announced. For his day on the lake, he'd chosen a slim-fitting pair of white shorts, a pink shirt with the top three buttons hanging undone and a pair of glinting aviator sunglasses.

'Is that a good idea?' Stephen asked. 'Surely the taxis would be more sensible.'

'Not a chance. How often do you get to drive a vintage Ferrari around the shores of Lake Garda?'

'Tosser,' Miles called back. 'You just want the photographer to get a shot as you pull up at the marina.'

'And what would be wrong with that?'

'Nothing at all. So long as I can ride shotgun.'

A small smile touched the corners of Laurence's mouth. 'I actually thought Robyn could ride with me. A jaunt around the lake sounds like the perfect opportunity to get to know each other a little better.'

Robyn shot Toby a nervous glance. His eyes narrowed.

'It's only twenty minutes to Riva,' Laurence teased. 'Fifteen, in this thing. Surely you can put up with me just for that?'

She looked again at Toby, who was now scowling, then around at the others. They were all watching, eager to get under way.

'All right.'

Toby frowned at her, and she gave her best nonchalant shrug. Fifteen minutes, she thought. What was the worst that could happen?

Laurence held the passenger door open for her, a gesture that only served to make her even more uncomfortable. When he closed it again, she had the sudden sense of being sealed inside. The interior, at least, was more spacious than she had expected. It was furnished with caramel-coloured leather, gleaming silver dials nestled in a dashboard as black as coal.

She reached for her seat belt, only to find there wasn't one. Spotting her alarm as he climbed into the driver's seat, Laurence gave a short laugh from behind his aviators before rumbling the engine into life. He grasped the steering wheel — wooden, and much larger than in any other car Robyn had been in — and they rolled towards the gates. With the Ferrari growling like a panther, she gave Toby one last fleeting look through the window before they moved onto the road.

For the first few minutes, they didn't speak, Laurence entranced by the road ahead. As they rolled down the hill and into town, Robyn saw bicycles and mopeds weaving between crowds of people, while delivery vans and taxis rattled down snug alleyways. Potted flowers lined the streets, trails of ivy pouring from the balconies and shuttered windows overhead. Every building was painted a different shade of either yellow, pink or orange, with each roof sharing the same terracotta tiles. They housed shops and restaurants on the ground floor, with apartments and hotels furnishing the upper storeys. And towering above it all, vast and imposing, were the mountains.

With one hand on the wheel and another resting on the gear stick, Laurence was clearly enjoying himself, relishing the sound of the engine and the admiring gazes they received from passers-by. Robyn shrivelled into her seat, feeling painfully out of place.

It wasn't until they'd passed through the town and were on the main road, heading north with the mountains on their right and the water on their left, that he finally spoke.

'The 250 GT Lusso,' he announced. 'D'you know, Ferrari only ever made three hundred and fifty of these.' He changed gear, building speed with every word. 'Back in 1963 this was the fastest road car in the world.'

Robyn nodded, hoping she looked suitably impressed.

'And you've bought it?'

He laughed again, tugging on the wooden steering wheel. 'Eva's father deals in classic cars. This is one of his. Took some real persuasion for him to let me drive it this weekend.'

Rounding a corner onto a sudden stretch of open road, he pressed down on the accelerator, the engine roaring in response. Robyn had to force herself to avoid looking at the speedometer, deciding it best not to know the speed they must be reaching.

'Look,' he said, raising his voice slightly to be heard above the engine. 'I think we may have got off on the wrong foot yesterday. Toby gets so serious about these things but we were only joking around.'

Robyn looked at him, not quite sure how he was expecting her to respond. She thought of the conversation between the two brothers that she'd interrupted on the patio.

She seems like a nice girl, but if she's encouraging you to keep going with this crazy idea of opening some bar, she's clearly a bad influence . . .

'It isn't that we don't like you,' Laurence explained. 'It isn't even that anyone disapproves of you. What Mum and I have a problem with is Toby's attitude. Everything Dad left us . . . HCM . . . He's shrugging it all off like it doesn't matter.'

'Perhaps he just wants to do something else.'

'Well, he doesn't get to make that choice. Dad founded HCM for us. Not just to set us up but for us to continue. To expand. Toby doesn't get to enjoy the benefits when it suits him – receive one of the most expensive educations in the world and then decide he isn't interested when it's time to do his share of the work.'

'I'd hardly say that he enjoyed Rushworth.'

'Then he needs to get over himself.'

They rounded a bend onto another stretch of open road, Laurence veering into the opposite lane in order to overtake a dusty Renault Clio that was trundling in front. In the absence of a handle, Robyn grasped the edges of her seat; the sudden burst of speed causing the engine to crescendo.

'What did he think of the job spec I left in your room?'

Robyn didn't reply.

'He didn't even look at it, did he?' Laurence gave a hollow laugh. 'Look,' he said again, steering back into the right-hand lane. 'This role would be perfect. Six-figure starting salary. As much or as little work as he'd like. He *has* to take it. Jeremy's going to speak to him about it over the weekend, but he's told me it's the last time he'll try. As far as he's concerned, Toby's a lost cause.'

He looked at her. 'I know his first instinct will be to say no. But he really needs to think about it. There's never going to be a cushier opportunity to get involved.'

The engine fell from a growl to a murmur, Laurence dropping his speed as the main road took them into Riva. Towering palm trees began to roll past, along with signs advertising boat trips.

'Why tell *me* this?' Robyn asked.

'I was hoping you could help to convince him. Make him see that it's in his interest.'

She was silent for a little while, listening to the rumbling of the engine.

'I don't see how I'd make a difference. He's adamant he won't ever work for HCM.'

'Well, I hope you'll at least try. Because when all's said and done he's my little brother and I love him. I just don't want him to waste his entire life behind a bar.'

Robyn resisted the temptation to point out how difficult it was not to take that part personally.

'I'll think about it,' she lied.

Laurence smirked, shifting down a gear as they neared the marina. 'We'll make a Heywood out of you yet.'

6

Regardless of how much she was dreading stepping aboard it, Robyn supposed it should come as little surprise that the yacht Laurence had chartered was obscenely impressive. Shaped like an arrowhead, it towered above the other boats in Riva's marina, a vast construction of sweeping white panels and tinted windows that seemed almost determined to outdo the stunning surroundings in which it sailed. Tourists gazed up at it, some even stopping to take pictures.

Robyn took one look and felt her nerves turn to nausea.

Laurence brought the Ferrari right up to it, the engine finally falling silent. Looking out at the surrounding piazza, Robyn saw pastel-coloured hotels and tables with umbrellas outside half a dozen cafés. A queue of tourists spilled from a nearby gelato shop, their heads all turned by the sound of the Ferrari announcing its arrival.

Two women were waiting for them, one of whom hurried straight over and began to fuss around Laurence as he stepped from the Ferrari. An iPhone was clutched in her hand, a pair of Ray-Bans perched on her nose and a tote bag slung over her shoulder. Robyn hoped she was lathered in suncream. She was pale as a sheet, her hair bleached white-blonde.

'I'm Harper,' she said cheerfully, bangles rattling on her wrist as she stuck out a hand for Robyn to shake. 'Eva's agent. And this is Cam.'

With a camera in her hand and a heavy bag slung over one shoulder, it was clear that Cam must be the photographer from *London Living*. Somewhere in her forties, she could have been dressed for a safari, wearing a loose-fitting T-shirt and cargo shorts, and with her hair tied back in a ponytail.

'Pleasure to meet you,' she said to Laurence.

He mumbled a vague pleasantry in response, his eyes fixed on the yacht.

'It's quite something,' said Harper. 'Cam's going to get some amazing shots once we're out on the water.'

Laurence didn't answer her. In the ensuing silence, a nearby clock tower struck quarter past, the bright chime sending a flock of pigeons scattering.

'You must have had an early start,' Robyn volunteered, seeing the enthusiasm ebb slightly from Harper's face. 'To have flown out this morning.'

'Oh, God no!' she said. 'No, I came last night.'

'And you didn't want to stay at the villa?'

'I suggested it, but Eva said there wasn't room. It's no trouble, though. I'm staying in a beautiful hotel. The view from my room was incredible this morning!'

Robyn frowned, convinced there would have been space for Harper in the villa. The room next to theirs was certainly vacant.

Before she could press the matter, though, the taxis began to pull up. Toby came straight over, glaring at Laurence as he looped an arm around Robyn's waist. 'All OK? What did he want?'

'It was fine,' she said quietly. 'It's that job. He wants me to help convince you to take it.'

Toby gave a weak laugh. 'Course he does.'

'Where's Eva?' Laurence called out.

'Right here.'

It was curious; Robyn had spent so much time scouring Eva's Instagram back in London that she felt as if she knew her already. But seeing her now, descending from the top deck of the yacht, was something else. The dark hair, the crimson lips, the deep brown eyes that were nestled in an almost heart-shaped face . . . Even the way she moved, brushing the handrail with a practised deftness. She was like a picture come to life.

And yet . . .

Toby hadn't explained what he'd meant the previous evening, when he'd snapped back at Laurence that Eva was a bad influence. Seeing how heated their conversation was at risk of becoming, Robyn had decided it best not to push him on it. But seeing Eva now, she suddenly wanted desperately to know.

Stepping off the yacht, she drew Laurence into a one-armed hug.

'I don't think that was quite dramatic enough, darling,' he said. 'Have you been waiting long?'

'Not too long. I've just been taking some photos of the boat before the others arrive.'

A shriek rang out, and two glamorous women hurried across the piazza. Seeing Chadwick and Miles share a knowing look, Robyn assumed they must be Eva's bridesmaids, Giulia and

Beatrice. Around the same age as Eva, they wore light summer dresses, broad hats and designer sunglasses. They pulled her into a hug, motioning excitedly towards the yacht as they spoke frantically in Italian.

Certain that she'd heard Eva had three bridesmaids, it took Robyn a moment to realise that there was indeed a third person with them. Trailing a few metres behind, she was younger – perhaps twenty-three or twenty-four – and sported features so closely resembling Eva's that they must surely have been sisters. She wore a nervous expression, quickly looking away when Robyn tried to offer her a smile.

Cheering and whooping, the group began to make its way on board, eagerly accepting glasses of champagne from two cabin crew in immaculate white uniforms. But as the others filed up the gangplank, Robyn noticed Cam touch Eva on the shoulder and bring her silently away for a photo with Laurence. She had them rest against the bonnet of the Ferrari, gazing adoringly into each other's eyes. The yacht was behind them, and behind that, the lake. Robyn was no photographer, but she could plainly see that it was going to be a breathtaking picture.

She noticed something else, however. Just a few feet away, Eva's sister was glaring at the happy couple.

'She doesn't look thrilled to be here.'

'Dina.' Toby squinted at her. 'I don't suppose she is. Laurence says there's some pretty bad blood there. Especially where the wedding's concerned.'

Seeing that Robyn was now even more curious, Toby grimaced. 'Dina was meant to get married last year. To her high-school sweetheart. But Eva wasn't happy about the colour she'd chosen for her bridesmaids' dresses.'

'Are you serious?'

'Apparently Eva wanted it one day for her own bridesmaids. And she was adamant that she and Dina couldn't both have it. As I understand it, she tried telling Dina to pick something different, but, to her credit, Dina stood up to her. Said no. So Eva went instead to the fiancé.

'She told him he had to make Dina change the dresses, but he refused. Things got heated and Eva started laying into him for a load of other stuff. She wasn't happy about the venue they'd chosen. The date. How many people they were planning to invite. Apparently she just let loose, telling him everything she wanted Dina to change.'

Toby shook his head. 'After that, the guy told Dina that maybe they should put the wedding on hold. Revisit it in a few months, when her family was more open to it all. But, of course, they didn't. After Eva's outburst, it just became too awkward. They struggled along for a few months until he decided to cut things off completely.'

Robyn looked at Dina, feeling an intense pang of sympathy. 'I'm surprised Laurence told you all of that.'

'He told the story slightly differently. He thinks Eva was completely justified. That nothing she said was out of turn and Dina's fiancé completely overreacted. But if you ignore his bullshit and read between the lines, you get a pretty clear idea of what actually happened.'

Robyn thought for a moment. 'The dresses. Eva hasn't . . . After what happened to Dina, she wouldn't still . . .'

'No idea. I haven't been brave enough to ask. But I guess we'll find out tomorrow. Laurence says the dresses Eva wanted – the ones she told Dina she couldn't have – were sage green.'

A member of the cabin crew approached with a tray of champagne glasses, and politely told them it was time to make their way aboard.

'How far are we going?' Robyn asked, taking a glass.

'All the way down to the southern shore. We'll be sailing at a gentle speed, to take in the landscape. Each way should take around two and a half hours.'

'Will we be stopping anywhere?'

'Not today, ma'am. We might pause for some swimming, but Mr Lambourne would like to stay on the water.'

Robyn gave a weak smile, trying to hide her discomfort at the thought of it being five hours before she set foot on solid ground again. For a split second, it was almost too much. She had to bite down on her lip to stop herself from telling Toby she couldn't do it.

Everything was going to be fine, she told herself forcefully. The yacht was huge and the lake was calm. If she were to take herself inside, she could probably fool herself into thinking she wasn't on a boat at all.

Toby motioned towards the yacht. 'After you.'

Robyn looked down at the gangway. The yacht itself might well be sturdy. But the narrow bridge she had to walk across in order to board it appeared anything but. It seemed to sway slightly, suspended a few feet above the water. Robyn forced herself not to think of the way it had just rattled as the others careered across.

'Rob?' Toby peered at her, his brow furrowing. 'Everything OK?'

Forcing a smile, she grasped the handrail and in three quick steps almost threw herself aboard.

7

Harper sighed.

She'd hoped that in her home country, on the weekend of her wedding and with a magazine shoot in tow, Eva might – for once – be in a good mood.

It hadn't taken long for those hopes to be dashed.

Meeting in the piazza, Harper had barely said good morning before being scolded for bringing a coffee with the wrong kind of milk.

'How could you get it wrong?' Eva had demanded. 'When I was last here I bought my coffee there every day. I ordered the exact same thing. They know me!'

Perhaps, when Eva was last in town, whoever had been working in the little café really had known her. But the confused young woman working behind the counter that morning certainly hadn't. And with Harper trying in the most basic Italian to place an order so complex that in London it intimidated even the most seasoned Starbucks baristas, she'd known immediately that the likelihood of starting the day on a sour note would be high.

Harper had then introduced Eva to Cam, before the next problem arose.

'Did you bring the kimono?' Eva asked.

Harper frowned at her.

'The kimono. From ASOS. I told you to bring it so I could get some pictures on the yacht. I emailed you last week!'

After Eva had stormed onto the yacht, Harper scoured her inbox. If such an email really had been sent, it had gone to someone else.

Harper gave another sigh. She'd known, of course, that she was only attending Eva's wedding as a glorified runner. It was just part of the job. To be an agent was to be a salesperson, an assistant and a cheerleader all at once. But even so . . . They were in Italy. She had been looking forward to food, wine and sun. In essence, for managing Eva to finally be something other than a complete nightmare.

Even the photographer seemed to want nothing to do with her. The previous evening, once they'd checked in to their hotel, Harper had noticed a few nice-looking bars nearby and suggested the two of them get a drink. But Cam had immediately turned her down, eager instead to sort through some photos she'd taken on a shoot that morning. As such, Harper had spent the first evening alone in her hotel room, with nothing for company but a view of a car park and a bottle of white wine purchased from the neighbouring *supermercato*.

It would be worth it, she told herself. It *had* to be worth it.

She thought of the rejection she'd read, just that morning, from yet another brand manager to whom she'd pitched Eva as an ambassador. There'd been so many now that they didn't come as a surprise any more. But that didn't make them any less disheartening. If anything, this one was worse. When it was a household name turning her down, Harper could at least

71

comfort herself – and, for that matter, try to comfort Eva – with the rationale that the competition was fierce. But there was no chance of making a case like that with this latest rejection, from some zero-sugar energy drink that was brand new to the high street.

Of course, they hadn't outright rejected Eva. Nobody ever did. It was always 'No available budget' or 'We aren't looking for new influencer collaborations right now'. But one way or another, it was always a rejection.

Although not for the reasons she was used to.

Eva had originally made her name in fashion and beauty – her content was excellent and her following strong – but the simple truth was that she was getting a reputation. As Harper knew only too well, she was difficult to work with. She was rude and demanding. And with the brand managers she relied on for work all attending the same networking events and industry conferences, Harper was convinced that word was getting round. Eva Bianchi was a problem. She looked the part, but unless you had the stomach for a rough ride, she was best avoided.

With leads drying up, Harper had advised Eva that they should shift their focus to health and well-being. It was new territory, where her reputation wasn't likely to get ahead of them, but it wasn't such a pivot that she would alienate the audience she had spent years building.

It had seemed like the perfect solution. But after months of trying, every door Harper knocked on remained defiantly closed. She almost wished one of them would tell the truth. That someone would just admit they couldn't place their brand in the hands of an influencer whose first desperate foray into their industry had hospitalised a teenager.

If she'd been with any other agency, Eva would most likely have been cut loose the moment the news broke. She'd gone rogue. Posted harmful content she had no business creating, and all without first consulting Harper.

But Harper's agency was struggling. They were haemorrhaging clients, with precious little in the way of new prospects. That year alone, two of her colleagues had already been made redundant. With one of Harper's clients being the latest to deliver their notice, and fearful of her own redundancy, she had petitioned to keep Eva on the books, promising to bring the situation under control.

'Give me two months,' she'd pleaded. 'By the time we've worked our notice period it'll have blown over, meaning that one way or another, we have to ride it out. Let me see if I can turn her around. If she's still causing nothing but trouble, we'll let her go. But there's no point losing her if we don't have to.'

The agency had agreed, and by the time her two months were over, Harper had been proved right. Within a few weeks, the news cycle had churned over and the hospitalised kid had disappeared from the mainstream press.

But the industry remembered. The brands Harper had been so reliant on welcoming Eva in – Nutribullet; Whey Protein; Huel – wanted nothing to do with her. And it was Harper's job to make them forget.

For months she made offers so low that they would practically have been working for free. And all the while, Eva was growing impatient for results.

Sometimes she wondered if redundancy wouldn't be better. The late nights, the weekends, the endless torrent of ungrateful messages . . . It surely wasn't worth it. The only thing keeping her hanging on — her only hope of finally turning a corner — was *London Living*.

If she was honest, Harper still couldn't quite believe the magazine had wanted it. A cover feature and a glossy, double-page spread . . . Sure, Eva was popular. An Instagram following of over five hundred thousand wasn't to be sniffed at. But all of this for her wedding? When she'd outreached to the major lifestyle magazines, offering them the story, she'd been going through the motions, no hope at all that one of them might actually respond.

'Must be the way things are going,' her boss had said upon receiving the news. 'Used to be actors and singers getting married in magazines. Now it's influencers.'

Maybe, Harper had thought. Or maybe it was the Italian castle that had done it. In any case, she hadn't complained. Right now, Eva was a nobody in the eyes of the brands she wanted to work with. Worse than a nobody, she was a liability.

But liabilities don't appear on the covers of national magazines.

Harper already had her strategy planned. She was going to buy fifty copies — more, if she needed — and post them to every name that Eva had ever asked to work with. She was going to offer Eva's services as a brand ambassador at half the usual cost. In short, she was finally going to start landing the opportunities they needed.

With Laurence and Eva having boarded the yacht, Cam looked to be taking some atmospheric shots of the Ferrari. Seeing the backdrop behind it — the lake, the mountains, the endless blue sky — Harper felt a flutter of excitement. The pictures were going to be stunning.

Once Cam appeared to be finishing up by the car, Harper picked up her camera bag off the cobbled ground. It was heavy. Still, she gave a broad smile.

'Can I take this for you? Might as well make myself useful.'

Cam turned. But where Harper had expected to see gratitude – maybe even relief – instead her eyes flew wide, and she snatched the bag from Harper's hands as if she had stolen her purse.

For a few seconds, Harper just stood, too taken aback to even respond. 'I'm sorry . . .' she said. 'I didn't mean to . . .'

Cam's expression softened. 'It's OK. There's just some delicate gear in here. It's best if I take it.'

'Of course.'

Cam gave her a nod, shrugging the bag onto her shoulder before tilting her head towards the yacht. 'Shall we get aboard?'

She didn't wait for a reply, leaving Harper on the cobbles as she stepped straight onto the gangway.

8

They boarded at the back of the yacht, its prow pointing out towards the lake. Two staircases led to the upper deck Robyn had glimpsed from the marina, while a pair of tinted glass doors led inside. Stealing a glance, she saw a lavish dining room, with soft chairs, sparkling tableware and a huge flat-screen TV. Much like the villa, it reminded her more of an upmarket London hotel than of Italian craftsmanship.

With trembling knees, she followed the rest of the group upstairs, finding that the deck was even larger than she'd thought. There was a table, half a dozen sun loungers and a U-shaped sofa, all furnished in the same shade of grey. Two silver ice buckets full of champagne had been put out, while a hot tub occupied the middle of the deck. It struck Robyn that Beatrice and Giulia must have had bikinis on under their summer dresses, as they were in the water already, posing with their drinks as Cam hurried to take a shot of them.

Robyn started at the sight of the photographer. She must have come up via the adjacent flight of stairs, but even so. Just a moment earlier she'd been taking pictures of Laurence and

Eva beside the Ferrari. Quite when she'd managed to move from the marina onto the yacht Robyn had no idea.

Laurence appeared on deck. Already holding a bottle of champagne, he had swapped his loafers for flip-flops, and if Robyn wasn't mistaken, had also undone two more buttons on his shirt.

'Ladies and gents,' he called. 'I suggest we get under way!'

A cheer rang out, although it was quickly swallowed as music began playing from a portable speaker. The sound of autotune and an aggressive beat blared across the deck, drawing disapproving looks from bystanders in the marina.

While the others milled around the hot tub and the sofa, Robyn went with Toby and leaned against the railing. She felt the engine hum beneath her feet, and within seconds, the yacht began to stir, slicing through the tranquil water as it picked up speed.

She tried to enjoy the beauty of it all, the lake glittering before her like a blanket of blue diamonds. But all she could think of was the prospect of five uninterrupted hours on the water.

She turned to look at the others. Harper hurried over to the hot tub with a bottle of champagne, ready to refill Eva's empty glass.

'Put this somewhere,' Eva said, holding out a handbag.

'Shall I hold on to it?' Harper asked. 'Put it inside, maybe?'

'Just put it somewhere safe. Where I can still reach it.'

Robyn watched as Harper did as she was told, tucking the bag neatly under the nearest deckchair.

'Harper seems nice,' she said. 'A bit much, perhaps. But still. Nice.'

Toby hummed. 'Eva's not so impressed, apparently. I heard Laurence telling Stephen over breakfast that she isn't happy with the leads Harper's been bringing in.'

'Why not?'

'Seems she's desperate to partner with some nutritional brands. Nutribullet. Whey Protein. Those sorts of guys. And she's seriously pissed off that Harper hasn't been able to make it happen.'

'What's stopping her? I've seen some of the fashion brands she's worked with; Harper must be doing something right to land partnerships like those.'

'Who can say?' Toby grimaced and tipped back what remained of his champagne. 'I'm fetching another. Want one?'

Robyn looked down at her own glass. Having barely touched it, she shook her head and he disappeared inside.

For a minute or two, she stood by the railing, screwing her eyes shut as she tried to will some enjoyment from how the sun warmed her skin. The breeze that brushed her hair. But no matter how hard she tried, all she could think of was the vast body of water beneath them.

'Are you OK?'

Opening her eyes, she turned to find the photographer hovering behind her, a concerned expression on her face.

'Fine,' she lied. 'Just a little too much wine with dinner last night. How are you getting on?'

'Having the time of my life. The people, the location . . . I mean, just look at where we are. It's difficult to believe.'

'It isn't usually like this, then?'

'God, no. Most days I'm shooting in an East London studio

with crap coffee and no heating. Significantly less glamorous.' She put out a hand and said, 'Cam.'

'Robyn.' She took the photographer's hand, feeling a sudden rush of relief at the prospect of speaking to someone ordinary. Someone who wasn't part of the Rushworth club. 'Cam,' she repeated. 'Short for anything?'

'Nope.' Cam shook her head. 'Just Cam.' She waved an arm, motioning at the deck. 'So what about you? Your first super-yacht or is this how you guys commute?'

Robyn's stomach lurched, threatening to turn at the thought of doing this on a daily basis.

'Definitely my first. If you come across a bartender who commutes like this, you'll have to let me know. I'll be taking it up with my boss.'

'Bartender? I thought you were all stockbrokers or something?'

'The others are involved in all that. I'm just here with Toby, Laurence's brother.' She motioned towards the camera. 'How are the shots coming out?'

'Amazing. Fancy a look?'

Cam lifted the camera and began to flick through the pictures. She must have taken well over a hundred already, the vast majority being action shots. They were good. Great, even. But eventually she stopped on the picture she'd taken in the marina; the shot of Eva and Laurence, each glowing like runway models. The Ferrari, gleaming in the midday sun. The yacht behind it and the mountains rising on either side of the lake.

'Your editor's going to adore these,' said Robyn. 'And some of those candids are incredible.'

Cam cocked an eyebrow. 'You know about this stuff?'

Robyn thought of the message from Jess, wondering if Cam might have done any work for *Cosmopolitan*. For a split second she even wondered if the two of them might somehow know each other.

'I have a degree in journalism,' she said, pushing the thought back down. 'We did a module on magazine production.'

Cam nodded, apparently approving. 'Well, I hope you're right. I had to really push for us to cover this, so I need to make sure I deliver. I'm not convinced it's the one, though.' Seeing the confusion on Robyn's face, she explained, 'I spoke a little to Eva before I flew out. She made it pretty clear she's looking for a perfect shot. The image of her career.'

Robyn didn't say anything. Despite her not having actually met Eva yet, it didn't require much effort to imagine her staging an entire wedding for the sake of a single perfect picture.

'You sure you're OK?' Cam asked. 'You're looking a little green.'

She forced a smile. 'Fine. I just . . . If I'm honest I just don't do so well out on the water.'

'Want me to see if the crew have anything?'

'No,' Robyn said quickly. 'Thank you. I'm trying not to tell anyone. Lake Garda . . . Multimillion-pound yacht . . . I don't think it would look great for the plus-one to make a scene.'

Cam nodded, seemingly understanding. She hoisted her bag up onto her shoulder, flicking a quick glance at the passing landscape. 'Would you excuse me? We're coming up on the castle. I *have* to get one of Eva and Laurence with it in the background.'

'No worries. Go get your shot.'

Cam began to walk across the deck. After a couple of steps though, she turned back, fixing Robyn with a warm smile. 'Hey, it was really nice meeting you.'

Robyn nodded in return, and watched as Cam approached the hot tub, tapping Eva on the shoulder as she'd done in the marina. The bridesmaids barely seemed to notice, not even pausing their conversation as Eva stepped away and followed her to the railing.

Robyn hadn't known what to expect from the photographer, but Cam had surprised her. She supposed she'd expected someone more like Harper. A bright, bubbly twenty-something, with a camera in one hand and a champagne glass in the other. In reality, Cam seemed more down to earth than anyone else on the entire yacht.

Turning back towards the water, she saw that Cam was right; they were nearing Castello Fiore. It was the closest she'd been to it yet. The stone walls, the looming tower . . .

Robyn looked at the distance from the castle to the shore, the body of water between the two, and began to feel uneasy again. She felt the wind tugging at her hair and imagined what it would be like tomorrow, to be travelling there for the wedding, on a boat considerably smaller than Laurence's yacht.

She took a deep breath. Then another. But it was too much. All of a sudden, she felt an overpowering need to be somewhere else. Crossing the deck, she hurried down the staircase. She would take herself inside for a moment. Sit in the dining room and pretend that she really was in some cold London hotel.

Closing the door behind her, she sat down at the dining table, where she closed her eyes and tried to steady her breathing. No sooner had she done so, however, than she heard the door open again. The air became heavy with the scent of perfume. Opening her eyes, she looked up to see Eva standing in the doorway, those heart-shaped features creased with concern.

'Robyn . . . What are you doing here on your own?'

She scrambled for an answer. 'I'm not feeling too well. Too much wine last night. I just needed to sit down for a minute.'

Eva sat at the table. 'Can I get you anything? Some water perhaps?'

Even her voice was beautiful, her accent wrapping itself like silk around the words. Robyn breathed in her perfume, looked down at the engagement ring as it glistened on her finger and tried not to shudder at the thought of what it must be worth.

'You know,' she said, leaning in close before Robyn could reply, 'I've been very keen to meet you. I wanted to get the measure of you for myself.'

'The measure of me?'

'Of course.' She leaned in closer still, so that Robyn could feel her breath on her skin. 'I wanted to see the girl who has managed to upset my fiancé so badly.'

A sense of dread began to make itself very much at home in the pit of Robyn's stomach.

'Laurence called me last night,' Eva continued. 'He thinks you're leading Toby astray. Telling him to open a bar when he should be working for HCM.'

'I'm not,' Robyn managed, her voice suddenly hoarse. 'I mean, I'm supporting him. He's passionate about it and I think he'd do an amazing job. But it's his idea.'

'Laurence says you're pushing him into it.'

'I'm not pushing him into anything!'

Eva fixed her with a sad, almost sympathetic expression. 'Listen to me, Robyn. Sooner or later, Toby will come to his senses and realise that he belongs at HCM. More than that, he'll realise it's for the best. The life he'll have if he settles for pouring drinks . . . Laurence struggles to express it, but that's why he's so worried. He only wants the best for his little brother.'

'And what do *you* want?'

'I want what's best for Laurence. This time tomorrow we'll be getting married. I want him to be happy.'

Robyn felt a sudden flush of frustration. With Laurence. With Eva. With this ridiculous yacht. But before she could answer, the concern on Eva's face vanished in an instant, her features becoming set.

'You're going to help Laurence,' she said. 'Convince Toby he has to finally come to HCM.'

'That's up to him.'

'No. If he wants to be part of this family, he needs to start acting like it.'

'Part of this family?' Robyn echoed. 'Eva, *you* aren't even part of their family. Not yet.'

Eva gawped, adopting an expression of such shock that Robyn might have just slapped her.

Robyn climbed to her feet. 'I'm trying my best to convince Toby to play nicely with you all, but it isn't for me to bully him into working for HCM. And quite frankly, I don't see how it's up to you, either. If Laurence and Jeremy want to speak with him, and if he decides after that discussion that he's going to work with them, I won't try to stop him. But until that happens, you all need to leave him be.'

She swore as she stepped out onto the deck, her heart pounding with a slight rush of adrenaline.

She shouldn't have pushed back like that. As good as it had felt to put Eva in her place, if only for a moment, it was no use insisting Toby be on good behaviour if she couldn't even keep herself—

She didn't finish her thought. She had no chance. No sooner was she through the glass doors than she heard pattering footsteps behind her. She tensed, feeling a quick shove in the small of her back. Before she even knew what had happened, she'd tipped forward and tumbled into the water.

9

Stephen was on the U-shaped sofa with Chadwick and Miles.

In the hour since they'd left the villa, the two of them had barely paused for breath. In the taxi it had been the Ferrari, joking about how likely Laurence was to stall it. On the yacht, it was the bridesmaids, debating which they would each most like to take back with them to the villa.

Not that Stephen had been contributing. Instead, he was looking at Abigail across the deck. She was in the hot tub with Eva and her bridesmaids, a glass of iced lemon water in her hand while the others sipped champagne.

She was putting on a show, just as she had in the villa, smiling and laughing with the other women. Once again, Stephen was grateful for how convincingly she performed. In his mind, he replayed the conversation they'd had the previous evening.

Things are different now, Stephen. It isn't just us any more. What if everything comes out when the baby arrives? What if you're arrested?

She was right. Of course she was right. They were going to be a family, the three of them. He couldn't have this hanging over them any longer.

'How's your speech coming along, Stephen?' Chadwick cut through his train of thought, holding up his champagne glass for a member of the crew to refill. 'Hope you won't be letting Laurence off lightly.'

'I'd roast him if it was me,' said Miles. 'The stories I'd tell, he'd never be able to look Margot in the eye again.'

'Maybe that's why it *isn't* you.'

Stephen couldn't say if he'd meant to sound so aggressive or if it had just slipped out. Either way, his disdain for the two groomsmen was clear in his voice.

'What's your problem?' Miles demanded.

'Nothing.'

'There *is* a problem, Stephen. You've been a bloody misery since the moment we arrived. I'm not putting up with you moping all weekend so just spit it out.'

Stephen took a deep breath, sweeping a glance around to ensure no one was in earshot. 'How can you be so calm?' he whispered. 'How can you just sit here, drinking champagne like nothing happened?'

Chadwick's brow creased. 'No idea what you're talking about, mate.'

'A man died! You killed—'

'Shut up,' Miles hissed. 'Shut the fuck up.'

A tense silence settled between them.

'How are you not scared?' Stephen demanded. 'How are you not terrified that someone's going to find out?'

'Because Laurence promised they wouldn't.' Miles took a deep breath. 'Look. None of us are proud of what happened. It was a mistake. But Jeremy made the police investigation go away. If *they're* not even looking into it any more, how's anyone else ever going to know?'

'The papers—'

'The papers ran out of things to say within a week. It's been months, Stephen. Don't you think that if anything new was going to come out – something they could actually report on – it would have happened by now? The way Laurence describes it, they had so little they could actually print that Jeremy didn't even *need* to do anything about them.'

Stephen didn't answer. They didn't understand. But then, how could they? Of the three of them, he was the only one with a newborn on the way. If the truth did make its way out, and they did all face charges, he was the only one who stood to leave a family unprotected.

It was then that they heard it. Over the din of the music, a sudden cry rippling from the back of the yacht.

10

The moment Robyn hit the lake, panic took over.

She thrashed about, water in her eyes and mouth. She couldn't see. She couldn't think. There was nothing except the vast expanse beneath her.

Hearing her cry out, the others hurried down from the upper deck, one of the crew diving straight into the water. He swam over with a few powerful strokes, gave Robyn his arm and guided her back to the yacht.

With everyone now gathered on the lower deck, Toby barged his way to the front and helped her onto the yacht. Eva hovered at the back of the group, and for a moment she and Robyn locked eyes. Robyn was too shaken to hold her gaze, although she noticed Toby frowning beside her as he caught the short exchange.

'Let's go inside,' she said.

Toby snatched an enormous white towel from an anxious-looking crew member and wrapped it around her shoulders before ushering her through the glass doors. She could hear water dripping onto the polished floor, although Toby didn't seem to care. He knelt beside her and began to rub her arms through the towel.

'*Signorina.*' A different crew member followed them inside. 'Are you all right? If you need first aid, we can carry it out on board. Or we can head straight to shore if you need a doctor.'

Toby looked at her, his concern plain for both of them to see. 'Are you OK?'

Robyn nodded, her voice trembling. 'I'm fine. I was just a little light-headed. The heat . . . I'll be OK.'

'We can continue?' the crew member asked.

'Yes,' Robyn insisted. 'Yes, we can keep going. There's no need to stop.'

The crew member was clearly not entirely convinced, his brow furrowed. But he didn't protest. With a nod, he stepped back onto the deck, closing the door as he went.

'What happened?' Toby asked.

Robyn was asking herself the same thing. Eva had pushed her. She had actually pushed her off the yacht.

She replayed their conversation in her mind, trying to think of any way Eva might have known about her fear – to confirm if she could have realised just how badly tumbling into the lake would affect her. She could think of nothing. Unless Eva had been able simply to *see* how uncomfortable she was on the yacht – which, given her conversation a few minutes earlier with Cam, didn't seem completely impossible.

Even so, it was an extreme reaction. All Robyn had done was refuse to help coax Toby into HCM. Although perhaps that wasn't what had prompted Eva's fury. Perhaps it had been her final jab before she stepped out onto the deck.

Part of this family? Eva, you *aren't even part of their family. Not yet.*

Realising her mistake, she shuddered. She wondered how many times Eva had been told no. How many times in her entire life she'd been spoken to in such a tone.

'I don't know,' she said, voice trembling. 'I must have slipped. Didn't realise how close I was to the edge.'

Toby looked towards the glass doors. 'You were down here with Eva.'

'Eva didn't do any—'

'What did she want?'

Robyn tried to reply – to protest – but it didn't work. Her lips moved aimlessly, attempting to produce words that simply weren't there. Admitting defeat, she took a breath. 'She was telling me to help get you into HCM.'

Toby's expression darkened. 'I'm going to kill her. Laurence too. I'm going to—'

'Don't.' Robyn grabbed his wrist. 'Please don't do anything. It really isn't worth it.'

'Robyn, I have to—'

'No, you don't. Please, Toby. I've already made a bad first impression on Laurence and your mum. I don't want to cause a scene out here, too. I'll dry off, then let's head back upstairs and just pretend it didn't happen.'

Over Toby's shoulder, the glass doors opened again, Laurence sauntering inside.

'Everything all right?' he asked breezily. 'No harm done, I hope.'

'Get out,' Toby snarled. 'Out! Just leave us alone!' He leapt to his feet, striding across the room with such urgency that

Robyn thought for a moment he might hit him. Apparently having the same thought, Laurence quickly retreated, disappearing again in the direction of the upper deck.

Toby closed the doors again and, for a little while, neither of them spoke. He was shaking, his anger radiating so powerfully that the air around him seemed to buzz. And there was a look in his eyes that Robyn had never seen before. A look that frightened her half to death.

11

On the top deck, Stephen stood with Abigail, Harper and Cam. Nobody seemed to know quite how Robyn could have fallen into the lake, although it hadn't escaped Stephen's notice that Eva had been nearby when it happened. And while no one had said as much, he would have been willing to bet the others had spotted this too.

Hearing footsteps on the staircase, Stephen saw Laurence climbing back up.

'Is she all right?' Abigail asked.

'She's fine. Toby's throwing a strop; nothing new there.'

'But what happened?'

Stephen looked to Eva. She and the bridesmaids had returned straight to the hot tub, although she had the grace to at least look shaken. Her face became a perfect picture of concern, lips parted and eyes slightly narrowed.

'I have no idea,' she said. 'The deck was wet. Maybe the heat was making her feel light-headed? I tried to catch her wrist when I saw she'd slipped, but I didn't make it to her in time.'

'There,' said Laurence. 'You see? Completely harmless. I'm sure she'll dry off and be back up here in no time.'

Brushing past the others, he went to the table and picked up the champagne glass he'd abandoned when they heard the scream. Abigail, meanwhile, was less satisfied.

'I'm going to check on her.'

'Leave her be,' said Laurence. 'She went swimming in Lake Garda – what a hardship! Stephen, come on. Can you tell your wife to stop fussing and just enjoy herself?'

Stephen met Abigail's eye, an instant, unspoken conversation passing between them. He could see in her expression that to side with Laurence now would cost him later. But this wasn't the place to make a scene.

'I'm sure she'll be fine, Abi.'

'Of course she will,' said Laurence. 'Now, let's put the music back on and open another bottle of something.'

12

Robyn insisted on showing her face again. It took an hour, but after she'd dried off and Toby seemed to have calmed down, she told him that they were going back up to the deck.

As they rejoined the group, most wore expressions of concern. Abigail, in particular, offered a half-hearted smile. The only exception was Eva. Instead, there was something distinctly unpleasant in the way she watched them cross the boards. She was in the hot tub, her face hidden by a pair of designer sunglasses, but Robyn could see it all the same. A quiet glimmer of amusement.

Taking a couple of sun loungers near the front of the deck, they watched as the landscape rolled by, the boat humming beneath them. For the most part, the rest of the trip played out as if nothing had happened. The group sipped their champagne. Music continued to blare across the water. The crew even served lunch, placing baskets of bread, bowls of salad and boards of cheese and meat onto the table.

The only moment that lifted Robyn's spirits was when, a few minutes after she and Toby had reappeared, a shadow fell over her. She immediately tensed, before realising it was Cam. The photographer was standing beside her sun lounger, carrying a bottle of spring water in one hand and a glass of champagne in the other.

'I wasn't sure which would be more helpful,' she said.

Robyn didn't want champagne, but she found herself so intensely grateful for the gesture that she eagerly took both. Cam flashed her a smile, then moved along, furiously snapping the others as they congregated around the hot tub.

When, towards the end of the afternoon, the yacht finally docked again in Riva, Chadwick and Miles announced that they should find somewhere for more drinks. Toby, however, took Robyn's hand and steered her immediately in the direction of a taxi rank.

'Toby,' Laurence called after them. 'Come on. This is ridiculous.'

Toby didn't reply, continuing instead to lead Robyn away. She heard Laurence calling out right up until Toby shut the taxi door behind her.

The villa was empty when they arrived, Margot and Jeremy seemingly still in town. Robyn wondered if they'd found the church he was hoping to visit.

After heading upstairs and changing into some clothes that hadn't been subjected to a dip in the lake, she joined Toby in the kitchen. He was leaning against the counter, staring into space. She went to him and pulled him into a hug.

'I'm sorry,' he murmured into her shoulder. 'I knew they'd give me a hard time. But I really thought . . . With you . . .' He straightened up and cleared his throat. 'I've checked for flights home. There aren't any more today, but there's one in the morning. Say the word and I'll get us a couple of seats.'

Robyn must have thought for the best part of an entire

minute before replying. She thought of all the effort she'd made in the twenty-four hours since they'd arrived. Riding in the Ferrari with Laurence. Boarding the yacht. Even playing along when Chadwick and Miles mocked her accent. She thought of it all, picturing Eva's smirk as they'd returned to the top deck, and a sudden determination overcame her.

'I don't want that,' she told him. 'I want us to go into town. Have a drink. And then I want to just get this wedding over with.'

Toby's features shifted. 'You're sure? I don't care what they think. If you want to get out of here—'

'I know,' she said. 'But I'm not having them think they've scared me off. Let's get through today. Tomorrow they'll all be so busy with the wedding that they won't have time to think about us. After that, we can go home and ignore them for the rest of their stupid married lives.'

Toby thought for a moment, before nodding. 'OK. But at the very least let's skip dinner with Eva's family tonight. The others will be so busy trying to make a good impression they probably won't even notice we aren't there.'

Robyn shook her head, summoning as much defiance as she could muster. 'We aren't skipping anything. If we're staying, we're going to do it properly.'

Toby's eyes fell to the ground. 'I don't know why you're putting up with all of this.'

Seeing him so defeated, her heart broke.

'Perhaps I'm just hoping that one day I'll break you down and send you to HCM. Become a lady of leisure and give away your fortune to a librarian's charity.'

He gave a quiet laugh. 'That's your plan, is it?'

'Might be.'

'It's a good one.'

'I thought so.'

Eyes closed, he pressed his forehead to hers. 'I love you.'

She thought back to the first time he'd told her he loved her. It had been during their first trip away. Seven or eight months after they'd started seeing each other, and with a rare weekend off work, they'd booked an Airbnb in Bath and caught the train from Paddington. He'd said it on the Saturday evening, as they'd walked through the cobbled streets. She remembered being taken completely by surprise. Remembered the brief flicker of panic in his eyes as he wondered if he'd miscalculated, then the visible relief on his face as she'd said it back.

'Love you too,' she told him.

He pulled her into another hug, planting a kiss on her head before setting off upstairs to change. Suddenly alone, she felt her determination begin to falter.

She still couldn't quite believe Eva had pushed her. The quick shove in the small of her back, the slap of the lake surface, the immediate sense of the vast chasm of water looming beneath her . . . Again, she wondered what had prompted such a reaction; her refusal to help Laurence or the slight against Eva herself. Whichever it was, she resolved to stay out of Eva's way as much as possible for the remainder of the weekend.

Eager for a distraction, she noticed a book sitting on one of the kitchen counters, recognising it as the one Jeremy had been reading when she came downstairs for coffee. Open on a familiar page, Robyn saw the bronze-hilted dagger that seemed to have caught his attention. She looked at the image for a moment, the jewel embedded in the dagger's handle gleaming on the page like a bright green eye.

Able to take a closer look than she had done that morning, she read the paragraph of text that accompanied the photo. It had a name, apparently. The Vincenzi dagger. Awarded by the Republic of Venice to the general who reclaimed Castello Fiore from French invaders in the sixteenth century; Robyn felt her eyes pop when she saw, at the bottom of the paragraph, how much money it was estimated to be worth.

She flicked through a few more pages, skim-reading sections about the castle's architecture and the various Italian nobles who had occupied it over the years. Much like the dagger, she began to get the impression that it had been more of a ceremonial sort of place than an actual strategic fortification. If anything, it seemed to be just a particularly impressive home for whoever happened at that time to be presiding over the region.

Once Toby had reappeared, she closed the book and they walked the short distance into town. Despite the half-mile from the villa being entirely downhill, they each worked up a sweat in the late-afternoon heat. Not that they complained. Robyn enjoyed London for its constant rhythm, but this place had an altogether different kind of vibrancy. They wandered around a market in an open square, before winding through narrow side streets, enjoying the shade as they perused the shops. There were tea towels and fridge magnets for sale, emblazoned with the outline of the lake. Racks in the street that were heavily laden with postcards, snorkels and bottles of limoncello.

After an hour of exploring, they stopped at a restaurant right beside the lake. Robyn had never seen water so clear. It was like looking through a window, dozens of tiny fish swarming above neatly arranged pebbles on the lakebed. Tearing her eyes away, she looked up and saw the castle, and before she could resist it, felt a pang of sadness that their time there — more than that, their first trip abroad together — was so completely overshadowed by the wedding. She took Toby's hand, wondering if he might be thinking something similar. She hoped he was.

She wasn't sure how long they sat there in the end. Despite being due in just a couple of hours to have dinner with Eva's family, they shared a bottle of wine and a plate of seafood. As they ate, Robyn watched the people milling around them. There were couples drinking wine on restaurant terraces. Families with young children eating gelato. Locals carrying paper bags full of groceries. She wondered where they had all come from, pondering over who was staying in an Airbnb apartment and who had a suite in a five-star hotel. Which couples were celebrating anniversaries and which had eloped with secret lovers.

It was the people their own age who she settled on the longest. With rucksacks on their shoulders and maps in their hands, she imagined where they might be going next. Rome? Milan? Or perhaps even further? She wished she could go with them, surprising herself with just how desperately she wanted it.

Not once did they speak about Eva, Laurence or the wedding. Instead, they let their imaginations run wild about Toby's bar. They discussed the decor, the menu, the name. Everything that would need deciding if his loan came through. With the conversation beginning to lull after a heated debate about whether Toby should offer traditional or strawberry mojitos, Robyn tentatively changed the subject.

'You told Laurence I'd studied journalism.'

Toby grimaced. 'Sorry. It was a few months ago. Every time I spoke to them they asked about you. One of the questions they kept on hitting me with was what school you went to. Whether you'd been to uni. I just needed something to get them off my back.' He paused. 'Do you wish I hadn't?'

Robyn shrugged. 'It just took me by surprise.'

Toby hesitated again, the silence lingering a little longer this time. 'And have you thought any more about Jess's message?'

'A little.'

'Come on, Robyn. You can't just pass up an opportunity to write for somewhere like *Cosmo*.'

'You mean an opportunity to write about Kardashian look-alikes and *I'm a Celeb*? It isn't exactly hard-hitting journalism.'

She forced a laugh, but Toby didn't return it.

'That seems a little harsh,' he said, frowning. 'Don't you think you should at least try it?'

Robyn didn't reply straight away. She knew he was being supportive. Perhaps he felt he had to return the enthusiasm she'd shown for the bar. But he just didn't understand. In fairness, how could he? She'd never told him the full truth of it all. As far as he knew, she'd applied for a few junior reporting jobs after university but just hadn't caught her big break. What she'd never quite managed to tell him was how she'd given up, her ambitions fading away with nothing to take their place.

She was adrift. Like the yacht that afternoon, she was out on the water with no real destination.

Apparently recognising that she wasn't going to share any more, Toby looked out over the lake again.

'You sure you don't want to skip this dinner?'

Robyn nodded, squaring her shoulders. 'We're going.'

'Come on, then.' He reached for her hand across the table. 'Let's get it over with.'

13

Harper doubted her mood could sink lower if she tried.

Walking from their hotel, she and Cam had made sure to arrive first at the restaurant Eva had chosen, waiting outside so that they could get shots of the wedding party arriving for dinner. The sun was just beginning to set, grazing the tops of the mountains and tingeing the clouds a dusky shade of pink. Even the water was changing colour, the shimmering turquoise they had seen that afternoon beginning to blush in the evening light. When the cars eventually pulled in, Cam sprang into action, furiously taking pictures of the soon-to-be bride and groom as they stepped from the Ferrari, then bringing them to stand by the water, the castle sitting proudly in the background.

Eva lived for the camera, shoving her handbag into Harper's hand the moment Cam approached. Not that Harper cared. With Eva posing in a sweeping midnight-blue dress and a glistening diamond necklace, she felt a flicker of excitement as Cam positioned her and Laurence for the various pictures.

This could work, she thought, imagining the magazine cover. It really might work.

After Eva and Laurence had disappeared into the restaurant,

Cam lingered for a moment on the waterfront, taking a few more shots of the lake.

'How's it coming?' Harper asked.

She approached tentatively, still wary of how Cam had snapped at her for touching her bag beside the yacht. It seemed she had no need to worry, though.

'Beautifully,' Cam replied brightly. 'Eva's a dream to shoot.'

Once Cam was satisfied, they made to follow Eva into the restaurant, only to find Margot Heywood standing in their path.

'No,' she said. 'This is a family occasion. You aren't taking any pictures inside.'

Harper affected her most dazzling smile. 'It's all right, Mrs Heywood. It's for the magazine feature. This is Cam. She's from *London*—'

'I know who she is. And while I can't tell Laurence not to have her at his wedding, she isn't welcome tonight.'

'You aren't even going to let her in?'

'I am not.'

Keeping her smile fixed in place, Harper carefully slipped a slight edge into her voice. 'Can I speak to Eva, please? This is important. She won't want—'

'You're taking pictures of Eva's wedding. Not of our family at dinner. I'm sorry, but she isn't coming in.'

Harper turned to Cam, no idea what to say.

'It's fine,' said Cam. 'I'll head back to the hotel. Start sorting through the pictures from the yacht.'

'Shall I come too?'

'You go ahead. One of us might as well get a nice dinner.'

Following Margot, Harper was shown by a waiter to the first floor, where an open terrace offered perhaps the best view of the lake she had seen so far. Not that she had a chance to appreciate it. The moment she stepped inside, Eva was on her.

'Where's the photographer?'

'Mrs Heywood sent her away.'

'What do you mean, sent her away?'

'She said we can take all the pictures we like of the wedding but not of a family dinner.'

Eva's eyes flew wide. 'And you let her go? What is *the point* of you?' She scowled, stalking away before Harper could reply.

Following the others to a long table laid out for them at the end of the terrace, Harper glumly took her place beside one of Laurence's friends, Chadwick. She caught his eyes flick up and down as she sat down, the corners of his mouth twitching into a small smile.

For a few seconds she thought about the possibility of taking him back to the hotel after dinner. He wasn't bad-looking. She might as well find something in Italy to enjoy.

Grimacing, she scoured the thought from her mind. She had to focus on the task at hand. Picking up one of Laurence's idiotic friends was hardly going to help Eva's career. Nor, for that matter, would it save her own.

An Italian couple approached the table, who Harper took to be Eva's parents. Rising to his feet, she saw Laurence march ahead to introduce Margot. Eva's dad, Vito, stepped forward and kissed Margot on both cheeks, greeting her with a broad smile and a thick Italian accent. Harper assumed that Paola,

Eva's mum, didn't speak much English, slowly saying how good it was to meet her. Margot returned the compliment, telling her that she had raised a wonderful daughter, and Vito immediately offered a translation.

Harper had to make a conscious effort not to laugh out loud. A wonderful daughter. If only they knew.

14

All things considered, dinner went smoothly.

Just as Robyn had hoped, Laurence and Eva seemed to have little interest in her, both being far too busy ensuring the first meeting between their respective parents went smoothly. She and Toby were actually seated at the far end of the table. Whether it had happened by accident or design, Robyn couldn't say. Nor did she particularly care. She was just relieved to be out of the way.

With ravioli to start, fish for her main course – described simply on the menu as 'lake fish' – and tiramisu for dessert, the food was by far the best Robyn had tasted since they'd arrived. Making quiet conversation with Toby, the only time that either Laurence or Eva seemed to even notice they were there was while the starters were being cleared.

'Are you feeling better, Robyn?' Eva had called sweetly down the table. 'I hope you're OK. You must be so careful in this heat, especially when you aren't used to it.'

A note of tension had hung in the air. Abigail, in particular, scowled, while Harper looked guiltily at her plate.

Robyn smiled back at her. 'Fine, thank you. No harm done. The heat will need to try harder than that.'

As the evening went by, Robyn became more and more intrigued by the dynamic between the two families. She heard Laurence boasting to Stephen and Jeremy about the classic cars Vito sold in his dealership, noticed Eva shunning her nervous-looking sister in favour of her glamorous friends and listened as Margot and Paola made brisk conversation about the wedding preparations.

The atmosphere between Eva and Margot, specifically, Robyn found to be surprisingly cold. With Paola's English seemingly limited, the two mothers used Vito as a translator, although Eva had to duck in from time to time when a particular word evaded him. When she did, she was especially curt, snapping at Margot with just a word or a phrase before returning her attention to Laurence or the bridesmaids.

Despite this, all seemed for the most part to go well. Laurence certainly looked pleased with how things were progressing. It wasn't until Robyn visited the loo, shortly after the coffee and brandy had been served, that she realised this first meeting between the parents might be less cordial than their conversation over dinner suggested.

The toilet doors were behind a thin wall, which Robyn assumed was to shield them from the diners' view. That was certainly the prevailing logic at the Willows. As her own manager had once grumpily told her, a customer paying ninety pounds for their côte de boeuf doesn't want to know every time someone uses the facilities. As such, the toilets in the Willows were so far away they might as well have been in a different building altogether.

But in that particular moment, what the narrow wall actually meant was that as Robyn stepped back into the restaurant, and heard Vito Bianchi speaking nearby in a low, frustrated tone, he had no clue that she was there.

'This is disgraceful,' he protested. 'Laurence is a good man and he will be a good husband to Eva. But I am in no need of his money. My business—'

'We're well aware of how your business is faring.'

It was Jeremy Lambourne who replied. He was speaking quietly, making it difficult to pick out every word over the sound of clattering plates and cheerful Italian voices. Robyn actually found herself grateful for his cut-glass drawl, which was so out of place it helped her to discern their conversation from the rest of the noise.

'Just as we're aware,' Margot added, 'of the sort of people from whom you've been accepting loans.'

They must have been huddling in the corner of the restaurant, right beside the toilets. Hovering behind the thin wall, Robyn knew that she should move, or at the very least that she should make a sound of some kind to let them know she was there. If she were caught eavesdropping she doubted she would ever be able to concoct an explanation that would satisfy Margot.

And yet she stayed exactly where she was. Emboldened, perhaps, by the bottle of rosé she and Toby had shared with their seafood, her curiosity ultimately won out.

'Loans?' Vito retorted. 'There are no loans.'

'There are loans, Mr Bianchi,' said Jeremy. 'I've made a detailed investigation into your affairs, so let's not either of us pretend that your dealership is in anything other than serious trouble.'

'An investigation?' Vito hissed. 'Into my business? How dare you? Is this how the English treat family? With insults and threats?' He swore in Italian. 'So what if there are loans? Is it not acceptable for a business to take out a loan?'

'From a bank,' said Margot. 'Not from the sort of organisations *you* have been dealing with.'

'We haven't shared this with Laurence,' said Jeremy, his voice, as always, perfectly level. 'Nor do we intend to. But rest assured that we will be watching closely, and if you imagine that he might one day be persuaded to ride to the rescue of his dear father-in-law – that you'll receive a single penny from this marriage – I strongly advise you to think again. HCM will never be available to you, nor the people to whom you're indebted. As long as I continue to breathe, you can be quite certain of that.'

Much as she wanted to keep listening, Robyn knew she had to move. If someone caught her on their way to the toilets, or if Toby started to wonder where she'd gone, the game would be up.

Pushing open the toilet door, she pulled it briskly closed again with a satisfying thump. As expected, she heard the conversation immediately stop. Stepping from behind the wall, she flashed them the most innocent expression she could manage as she came into view, trying even to feign some surprise at seeing how they were huddled. She didn't wait to see if her efforts were successful, instead hurrying straight back across the terrace.

As she neared the table, she saw that Toby was looking at his phone. Probably scrolling through Twitter, she assumed, in an effort to avoid making conversation with the others while she was away.

But as she grew closer, she became less convinced. He wasn't idly scrolling. He was reading something, his features etched into an intense frown.

Seeing her approaching, he quickly put the phone away, a smile snapping into place.

'All OK?' she asked.

'Fine,' he said. 'Just a work thing. Someone's left us a bad review on TripAdvisor and the owner's pretty pissed off.'

'About a TripAdvisor review?'

Toby nodded, lifting the wine bottle from the table. 'Pour you another glass?'

Robyn didn't reply straight away. In the year they'd been seeing each other, Toby had never lied to her. At least, not that she was aware of. And while she struggled to believe that he ever would, this exchange just didn't sit right. His stern expression had vanished just a little too quickly. His tone was slightly too bright. His attempt to change the subject too eager.

She locked eyes with him, considering the possibility of challenging him. But after a moment's thought, she decided not to push it. She trusted him. And regardless of whether his boss actually was giving him grief over a TripAdvisor review, she wasn't prepared to call him out in front of the Heywood clan.

She nudged her wine glass towards him. 'Sure. Thanks.'

As he began to pour, Robyn turned her mind to the conversation she'd overheard, debating whether to share it with Toby. Eva's father was clearly in financial trouble. But did Eva know? Robyn doubted it. If Margot and Jeremy had their facts straight, it seemed Laurence certainly didn't.

She wondered what Margot had meant; that Vito was in debt

to someone other than a bank. Could he have borrowed money from family, perhaps? Friends, even?

There was no way of knowing. At least, not from what little she'd heard.

As she weighed up her options, she resolved to keep this nugget to herself. While she didn't want to make a habit of keeping things from Toby, she could far too easily imagine him using it as a weapon when he and Laurence next fell out. And if it emerged that he only knew because of what *she* had over-heard, she suspected any chance of the Heywoods tolerating her presence would completely evaporate.

Her train of thought was interrupted by a glug of wine splashing onto the table in front of her.

'Sorry,' Toby murmured. 'Must have had a couple too many.'

He tried to laugh it off, but Robyn wasn't convinced. She couldn't remember a single time she had ever seen him spill a drink. He could pour a perfect measure by sight alone. Looking closer, she noticed now that his hand was trembling slightly.

But before she could question it, Eva's voice rang out across the table.

'Where's my bag?' she demanded. 'I need my mirror, Harper. Where's my fucking bag?'

Robyn watched as Harper passed a small handbag across the table. Rummaging inside, Eva fetched out a small mirror and carefully prised a fleck of salad from between her front teeth. As she went to replace the mirror, however, she frowned, drawing out a folded slip of paper. One of the bridesmaids asked her something in Italian. Eva shrugged, shaking her head as she unfolded it.

'What is it, darling?'

Laurence scooped up a wine bottle and refilled her glass. But Eva didn't reply. She gave no sign that she'd even heard him, her eyes glued to whatever it was that had been tucked inside her bag.

'Eva?' Laurence's brow creased with concern. 'Eva, what is it?'

She took a breath. And another. Then, her eyes still not straying from the paper, she spoke in a low, menacing tone.

'Who's done this?'

Suddenly, her eyes flicked up. Looking down the table, she met Robyn's gaze with a look that could have killed. She moved next to Toby. Then to Abigail. And finally to Harper.

'Who the fuck has done this?'

Her voice rose this time to a near shriek, drawing the attention of almost the entire restaurant. Trying desperately to calm her, Laurence snatched the scrap of paper from her hand. The instant he looked at it, and saw whatever it contained, his own face lit up with alarm. He stared for a few seconds at the paper, looked at Eva's bag and then back at the paper again.

'What is it, Laurence?'

Toby called down the table, but Laurence didn't answer. Instead, he slapped the note down on the table. It was a short message. Two sentences printed in bold type.

I know what you did. The secret you've locked away.

15

Vito Bianchi couldn't believe what he was hearing.

For the best part of a year, he had managed to hide his debt.
A year of lying. Of scraping and clawing to keep his family
blissfully in the dark. Now, on the day before he would set
things straight, Margot Heywood and Jeremy Lambourne had
arrived, and revealed that his darkest secret was in fact no secret
at all.

He simply couldn't fathom it. They had been at a family
dinner. The night before their children's wedding, for God's
sake.

How had they even known? This investigation into his
affairs . . . What had they been looking for? He could understand wanting to protect their family's interests, but it beggared
belief that they would go so far as to formally investigate him.
It must have been thorough, too. The people he was indebted
to didn't exactly advertise their services.

Over Jeremy's shoulder, Vito saw Paola approaching and
felt a stab of panic.

'*Va tutto bene?*' she asked brightly.

He forced a smile. 'It's fine,' he told her in Italian. 'We just

can't quite agree on who's paying the bill. I'm insisting that as the parents of the bride, it would be our pleasure. But Mrs Heywood and Mr Lambourne are putting up quite the fight.'

He quickly offered an English translation, prompting Margot to adopt an expression somewhere between a smile and a grimace.

'You're both far too generous,' she said. 'I insist we pay half.'

Vito felt his fear turn to hatred. Thank God they had at least spoken to him alone. For Paola to discover the danger they were in would be disastrous.

One day. In just one day his debt would finally be cleared. The means by which he was going to achieve it frightened him half to death. But there was no other option. He had long accepted that with the interest these people were demanding, he couldn't pay them back. If he didn't do this, they would come to his home. They would come for his family. He couldn't allow that to happen.

But could he even still go through with it? Surely, Margot and Jeremy's knowledge of his predicament changed everything. If something went wrong ... If, somehow, he was caught, wouldn't they immediately see what had happened?

It didn't matter. His debtors were hardly going to let him back out. And even if they did, what good would it do? Better he be caught trying to make things right than let his family suffer the consequences of doing nothing.

There was no other way. When they were inside the castle, and the time came, he would simply have to make a success of it. And if Margot Heywood or Jeremy Lambourne tried to stop him . . .

He supposed he would just have to make sure they failed.

They were interrupted by a sudden commotion coming from the table. Looking over, Vito saw Eva rising abruptly to her feet. Her voice rose too, although from across the terrace he couldn't hear exactly what was being said.

He turned to Paola. 'What's happening?'

She shook her head, apparently none the wiser.

'Eva,' Laurence called after her. 'Eva!'

He stood as well, watching as she marched from the terrace, her bridesmaids scurrying after her.

Vito looked to Margot and Jeremy, hoping they might somehow explain. But the two of them simply watched, a slight narrowing of Margot's eyes the only sign they'd seen anything happen at all.

Returning his gaze to Laurence, Vito was just in time to see him snatch something up from the table, stuff it into his pocket and hurry after his fiancée. Those he left behind – the grooms-men, his brother and Eva's agent – looked just as bemused as Vito himself felt.

'I think,' said Jeremy, 'that perhaps dinner might be over.'

16

The mood when they returned to the villa was bleak.

After Eva had stormed from the restaurant, loudly declaring that she was returning to her hotel, those left at the table agreed that taxis should be called.

Laurence was the first to leave. Clearly furious with how the evening had turned out, he was eager to drive back in the Ferrari, but Jeremy just about succeeded in convincing him that he'd drunk too much wine to get behind the wheel. Reluctantly agreeing, he climbed instead into the back of a slightly beaten-up Vauxhall with Chadwick and Miles. Stephen and Abigail joined Margot and Jeremy in the next taxi, after which Vito, Paola and Harper all left on foot, their hotels apparently just a few minutes from the restaurant. Robyn and Toby took the last car, the driver speeding them back up the hill as they left the town behind.

Inside, the villa was completely silent. No dance music blared. No boisterous laughter echoed from the lounge. Instead, Robyn could see Margot and Jeremy speaking quietly on the sofa, while Chadwick and Miles paced back and forth on the patio. There was no sign of Laurence.

Toby went straight to the kitchen.

'Aren't you coming to bed?' Robyn asked.

'In a minute.' Heading to the fridge, he withdrew a bottle of wine. 'Drink?'

She didn't reply straight away. But it wasn't just that she couldn't imagine anything she wanted less in that moment than another drink. It was him. Something was off, and for reasons she couldn't fathom, he wasn't going to explain it to her.

Whatever it was, she couldn't attribute it to their afternoon on the yacht. By the time they went for dinner his mood had lifted, bolstered by their trip into town. Nor could she simply put it down to what had happened in the restaurant. She thought of the minutes before Eva found the message in her bag, remembering how he'd been staring so intently at his phone. The way his hand had trembled when he poured her another glass of wine . . .

'Toby . . .'

He looked at her, waiting. But the words just didn't come. If he wasn't going to tell her in the restaurant what was going through his head, she doubted he would now. So what could she ask him? If he was OK? She knew already that he wasn't.

He held up the bottle. 'You sure you don't want a glass?'

She shook her head. She was aching for sleep, her conversation with Jeremy when she rose early to make coffee feeling like days ago. Perhaps that was what bothered him, too. Perhaps he was just tired. Worn out after twenty-four hours with his family. He had, after all, been prepared just a few hours ago to get on a plane and fly home.

She looked at the clock. No wonder she was so exhausted; it was coming up to midnight. With a jolt, another thought

116

occurred to her. The wedding was taking place at midday. In just twelve hours they would be there, inside the castle.

Robyn climbed the stairs alone, her sense of unease beginning to grow.

I know what you did. The secret you've locked away.

What, exactly, had Eva done? Robyn suspected it was a question with a variety of unappealing answers. Just that afternoon she'd pushed a woman she'd known for all of two minutes off a moving yacht.

But what, in the context of this message, had she done? And who had given it to her? They had all been in the restaurant. And yet, it seemed Harper had been holding onto Eva's bag for the duration of the meal. Could she have put it down for a moment? Left it unattended to visit the ladies' or the bar? Harper seemed so attentive that Robyn struggled to imagine it. And yet, she must have done. How else could it have happened?

It also wasn't lost on Robyn that the message hadn't been handwritten. It had been printed. And with no printer in the villa – certainly not one in the restaurant – it must have been prepared ahead of time. The only conclusion she could draw from that particular assumption was that someone had *planned* to show it to Eva. It hadn't been a spur-of-the-moment decision. Someone had brought it to Lake Garda with the intention of her reading it.

Opening the bedroom door, she felt a presence behind her. Expecting to find that Toby had followed her up the stairs, instead she saw Abigail. Sweeping a nervous glance up and down the landing, she ushered Robyn inside and quickly closed the door.

'Tell me it wasn't you.'

Robyn peered at her, so confused that she had no reply.

'That message,' Abigail said. 'In Eva's bag. Tell me it wasn't you.'

'Why would it have been me? I don't even know what it meant!'

Abigail stared at her. 'Look,' she said. 'I wouldn't blame you. Pushing you off the yacht today, and after the boys were so rude to you yesterday . . . I'd want to shake Eva up too. But this is too far. If it was you, you have to tell me.'

For a few seconds, Robyn just watched her. She saw the fear in Abigail's eyes. Heard the slight tremor in her voice. She was deadly serious.

'I swear. I didn't do it.'

'So it was Toby.'

'Why would Toby—'

Abigail grabbed her wrist. 'No one else at that table would give Eva that message. Do you understand? *No one*. So if it wasn't you, it had to be Toby.'

'But why would Toby do that? Abigail, what did it even mean?'

For a moment, it looked as if Abigail might cry.

'I want to believe you,' she said quietly. 'I really do.' Her grip tightened on Robyn's wrist. 'It was one of you. I know it. The others will all know it. And while I really, really hope it was Toby, I'm going to tell you this too. Because you need to know how serious I am.'

She leaned in close, dropping her voice so low it was barely more than a growl. 'I know they've been horrible to you. But you've made your point. You've freaked Eva out. Now drop it. Or if you're planning to do more, keep it between you and her.

Because if you try to threaten my family – *my* family – I'll make sure it's more than a dip in the lake that you'll have to look forward to.'

Before Robyn could reply, Abigail leapt to her feet and barged from the room.

For a long while after she'd gone, Robyn sat on the bed, heart racing as she tried to unpick what had just happened. She couldn't speak. She couldn't even move. She was so utterly confused by whatever Abigail had been suggesting that she simply didn't know what to do.

After a few minutes had passed, Toby came into the room. Gently closing the door, he saw Robyn perching on the edge of the bed and fixed her with a quizzical look.

'You OK?'

She nodded. 'Yes. Sorry, yes. Just . . . thinking.'

Toby hovered for a moment, clearly struggling to believe her. But he didn't push. Instead, he moved into the room and began silently getting ready for bed.

'Toby . . .' she said. 'What did that message mean?'

His back was turned. Even so, he hesitated, pausing for just a second too long. 'I don't know.'

'You didn't . . .' She tailed off, almost too afraid to ask. 'After what Eva did on the yacht today. It wasn't . . . ?'

His turned to face her, eyes wide. 'You think it was me?'

'I don't know. But if it *was* . . . If it was some way of just freaking Eva out. Getting her to back off and leave me alone—'

He sat beside her on the bed, taking her hand. 'I promise. I don't know who gave Eva that message. But I swear to you, it wasn't me.'

She didn't believe he would lie to her. But nor did she doubt

Abigail. She could still feel her grip on her wrist. Hear the fear in her voice.

No one else at that table would give Eva that message. Do you understand? No one.

They didn't talk about it any further, getting into bed and turning out the light with barely a 'goodnight'. But by the time Toby had fallen asleep, Robyn was wired. Her mind raced, the question of the message nagging like an itch she couldn't reach.

Leave it, she urged herself. Just leave it.

But she knew that she couldn't. She was rolling down a slope, scrambling for handholds that just weren't there.

With the prospect of sleep now seemingly long gone, she reached for her phone and opened Instagram in a desperate bid to distract herself. She realised her mistake the second the app opened. Right there, at the top of her newsfeed, was a picture from the yacht. Eva and her bridesmaids, leaning against the railing with Castello Fiore in the background. Posted at midday, the caption simply read: *Twenty-four hours to go . . .*

Opening Eva's Instagram profile, Robyn began to scroll aimlessly. She whipped through months' worth of brightly coloured photos taken in parks and cocktail bars; past dozens of carefully curated pictures spotlighting fashion labels, jewellery brands and upmarket restaurants.

She must have scrolled for a good few minutes before one picture caused her to stop. Eva and Laurence, both beaming, with a group of friends at a swanky restaurant in Chelsea. The caption read: *The most beautiful dinner tonight for Olive's birthday. Thirty, flirty and thriving! Grazie mille @DolceVitaRestaurant for looking after us so well. This Italian is very impressed.*

Robyn couldn't say why this picture had caught her eye.

There was nothing special about the caption, nor, from what she could see, about the restaurant. After peering at it for a few moments, though, she realised why it had struck her as odd.

She must have just looked at well over a hundred pictures. And yet, she was fairly certain this was the first to include Laurence.

She went to the post in which Eva had announced their engagement. Even in that one, Laurence was nowhere to be seen. The picture was of Eva's engagement ring, sparkling on her outstretched hand.

Beside her, Toby stirred, murmuring something unintelligible in his sleep. Worried that the light from her phone would wake him, Robyn quickly switched her screen off, only turning it on again once she was satisfied that he was still asleep.

Her mind fizzed, Eva's Instagram having given her a new idea. Over the course of Eva's career, Harper had clearly managed to land some significant brand partnerships. And yet, Toby had said on the yacht that none of the nutritional brands she wanted to work with would touch her. Robyn couldn't imagine what she could have done both to upset a nutritional company and to earn the note she'd received at dinner. But however tenuous it might be, it was the only lead she had.

Abandoning Instagram, she went instead to Google, clicked *News* and searched *Eva Bianchi nutrition*.

She scrolled through the resulting headlines but none looked particularly promising. Eager not to give up, though, she thought again of the conversation she'd overheard on the patio.

A bad influence? Toby had protested. *That's pretty rich, considering what Eva had you—*

Returning to her phone, Robyn searched instead for *Eva Bianchi nutrition influencer*.

Halfway down the first page, she found it. An article from the *Guardian* that stopped her in her tracks.

Heart pounding, she took a deep breath, tapped the link and began to read:

INFLUENCER BLAMED AFTER TEENAGER FOUND UNCONSCIOUS

Owen Lock, Lifestyle Correspondent

An ambulance has been called to a home in Reading after a teenager who had been sustaining herself on meal replacement supplements advertised on social media was found unconscious by her parents.

Rachel Carlisle, 15, was treated by paramedics after fainting in the family home. They reported her blood pressure as being dangerously low, while her friends revealed that for several days she had sustained herself solely on a line of ultra-low-calorie meal replacement shakes. Rachel had seen the shakes advertised on social media and been feigning sickness, as well as claiming to have eaten elsewhere, in order to avoid meals at home.

Rachel's parents, Mark and Susan Carlisle, place the blame for their daughter's experience on Eva Bianchi, a London-based influencer from Bologna, Italy. Ms Bianchi shares content revolving around her life in the city with over 500,000 followers on Instagram.

'There are children viewing this material,' Mrs Carlisle has said. 'Eva Bianchi spoke about rapid weight loss to an audience that includes impressionable, vulnerable people, without also sharing any of the associated science or potential dangers, and my daughter has required emergency medical attention as a result. It's obscenely irresponsible.'

Ms Bianchi was contacted via her agent regarding Mrs Carlisle's claims but declined to comment. After spending a night in hospital under observation, Rachel is now home.

Slim-Shake has condemned all of Ms Bianchi's material featuring its products, stressing that the company had no involvement and that the shakes are intended as part of a balanced, nutritional diet.

Reaching the end of the article, Robyn set down her phone.

She supposed this explained why there were no nutritional brands willing to provide Eva with work. How was Harper supposed to convince a company that made its name off the back of health and well-being to partner with an influencer whose fasting advice had put a teenager in hospital?

But did it explain what had happened at dinner?

Robyn doubted it. She couldn't see why anyone at the table would be so offended by what had happened to Rachel Carlisle. And even if they had been, this was hardly a secret locked away. It had been reported on by a national newspaper.

Toby stirred again. This time, Robyn put the phone on the bedside table.

She looked at the back of his head, listening to his rhythmic breathing. He knew what the message had meant. She had no doubt of that. Just as she had no doubt that he hadn't simply been reading a scolding from his boss when she returned to the table. The question was why he would keep any of it from her.

She thought again of her conversation with Abigail. Could she be right? Could the message have been Toby's?

That, in itself, would raise questions Robyn couldn't answer. If she was right – if someone had had the foresight to bring the message with them, potentially even from the UK – then Toby planting it in Eva's bag couldn't be a simple case of reacting to her behaviour on the yacht.

Lying on her back, Robyn stared up at the ceiling.

She wanted to call him out in the morning. To tell him that she knew he was holding back, and wouldn't settle for anything less than a full explanation. But on the morning of the wedding . . . ? Tensions were already high enough.

Begrudgingly, she accepted that she would have to leave it. As painful as the thought of Toby keeping something from her might be, she couldn't afford to fall out with him on the day of the wedding.

For now, at least, it would have to wait.

The day of the wedding

17

Having recently turned twenty-six, it sometimes seemed to Robyn as if every other week another of her friends was either getting married or engaged, her summers rapidly filling up with engagement parties, hen weekends and of course wedding days.

At the weddings she'd attended before, the hours getting ready in the morning had almost been as exciting as the event itself. The anticipation over the venue, the party, finally putting on the outfit she'd spent so many weeks choosing . . .

Not so, that morning in Lake Garda.

For one thing, the heat was the most intense it had been since they'd arrived, the air conditioning inside the villa working so hard Robyn thought she could hear it beginning to rattle. But the simple truth was that the mood hadn't recovered from the previous evening.

In fairness, Laurence tried. He bounded into the lounge, his voice filled with enthusiasm. 'Bloody hell, everyone. Let's look like we're pleased to be here, shall we? I'm getting married today!'

Robyn wondered if it was an act. If so, it was convincing. But she remembered the panic in his eyes as he'd tried to follow

Eva from the restaurant. Whatever had been meant by the message in her bag – the secret she'd locked away – Robyn was willing to bet it had frightened him just as much as it had his fiancée.

Then there was Toby.

He'd been in a subdued mood since the moment they woke, responding to any attempt at conversation with one-word answers and carrying himself more as if he were about to face some gruelling doctor's examination than his brother's wedding.

Robyn tried to remind herself of how strained the relationship between the two brothers seemed to be becoming. He'll be fine, she told herself. Once the wedding's over, and there's some distance between them again, he'll bounce back.

And yet she couldn't dismiss all that had happened the previous evening. Abigail's certainty that he must have been the one to slip Eva the message. The way he'd seemed so nervous just before she found it. Even the news report Robyn had read on Rachel Carlisle.

Whether any of it suggested that Abigail was right – that the message must have been Toby's – Robyn had no idea. Whether it was even all connected, she was less sure still. She was willing to bet that Eva inadvertently hospitalising a teenager went some way towards explaining why Harper was struggling to win her work in health and well-being. But she struggled to believe it was the secret Eva had supposedly locked away, let alone that bringing it up would cause as much upset as it had.

After a tense breakfast of pastries and fruit, they all retired upstairs to change. Robyn had bought a pale blue dress for the wedding. Carefully chosen, it was the most lightweight material she could find, and her shoulders would be shielded from the sun. It was an appropriate colour for the occasion and the setting, but subtle enough that there was no risk whatsoever of her outshining Margot, the bridesmaids or – heaven forbid – Eva herself.

Toby, meanwhile, had put considerably less thought into his attire. He owned just one suit, a three-piece number in a shade of blue so dark it might as well have been black, and while Robyn had tried for several weeks to convince him to pick up something a little lighter, her pleas had fallen on deaf ears. The explanation he'd given for his stubborn refusal was that he had no need of a second suit. In reality, Robyn suspected that had this been any other bride and groom, he would happily have made the effort.

Making their way back to the lounge, they found that the mood was gradually beginning to lift. Dressed in matching cream-coloured linen suits, Laurence, Chadwick and Miles were exchanging jokes and sipping from glasses of whisky. It seemed they were going open-collar in the heat, each displaying a triangle of tanned skin in place of a tie. White flowers were pinned to their lapels, ankles showing above what looked like brand-new loafers.

As Robyn and Toby joined the group, Laurence held out another whisky. 'One for the road,' he said. 'Toast your big brother before he signs his life away.'

Robyn tensed, expecting Toby to turn him down. But she breathed a silent sigh of relief when he did accept, raising the glass to his soon-to-be-married brother.

Stephen and Abigail were there too, although they appeared considerably more reserved. Stephen seemed not to have touched his whisky, while Abigail loitered on the edge of the group. For a split second, she and Robyn locked eyes. Offering her a smile, Robyn saw Abigail quickly look away, her gaze dropping to a glass of lemon water.

Margot and Jeremy were the last to join them. Like the groomsmen, Jeremy had also chosen a linen suit, although his was pencil-grey. Margot, meanwhile, wore a stunning violet dress, accompanied by what was perhaps the largest hat Robyn had ever seen.

A few minutes before eleven o'clock, a pair of taxis rolled up to the villa and ferried them the short journey into town. Looking out of the window, Robyn saw the market in the square, crates of fruit and light silk scarfs being sold from wooden stalls. For a moment, she fantasised about telling the driver to stop. About jumping from the taxi and spending the day exploring the town, just as she had with Toby the previous afternoon.

It was a pleasant image, but she didn't allow herself to linger on it. Instead, she reminded herself that they were nearly done. That once this day was over with, they would be heading home.

Turning away from the market, she looked instead to Toby. 'Are Harper and Cam meeting us in the harbour?'

He shook his head. 'Laurence says that Eva and the bridesmaids have been on the island all morning. Cam went with them, to take some shots of them all getting ready. I guess that means Harper went too.'

Arriving in the harbour, they met a group of Italians, who it emerged were Paola's brother and his wife, two cousins and a couple of Eva's old friends from school. None seemed to speak much English, resulting in an exchange of slightly awkward smiles, nods and '*buongiorno*'s as the two parties waited to be ferried to the island.

Two strangers were also there, lingering on the edge of the group. They intrigued Robyn most. Both were lean, with dark suits, dark hair and even darker eyes. One had a light beard and a small ponytail tied tightly behind his head, while the other looked as if he should be starring in a teenage romcom, fresh-faced, with his hair hanging loose at his shoulders.

It was curious. At first glance, there appeared to be quite an age gap between them. But the more Robyn studied them, the more she began to suspect they must be around the same age. Late twenties, perhaps. Only a year or two older than she was herself. It was the way they carried themselves, she realised, that distinguished them. The bearded man was radiating an almost ferocious kind of energy, his brow creased and his eyes twitching around the harbour. His fresh-faced companion seemed less confident. Nervous, even.

'Nice to meet you,' Laurence announced, striding towards them with his hand outstretched. 'And who might you be?'

It seemed the two men didn't speak much English, and while Robyn didn't quite catch their names, she heard them just about manage to communicate that they were brothers – cousins of Eva's, on Vito's side of the family. Their father, they explained – Vito's brother – was ill and couldn't travel. They hadn't seen Eva in some years, but they had come to attend the wedding in his place.

'Well, it's good to have you,' said Laurence, clapping them each on the shoulder. 'I'm sure it means a lot to Vito. And to Eva, as well. I'll look forward to us all getting better acquainted after the ceremony.'

Despite her strategic choice of dress, Robyn felt as if she could be standing inside a sauna. A few metres away, she saw a barrel of flowers beginning to wilt, their heads drooping in the heat. She imagined she must look in a similar state. She certainly felt it. Glancing around at the others, she saw that they too seemed to be struggling. Abigail, in particular, had already gone red, her cheeks flushed. Even Laurence and the groomsmen were beginning to sweat inside their linen suits.

The heat was growing so intense that Robyn was almost relieved to see the boats, when, shortly after quarter past eleven, they moved cleanly into the harbour. There were two of them, sleek vessels with polished wooden hulls and crimson canopies to shelter passengers from the sun. Seeing the pace at which they approached, Robyn didn't think it would take much more than ten minutes to ferry them to the island. Even so, it was ten minutes too long. After her experience on the yacht, she suspected it would be years before she willingly boarded a boat again.

Having quickly tied the boats in place, the skippers stepped onto the harbour wall and helped Eva's team of hair and make-up artists disembark. Their role in the day's proceedings now over, once they were clear the guests began to climb aboard.

With no seats left for them in the Heywoods' boat, Robyn and Toby found themselves sharing with the Italians. The last to step aboard, when it came to Robyn's turn her stomach lurched. Placing one foot inside the boat, she felt it rock gently beneath her, her knees turning to jelly, and she caught herself wishing that she had taken Toby up on his offer of leaving early. That instead of Castello Fiore, they had been en route to the airport.

Scolding herself at the thought of Eva thinking she'd frightened her off for the sake of ten minutes on the lake, she practically launched herself into the boat, climbing aboard before she could think about it any further. As she did, a sudden ripple on the surface of the water caught the side of the vessel, robbing her of her balance.

She looked for Toby, but he had ushered her onto the boat before him and was now too far away to help. Instead, seeing that she was about to fall, the younger-looking of Eva's cousins leapt to his feet, reaching out and catching her hand.

They stood there for a moment, the panicked expression on his face suggesting he was just as surprised as Robyn that he had sprung up to help her.

'Thank you,' she said, letting go of his hand.

He nodded, looking away as if suddenly embarrassed. '*Prego.*'

She planted herself firmly on a cushioned bench while Toby hurried onto the boat and settled next to her.

'You OK?'

'Fine,' she muttered. 'Just lost my balance.'

With everyone aboard, the boats set off again, turning neatly in the harbour and heading back onto the lake. As they did, Robyn looked over her shoulder. The young man who had leapt up to help her now seemed hopelessly unsure of himself, giving her an awkward smile before dropping his eyes to his feet. His brother, meanwhile – the bearded man – wore an expression that took her completely by surprise. He was glaring at his companion. If she had to guess, Robyn would have said he looked livid.

Despite the impossible beauty of their surroundings, Robyn spent most of the ten-minute journey to the island looking squarely down at her lap. She knew she was being irrational. The boat might be less than a fraction of the size of Laurence's yacht, but it was clearly a sturdy vessel.

It was no good, though. Not when she could still hear the slap of the water as she tumbled from the yacht. Feel it filling her eyes, her nose, her mouth. The fact that she and Toby were sharing their boat with the Italians, therefore making it easier to hide her discomfort from Laurence and Margot, was at least a slight source of relief.

She risked a glance at the lake, the water shimmering beneath them. Slightly ahead, on the other boat, she saw Laurence. He was standing at the front in his linen suit, his gaze fixed on the castle like an explorer watching a newly discovered continent drift into view. Robyn half-expected him to pop one of his feet up onto the prow and adopt some kind of heroic, Columbus-esque pose.

She turned to Toby, sitting stoically beside her.

She hadn't told him about Abigail's visit to their room, nor her certainty that the message in Eva's bag had been his. She'd told herself it was because she would only be creating more drama. That whoever had actually planted it would only bene-fit from her causing a stir.

But the truth . . . With his curious behaviour in the moments before the note was found, the truth was that she was scared stiff of the possibility that Abigail might be right. That the message had been a way of telling Eva, after pushing her into the lake, to back off and leave them alone.

Someone had *planned* to show that message to Eva. They had printed it and brought it with them to Lake Garda. It seemed a stretch for Toby to have done that just to have up his sleeve. Something he could whip out if he needed to give Eva a fright. So if Abigail was right – if it really had been his – when would he have planned for her to see it? At the wedding, perhaps? If the goal had simply been to upset her, that would have been particularly effective. But after what had happened on the yacht, he could have decided not to wait. Back off, he might now be saying. Leave Robyn alone.

She looked down at her lap again. It was an uncomfortable theory, and one that she was trying hard not to nurse too readily. They had all been in the restaurant. And if it was in any way related, they presumably all knew about what had happened to Rachel Carlisle. If Toby could have sneaked that message into Eva's bag, then so could any of them.

And yet she couldn't help but think of Abigail's frantic plea.

No one else at that table would give Eva that message. Do you understand? No one.

She wished Abigail had said just a little more. Wished she had explained what it meant. But it was too late now. And as much as Robyn wanted to, questioning her further wasn't an option. Not when she seemed to believe that, if the message hadn't been Toby's, it could just as easily have been *hers*.

Robyn closed her eyes, trying to take some comfort from the knowledge that the wedding would soon be over. That in twenty-four hours, she and Toby would be at the airport. Once they were away, there would be all the time in the world to ask him what was going on. To *make* him tell her, if she had to.

For now, all she needed to do was grin and bear it.

18

On the other boat, Stephen watched the castle growing closer. He imagined somehow going back in time, to before Rushworth, and telling himself that he would one day be there. In a place more beautiful than he could have imagined, among people wealthier than he could have comprehended.

He would tell his younger self to run for the hills.

Turning to Abigail, he offered her a weak smile. She didn't return it.

They'd had a vicious argument the previous evening, after she'd emerged from Robyn and Toby's room.

'What are you thinking?' he'd demanded. 'We can't be sure it was them.'

'Of course it was,' Abigail had hissed, ushering him into their own room so that nobody would hear. 'The secret Eva's *locked away*. No one else at that table is going to dredge this back up. We all just want it to go away. So who else could it be?'

Stephen's mind raced. 'Look. If it was someone at that table, then yes. At first glance, it does make sense it would be Toby or Robyn. But why? It's not as if they can blackmail all of us. If they so much as tried, Jeremy would *destroy* them. So what would be the point?'

'They're trying to frighten us. They're pissed off with how Eva behaved on the yacht and now they're letting us know they have dirt.'

Stephen didn't reply.

'Do you have another theory?'

'No. But it just doesn't add up. I get that Laurence and Toby don't see eye to eye, but this would be *such* an overreaction.' He looked at the door. 'How would Robyn even know?'

'How do you think? Toby told her.'

'But would *he* know? It isn't as if Laurence would have told him.'

'Could he have worked it out?'

Again, Stephen didn't reply, thinking instead of his conversation with Chadwick and Miles on the yacht.

The papers ran out of things to say within a week . . . The way Laurence describes it, they had so little they could actually print that Jeremy didn't even need *to do anything about them.*

'No,' he said. 'No, I don't think so. I mean . . . There were the initial reports when it happened. I remember the *Guardian* ran something announcing the death. But they had nothing that could trace it back to us.'

'So how do they know? Whether it's one of them or both of them, whoever gave Eva that message *must* know.' She took a deep breath. 'We have to talk to Laurence.'

'No.'

'Stephen, we have to.'

'Don't you think he's having exactly the same thought?

Everyone must be thinking it.' He took a step closer, putting his hands on her shoulders. 'If it really was Robyn or Toby, they know now that we're on to them. They won't risk trying anything else. And when the wedding's out of the way, I'll talk to Laurence and Jeremy about how we deal with it.'

Abigail had glowered at him, tears welling in the corners of her eyes. 'And what are *you* going to do? Once the wedding's over? How are *you* going to keep us safe? I can't do this any more, Stephen. I can't go on, wondering who might find out. Waiting for the day the police finally take you all away.'

She took a deep breath. 'It isn't enough any more to just rely on Laurence and Jeremy. I'm not having our baby grow up without a father because you've gone to prison for Laurence Heywood. We need them out of our lives. Laurence *and* Eva.'

He hadn't had an answer to that. He'd stayed up thinking about it for half the night, and when Abigail slept, he had cried.

He cried burning tears of frustration. Frustration with Eva for making it happen, and frustration with Laurence for dragging him into it. He cried with the guilt, so overwhelming he thought it might drown him. He cried for the innocent man who had lost his life. And he cried for Abigail. Because in much the same way that he now knew his life would have been better if he'd never met Laurence, he was equally certain that hers would be better if she'd never met *him*.

Come on, mate. You know I can't let you leave.

Those had been Laurence's words, the last time he'd tried to break away. And yet Abigail was right. He owed it to her – and to the baby – to somehow get Laurence and Eva out of their lives.

He looked up at Laurence, standing at the front of the boat as the island grew closer.

He had to get them out. He didn't know how. But he *would* get them out.

19

Usually, in Robyn's experience, it was the groomsmen who ushered guests into the venue.

Not today. Not only was there the small matter of Stephen, Chadwick and Miles being among those about to set foot on the island for the first time, but Eva had apparently been vocal in her opinion that they couldn't be relied on to ensure things went perfectly. As such, when the boats moored alongside a wooden jetty, the bridesmaids were waiting for them instead, along with three members of staff.

Two were young men in gleaming white polo shirts who appeared immediately out of place. Robyn had no idea what she'd expected, but they looked as if they should be parking cars at a golf club in Surrey, rather than representing the ornate castle that sat behind them.

The third, however, looked like the real deal. Mid-forties, wearing a tapered cream dress and with a complexion that spoke of a lifetime in the Mediterranean sun, she approached the boat as if she might just have stepped off a fashion show catwalk and spoke rapidly in Italian, before turning to Toby and Robyn and introducing herself in flawless English as Sofia.

'I'm the wedding planner at Castello Fiore,' she told them with a broad smile. 'Please make your way inside. The ceremony will begin promptly at twelve o'clock. You will find staff in the courtyard, who will help with whatever you may need. But if there is anything I can do personally while you're on the island today, please let me know.'

Just as Robyn had seen from the villa, a short path flanked by a dozen palm trees sloped from the jetty up to the castle. She was desperately grateful for the shade, the midday heat now so intense that even the brief walk to the gate left her with beads of sweat on her forehead.

Inside, the castle gates opened directly onto a courtyard, stretching ahead like a cobbled playing field. There were wooden benches, a few strips of neatly tended lawn and easily a dozen enormous flowerpots, all containing small palm trees or sturdy-looking bushes. To the left was the old guardhouse, or the casermetta, as Robyn had seen it referred to in Jeremy's guidebook. Larger by far than any house Robyn had ever lived in, it was beautiful, two storeys high with sand-coloured walls and brightly painted shutters. Much like the boats on which they'd just sailed, it embodied Italian tradition a great deal more than the Heywoods' glass-fronted villa. To the right, a vast wall loomed over them, a smooth face of ancient brickwork with two sweeping stone staircases leading to upper levels. The watchtower stood proudly above, and at the far end of the courtyard, the wall dipped to waist-height, offering a raised view of the glittering water.

Robyn could see why Eva had been so insistent on this place. Likewise, why *London Living* had been so eager to cover it. For a moment, she simply stood, completely in awe.

They were the last inside, Laurence's boat having arrived first, and the congregation was already busy mingling in the centre of the courtyard. Everyone looked to be there. That is, everyone but Eva. No doubt saving the reveal of her dress for the moment she walked up the aisle.

After a few minutes, two more staff in white polo shirts — Robyn now counted four in total — began to direct them towards the broader of the stone staircases. The ceremony was to be performed on the castle's terrace, overlooking the lake, and it was time for them to find their seats.

Taking out her phone, Robyn checked the time. Quarter to twelve. Fifteen minutes to go.

Toby placed a hand on the small of her back. 'You go ahead. I'll catch up.'

'Where are you going?'

'I need some water before this thing begins. I'm burning up.'

He did look to be struggling, his cheeks having turned a troubling shade of red. Robyn held herself back from pointing out how many times she'd told him that exactly this would happen if he insisted on his dark suit.

'I'll come with you,' she said.

'Don't worry. You find our seats. I'll join you in a minute.'

She opened her mouth to protest, but he broke away without waiting for an answer, crossing the courtyard and heading straight inside the casermetta.

Robyn stood, perplexed. For a moment she considered calling him back, but before she could, Dina appeared in front of her.

With one look at her, Robyn's heart sank. She had seen Dina on the jetty, but with everything else that had been on hand to distract her – her discomfort at being on the lake, seeing the castle up close, Sofia ushering them briskly inside – she hadn't realised what Eva had done. Now that it was just her and Dina, face to face, it dawned on her.

Sage green. The bridesmaids' dresses were sage green.

Robyn couldn't believe it. Eva was heartless. That much was plain. But to treat her own sister so cruelly . . .

'Please,' Dina said, looking distinctly uncomfortable as she motioned towards the staircase. 'The wedding will start soon.'

At first, Robyn didn't move, instead looking a little longer at the door through which Toby had just disappeared. Again, Abigail's assessment echoed in her mind.

No one else at that table would give Eva that message. Do you understand? No one.

She had to move. Much as she would prefer to wait for Toby, Dina was still standing there, trying to usher her towards the stairs. Doing as she was asked, Robyn turned away, begrudgingly accepting that she would just have to meet Toby on the terrace.

*Fifteen minutes before
the wedding*

20

From the upper floor of the casermetta, Vito looked into the courtyard, watching as the guests made their way up to the terrace.

When he received his instructions, just a fortnight before the wedding, he had thought that once the task was completed he would feel a sense of relief.

Place the dagger in the cove. That was all. The display case would be unlocked, the CCTV camera turned off. He didn't need to know how these feats had been arranged. Nor did he need to know what would happen to the dagger next. All he had to do was make the swap, replacing it in the museum with the fake he had been provided. Do this before the guests arrived on the island – before the wedding began – and his debt would be cleared. His family would be safe.

The shame of using Eva's wedding day in such a way would hang over him for ever. But he had consoled himself with the knowledge that no one would ever need to know. The shame would be his to carry alone.

Now that the moment was here, though – his task completed – it wasn't relief he felt. Instead it was terror.

Yes, he had been successful. He had done what was asked; the dagger now lay in the cove. But he had also been caught.

The look in Eva's eyes when she saw him leave the museum – when she realised what he'd done – was branded onto his memory. The way her confusion had given way to hurt, before being swallowed entirely by her anger.

Eva had always been strong-willed. Even as a child, she'd had a formidable temper. But Vito had never before seen her so furious. The things she had called him . . . The promises she had made to never forgive him. The only small mercies were that it had happened before the guests arrived, and that she had agreed to keep his betrayal from Paola.

Still looking out of the window, his eyes settled on the two strangers.

He hadn't seen either of them before. But then that was always the way. Whenever they came to the dealership, making threats and demanding that month's payment, they were always in pairs and it was never the same men twice.

One certainly looked the part. With a beard and a ponytail, his eyes were darting around like a wolf in search of prey. And the other . . . Christ, the other was so fresh-faced he looked like he might still be a teenager.

Vito felt a swell of resentment at the sight of them. This was meant to be one of the most joyful days of his life, and yet there they were. Attending his daughter's wedding. Mixing with his family.

He had to keep Paola from seeing them. She knew that something was wrong. She hadn't yet called him out, but with over thirty years of marriage under their belts, Vito knew when his wife was growing suspicious.

'Was it really just the bill that you were discussing?' she had asked gently, the previous evening in their hotel. 'With Margot and Mr Lambourne?'

'It was, my love. They wanted to pay for dinner, but I wasn't having it.'

'It looked rather intense.'

'The English are stubborn.'

They had locked eyes, a slight frown taking form on her face.

She knew that he wasn't telling her the truth. Or at least, not the full truth. He could see it. She didn't press him on it, though. Her expression softened, the frown melting away.

'They'll need to be stubborn, if Eva's going to become a Heywood. For a moment I thought you might be talking about the photographer from this London magazine. She was furious Margot wouldn't allow photos at dinner.'

Vito had given a small laugh. 'I wouldn't dream of it. Eva can fight that particular battle far more fiercely than I ever could.'

Still watching the two strangers as they milled in the courtyard, he wondered what they had said to the other guests – how they had managed to talk their way onto the boats. Then his thoughts strayed to what their next move might be.

When the instructions had come to the dealership, hand-delivered by another anonymous young man who Vito had never seen before and hadn't seen since, all he'd received were the details of his own role. But he had his theories. The fact that the dagger must be placed in the cove before the guests arrived suggested they were planning to collect it during the ceremony. It surely made the most sense. A half-hour stretch in which all of the guests and most of the staff would be distracted.

After that . . . He couldn't say. If he was right, he hoped they would leave the island during the ceremony too. Take their prize and run, before anyone had a chance to notice they didn't belong.

Except it seemed that wasn't what was happening. Vito watched, frowning as a member of staff – a woman in a white polo shirt – approached the younger-looking man and motioned towards the staircase.

She was ushering him towards the terrace. Up to the wedding.

The stranger hesitated, speaking so quietly that Vito couldn't hear what was being said. Then, making her own way towards the terrace, Margot Heywood appeared. She paused, watching as the stranger seemed to protest to the young woman.

Realising that they were being observed, the stranger stopped. He looked at the staff member, then to Margot, and then back again. Relenting, he nodded and made slowly towards the staircase. A moment later, his bearded companion hurried after him, and together they continued to the terrace.

Vito felt a flicker of panic.

They were joining the wedding? So when would they take the dagger? How long would they be on the island?

He closed his eyes, taking a deep breath to steady his nerves.

All would be fine, he told himself. He had done his part. Now the rest was down to them. Whatever they were going to do, they surely couldn't be planning to stay on the island for long.

Turning away from the window, he checked his watch.

Eva was away somewhere, presumably having some last-minute photos taken before the wedding got under way. She would be back soon, and when she appeared, he would walk her up the aisle.

He focused on that. Tried to wash all thoughts of the dagger, of the strangers and of his argument with Eva from his mind.

They would talk properly after the wedding, and in time she would understand why he had done it. For now, he would just have to hope that as they walked together, arm in arm, all would be forgiven, if only for a moment.

21

Music drifted across the terrace, the string quartet gently playing as the guests waited for the ceremony to begin. At the front of the congregation, standing at the head of a white carpet scattered with rose petals, Laurence and Stephen chatted with the celebrant. Behind them, the lake stretched into the distance, twinkling as it caught the light. If Robyn strained her neck, she might just be able to see the jetty, and the path she had walked up to reach the castle.

Not that she noticed. Having sat now for several minutes in the sun, she instead found herself growing increasingly jealous of the canopy under which Laurence and Stephen stood. A paper fan had been left on each seat, although she'd quickly given up on trying to use hers. Even the chair was hot. She could feel the metal, warm against her back through her dress.

Looking out across the lake, she almost wished the island had been further from the shore. Being close enough to just make out the windows on the buildings, the cars trailing neatly along the road . . . It made knowing she would be there until midnight, when the boats finally came to collect them, even more insufferable.

In the corner of her vision, Cam appeared, her camera held aloft as she snapped away. Robyn smiled as she passed, but the photographer ignored her, a serious expression fixed in place behind her sunglasses. Fair enough, Robyn supposed. She was working, after all. This moment was the reason she was there.

She watched the water for a little while, focusing on the boats as they drifted past, until she eventually settled on a small white speedboat.

There wasn't anything particularly distinctive about it. She must have seen dozens like it moored in the marina at Malcesine. As for the man who was steering it . . . Robyn stood no chance whatsoever of making out his face, but she could just about see dark hair, and a yellow shirt fluttering as he whipped across the water.

The boat carried on, disappearing from view as it moved around the back of the island. But a minute later, it was there again, following exactly the same route. Had it just circled the island? Either that or Robyn was hallucinating. In this heat, that wouldn't have surprised her.

The boat disappeared again. Then, a minute later, it passed a third time.

Robyn leaned forward in her seat, peering at the boat. It was circling the island. She was certain of it, although she couldn't imagine why.

It wasn't carrying tourists on a sightseeing tour – Robyn could see that the skipper was definitely alone. Could he be a curious local? He'd noticed some hubbub and wanted a closer look? That didn't make sense either. As Jeremy had said, Castello Fiore was a popular wedding venue. There was surely nothing extraordinary – at least from the distance at which the skipper was observing them – about Laurence and Eva's wedding.

Robyn watched a little longer, expecting the boat to disappear behind the island and come around for a fourth time. Instead, it broke off, deviating from its loop and speeding towards the shore. As she watched it go, Robyn struggled to withhold an intense flash of jealousy.

She took out her phone, checking the time. Twelve o'clock. Fifteen minutes had passed since Toby went into the casermetta. If he took much longer he was going to miss the beginning of the ceremony. Then again, perhaps that was exactly his plan.

In the row of seats ahead of her, Jeremy sat down beside Margot. She fixed him with an iron-clad look.

'Well?'

He shook his head, his expression grave.

Margot didn't reply, pausing for a moment before pursing her lips and returning her attention to the lake.

It was a curious exchange, although Robyn didn't have the chance to consider it further. Hearing movement beside her, she turned to see Toby dropping into the neighbouring seat. He tugged at his collar, his cheeks flushed.

'Where were you?' she hissed.

'Nowhere. Sorry. Couldn't find a bloody glass.'

She frowned at him. Of all the places someone might struggle to find a glass, a wedding venue seemed an unlikely contender. Especially with staff on hand to help.

Without intending to, she thought again of her conversation with Abigail. Of her certainty that Toby had been the one to plant the message in Eva's bag.

Forcing the thought from her mind, she looked once more towards the front.

The minutes began to creep by. First five. Then ten.

Robyn felt her heart begin to beat a little quicker. What was Eva doing?

She briefly wondered if there might still be some pre-ceremony photos being taken. Only that couldn't be the case. Cam was right there, waiting with the rest of them.

She sat a little straighter in her seat, craning her neck as she looked around the terrace for some indication as to what could be happening.

Toby gave her a quizzical look. 'You OK?'

She didn't answer. She wasn't someone who dealt in hunches. But in that particular moment, she was willing to make an exception.

The delay. The boat. Even Toby and his sudden disappearance into the casermetta.

This wasn't simply a case of a bride running slightly behind. Robyn was suddenly sure – convinced, even – that somewhere on the island, something was deeply wrong.

She didn't have to wait long for her suspicions to be confirmed. Because at that moment a breeze drifted onto the terrace, carrying with it a piercing, blood-curdling scream.

22

The congregation sprang to its feet. The music stopped, the sweltering heat immediately forgotten as everyone looked frantically around, trying to determine the origin of the scream.

Laurence ran the length of the aisle, panic on his face as he dashed towards the stone steps, Chadwick and Miles hot on his heels. Robyn locked eyes with Toby and shook her head, pleading silently with him to stay on the terrace.

She had no idea if he'd failed to understand or if he'd simply ignored her. Either way, he turned and followed them from the terrace. Robyn tried to call him back, but it was too late. Cursing under her breath, she hurried after him.

At the bottom of the steps, in the courtyard, they began breaking off into smaller groups. The groomsmen followed Laurence into the casermetta, while a pair of Italians flew up a second, narrower staircase.

Toby made to follow Laurence, but Robyn grabbed his hand.

'Wait. What about over there?'

He looked in the direction she was pointing, settling on a modest wooden door standing slightly ajar at the far end of the courtyard.

He ran to it at full pelt, Robyn hurrying to follow. Barrelling through the door, he hurtled down a winding flight of cobbled steps, moving so frantically that Robyn was convinced he would slip and go flying. She followed as quickly as she dared, terrified of falling in her heels. The staircase hairpinned a couple of times, a pair of low stone walls hugging it closely on either side. The air smelled sweet, bushes adorned with brightly coloured flowers growing from the rockface.

At last, they reached the bottom, the staircase ending between two hulking pieces of pale rock, and they emerged into a small cove. Water lapped quietly at the shore, so clear in the shallows that Robyn could see each pebble resting on the lakebed. In the distance, a sailing boat cruised by, the mountains looming behind it.

It should have been beautiful. But in that moment, it was the scene of the most horrific thing Robyn had ever laid eyes on.

Toby stood with his back to her, staring at his discovery. Dina – the source of the scream, Robyn realised – was heaped upon the ground. Her sage green bridesmaid's dress was peppered with sand, and she was murmuring frantically in Italian between deep, shuddering sobs.

As for the bride herself . . .

'Oh, God . . .' Robyn whispered.

Eva lay on her back, splayed across the shingle. Her eyes were hollow, her final expression a vacant look of surprise. Her white dress, pristine as a layer of fresh snow, was now stained with blood. And buried in her heart, pointing towards the sky, was a bronze-hilted dagger bearing a glittering green jewel.

23

'Eva!'

Robyn turned to see Laurence hurrying down the cobbled steps, with Stephen, Chadwick and Miles close behind.

'Eva!' he cried out again, his polished shoes slipping on the loose stone as he scrambled onto the beach. He stood over the body of his fiancée, taking in the dagger, her pale skin, the white dress now stained with blood.

For several seconds, nobody moved. Even Dina lifted her face from her hands, looking up at him with fear in her eyes.

Laurence tore his eyes from his bride. He looked at Dina, still kneeling on the shale. He turned to Robyn, then finally to Toby.

'What have you done?' He sprang forward, his voice rising as he seized his brother by the lapels. '*What have you done?*'

'It wasn't him!' Robyn shouted. 'Dina found her. We just followed the scream.'

At first, she wasn't sure if Laurence had heard. He stood there, knuckles turning white as he gripped Toby's jacket. Then, after several painstaking seconds, he let go and dropped to the ground.

'Eva,' he murmured, his voice cracking. 'Jesus Christ, Eva . . .'

The rest of the wedding party was beginning to gather now. Behind Laurence, Robyn saw the wedding planner, Sofia, her face a picture of pure horror.

'*Oh, Madonna*,' she murmured, a hand flying up to cover her mouth. 'I'll call the police.'

She hurried from the cove, brushing Chadwick and Miles aside as she dashed back up the cobbled staircase. Robyn, meanwhile, took Toby by the arm, trying gently to steer him away.

'Come on,' she said. 'We shouldn't be here for this. Let's go back up to the castle.'

He nodded, but he didn't move. He didn't even reply, his eyes glued to Eva's corpse.

Robyn took his hand, weaving her fingers between his as she doubled her efforts to tug him gently towards the staircase. Before they could move, though, there came a terrible howl. Turning to face it, she saw Eva's parents arrive on the beach. Vito ran the short distance to his daughter's body, speaking desperately in Italian. As he looked down on her, and his eyes settled on the dagger, he gave a primal cry of pain, sinking to his knees beside Laurence.

Robyn turned away, feeling like an intruder.

Giulia and Beatrice were on the beach now too. Midway up the steps, she saw Margot and Jeremy standing together, surveying the scene with completely unreadable expressions. A short way behind them stood Harper and Cam, and at the very top were the two cousins who had shared their boat. No one moved. They all stood, watching like spectators of some gruesome performance.

'When was she last seen?' Stephen called out.

Nobody spoke. There wasn't a sound to be heard except the gentle lapping of the water against the shore.

'One of you has seen *something*,' Laurence said, his voice straining. 'Someone must know who's done this!'

Still, nobody spoke. Robyn looked around at the group, taking in each of their faces in turn. Nobody did anything to betray that they might have something to share. Laurence. Dina. Stephen and Abigail. Margot and Jeremy. Even Toby. They all remained completely silent.

She looked back up towards the castle, trails of vivid green foliage creeping up the side of the cliff.

There might be someone hiding inside. Someone who wasn't part of the wedding. If so, the island wasn't huge. They wouldn't stay hidden for long. In any case, Laurence must be right. Someone knew what had happened to Eva. Someone was responsible. And whether they were there on the beach or hiding within the walls of the castle, there was no denying that they were, indeed, among them.

24

Sofia ran across the courtyard, brushing past two of her staff. They tried to ask what was happening, but she didn't stop to answer them. She was heading straight for the gatehouse, the little stone hut beside the castle gates that contained her office.

How had this happened? However much she'd resented them, the instructions had been simple. Ensure the display case was unlocked and that the museum's CCTV camera wasn't recording. The rest would be taken care of.

She'd told them – whoever they were – that they were taking a huge risk. As soon as someone noticed that the dagger was gone, the police would be on to her in moments. They would inspect her phone records. Check her movements. There wasn't a chance of the search ending with her. Everyone who had been in contact with her, however secretive they might try to be, would ultimately be found.

But they had been insistent. The police wouldn't investigate, because the dagger would still be in place at the end of the day. She didn't need to know what was happening while the camera was off. All she had to do make was sure it was.

Had she believed them? She had no idea. Part of her had

been certain that she would find the case empty. The thieves would be gone, the dagger with them, and she would be en route to prison for the rest of her life.

What she hadn't expected was for it to next be seen buried in Eva Bianchi's heart.

Throwing open the door to the gatehouse, she went straight to her desk and lifted the phone.

'What are you doing?'

A voice called out to her in Italian, and she turned to see that one of the guests had followed her. He was from the bride's side, presumably. A man with olive skin, a ponytail and a neatly styled beard.

'It's all right,' she said. 'I'm calling the police. They'll be here soon.'

'No police.'

'Soon, sir. They'll be here soon.'

The stranger cleared the little office in two strides, snatched the phone from her hand and pressed it back into the cradle.

'*No police.*'

Sofia stared at him, heart racing. Over his shoulder, she saw a second, younger-looking man. He was just standing, watching.

'Who are you?' she said, so quietly it was practically a whisper.

Still standing just inches away, the stranger looked her in the eye. 'Who do you think?'

As she finally realised what was happening, Sofia swallowed back a lump, her fear beginning to grow. 'You killed her?'

The bearded man slowly shook his head, fury in his eyes. 'We wanted the dagger. To take it away and sell it. We can hardly do that now it's turned up inside the fucking bride.'

'I have to call the police.'

'No. No police until we've gone.'

'And how long will that be?'

'Soon.'

'How soon?' Panic crept into her voice. 'A woman's been murdered. The bride, of all people. At her own wedding! I can't just decide not to call the police.'

The stranger loomed over her, so close now that she could smell his aftershave.

'Two weeks ago,' he said, 'we killed a man in Verona. A restaurant owner who thought he could escape his debt by helping with a police investigation. We murdered him for it. Went to his place, shot him straight through the head in his own kitchen. So you can understand, I expect, why we would be keen to leave this island before they arrive.'

Sofia was unable to speak, her fear threatening to overcome her.

'There's a man with a boat,' he continued. 'He's waiting for us. Once we've made the call, he'll come straight here and we'll be gone. *Then* you can call the police.'

'And what do I do about the guests?' Sofia's voice was now paper thin. 'I can't watch all of them at once. What if someone gets tired of waiting? How am I supposed to stop them from just calling the police themselves?'

'Convince them that help is coming. Tell them you've made the call and someone will be here soon. Tell them whatever you want. Just remember what's at stake if you fuck this up.'

Sofia didn't answer. There was no argument to be made.

They left her in the office, closing the door behind them. The instant they were gone Sofia went straight to the desk and fetched out a bottle of brandy. She put it to her lips, taking a large swig, then sank into her chair.

She sat there for a few moments, swearing under her breath as she tried desperately to bring her trembling body under control. Then, with the desk drawer still open, she reached inside and slid out a photograph. In the centre of the shot, her son sat on the edge of his bed, a look of defiance etched into his features as the camera was held up to the bars of his cell.

It had been sent two weeks ago, her phone ringing just minutes after the envelope landed on her desk. Whoever was on the other end had made their demands crystal clear. On the day of Eva Bianchi's wedding, the museum case containing the Vincenzo dagger must be unlocked and the security camera switched off.

How the picture had been taken, she couldn't imagine. By all accounts, the state prison in which her son was held enforced its no-phones policy militantly. All that mattered, though, was that it *had* been taken. Even in custody, serving a sentence for petty theft, it seemed he was within their reach. And she would much sooner join him behind bars than receive what had been promised if she didn't do as instructed – a second picture, of the same young man in the same cell. But this time with his throat slashed.

The caller didn't even wait to hear her answer before hanging up. They seemed to know just as well as she did that if helping to steal the dagger kept her son alive, she would do it without a second's hesitation.

Only the dagger hadn't been stolen. She had made her peace with being an accessory to theft. But to murder?

She thought of the young woman lying dead in the cove. It

must have been them; the two criminals who had just ambushed her in the office. No one else knew that the dagger was accessible. She wondered what the motive had been. Were the Bianchis in debt to these people? Were they part of a rival organisation?

But why would they lie? Why freely admit to taking the dagger – to killing a man in Verona and being prepared to kill her son – and then try to claim they were innocent of Eva Bianchi's murder?

She looked at the clock, mounted on the wall above her desk. Soon, they had said. They would be taken away soon. That was all that mattered. And the minute they were gone, she would call the police.

25

They made their way slowly back up the cobbled staircase.

Laurence and Vito had wanted to carry Eva up to the castle, but Jeremy quickly intervened, pointing out that the beach was now quite clearly a crime scene. If they wanted to see justice done, the body and the surrounding environment should be disturbed as little as possible.

Reluctantly, they had agreed, with Jeremy then appointing the two young men who had met them on the jetty to watch over the cove until Sofia had managed to bring the police to the island. Margot nodded her approval and instructed Laurence to go back to the castle with his groomsmen. Vito and Paola gathered up Dina, who was still sobbing on the shale, and the three of them were taken gently away by Giulia and Beatrice.

It was nearly half past twelve, the midday sun pressing down mercilessly as they climbed the twisting cobbled staircase, and Robyn was grateful for the shade of the castle walls once they had returned to the courtyard. She felt nauseous, and the heat wasn't helping. She liked to think she had a reasonably strong stomach, but even so . . . She had never seen a dead body before, let alone the corpse of someone who had been so brutally murdered.

She tried – and spectacularly failed – not to think of the scene in the cove. Tried not to picture the bloodstained wedding dress. Eva's wide, unblinking eyes. The dagger, buried in her chest.

That dagger . . . With its twisted hilt and glittering green jewel, she had recognised it immediately as the weapon from Jeremy's guidebook. He'd mentioned, when they spoke in the villa, that the castle had a museum. Could it have been taken from there? Stolen with the intention of plunging it into Eva's heart?

With the cove now completely vacated, except for the two poor staff members who had been left to stand guard over the body, Robyn looked around the courtyard. The bridesmaids took Vito, Dina and Paola straight inside the casermetta, with the Italian family members Robyn had first seen in the harbour following closely behind. Laurence sank onto a stone bench, Margot and Jeremy looking on as Chadwick and Miles planted themselves either side of him. On a thin stretch of lawn, Harper was speaking to Cam, her face grave.

The staff seemed completely at a loss without Sofia to direct them. A man and a woman wearing aprons, who Robyn took to be the chefs preparing the wedding breakfast, had emerged from the casermetta to see what was happening, while two young women in white polo shirts looked completely shell-shocked. In fairness, Robyn suspected that of the many ways a wedding could go wrong, no one had prepared them for the possibility of a murdered bride. She flicked a glance up towards the terrace. The celebrant and the musicians had remained where they were, but were peering nervously over the balustrade at the growing crowd.

Finally, she looked at Toby. He seemed to be just as shaken as she was, his expression distant and his skin sheet-white.

And yet . . .

Catching her staring, his eyes narrowed slightly. 'What?'

'Nothing.' She looked away, casting her gaze to the cobbled ground.

'You sure?'

She didn't reply.

Where had he been? Fifteen minutes he'd been gone, claiming to fetch a glass of water, only to slide into his seat on the terrace just moments before Eva's body was found.

She thought of how angry he'd been on the yacht. How nervous in the restaurant. She thought of the warning in Eva's bag and Abigail's insistence it had been Toby who placed it there.

I know what you did. The secret you've locked away.

She gritted her teeth, trying hard to convince herself she was being ridiculous. Yes, he'd been acting strangely. But there was absolutely no way Toby could have slipped away to kill Eva. He had sprinted into the cove, following the sound of Dina's scream. And she had seen the horror on his face when they found Eva's body. That couldn't have been an act. It had been far too convincing.

But then, isn't that exactly what you'd do? Wouldn't you make it seem convincing?

She looked around the courtyard, taking in each of the others in turn. Then she met Toby's gaze, concern swimming in his eyes.

'It was someone here,' she said. 'It has to be.'

She watched him closely, looking for any hint – any flicker whatsoever – that he was frightened to hear her thinking in such a way.

'One of the wedding party?' he said. 'You really think so?'

'I guess it's possible that someone else is hiding inside the castle. Or that they might just have made it in and out of the cove by boat without being seen from the terrace. But, realistically . . .'

She tailed off. A boat . . .

For the most part, the cove had been enclosed, with thick faces of pale stone shielding the beach from the lake. But with a small enough boat, Robyn imagined it would just be possible to access it from the water. A boat, for instance, about the size of the vessel she'd seen circling the island from the terrace.

Could that be it? Had the skipper steered his boat into the cove, killed Eva and then fled? But why circle the island afterwards? She'd seen the moment he turned and headed back to shore. He'd looped the island at least three times before speeding away. If he'd been involved, wouldn't he have vanished the moment he was clear?

Her imagination really was running away with itself now. She needed to talk to someone. To voice her thoughts out loud. She needed Toby . . .

They were supposed to be a team. She was supposed to be able to tell him anything, to trust him implicitly. And in that moment, she wanted desperately to trust him. She wanted to describe how she'd heard Margot and Jeremy threatening Vito in the restaurant. About Abigail and the message.

She wanted to tell him all of it. But until she knew where he'd been — knew exactly what it was that he was so clearly keeping from her — she felt as if she couldn't say a word.

There was a flicker of movement in the corner of her vision. Turning to meet it, she saw Sofia emerge from a small stone hut beside the castle gates. Robyn hadn't seen inside, but considering

Sofia had said she was calling the police, she assumed it must house an office.

'Did you get through to them?' asked Toby.

Robyn peered at him, her eyes narrowing as she heard the urgency in his tone. Was he asking out of concern for Eva? Or for himself? She began to feel even more sick, the thought of even entertaining such a question causing her head to spin.

Sofia nodded, her face pale. 'They're coming.'

'They understand what's happened?'

'I told you I have called them.'

She snapped at Toby so fiercely that he recoiled, panic flashing across his face. She then threw a hand into the air, waving him away like a bad smell, before marching in the direction of the terrace, murmuring to herself in Italian as she went.

As Robyn watched her go, a sudden rush of nausea hit her. Closing her eyes, the sight of Eva's body rushed back like a slap in the face. The bloodstained wedding dress. Her wide, empty eyes. The bronze-hilted dagger . . . She was convinced it had been the dagger from Jeremy's book. And that if it was, it must have come from the museum he'd mentioned. But she had to know for sure. Had to confirm it.

Without a word to Toby, she turned on her heel and began striding towards the narrower of the two staircases. She was vaguely aware of him behind her, hissing – almost whispering – her name.

'Robyn. Robyn!' He caught her wrist. 'Robyn . . . What are you doing?'

His face was a picture of . . . She wasn't sure what, exactly. Confusion. Concern. Fear, perhaps. She looked down at his hand. At his fingers clamped tightly around her wrist.

'Let go of me, please.'

'But why? Where are you going?'

'I just . . . I want to see something.'

'See what? Robyn, come on. You're being really weird . . .'

'Someone is dead,' she said. 'I've just seen a corpse for the first time in my life, and unless the killer has managed to get off the island without anyone noticing, it looks very much as if someone here – someone we've spent the last few days with – is responsible. So *don't tell me* I'm being weird.'

He stared at her, his eyes wide. In the year they'd been together, neither of them had once spoken to the other so sharply.

'I'm sorry,' he said, meekly relinquishing his grip on her wrist. 'I didn't mean to . . . I only thought that, until the police get here, we probably shouldn't go wandering off alone.'

For what felt like an eternity, they stood there, looking at each other.

Did she believe that Toby could have killed Eva? Did she actually, truly believe it?

She wanted desperately not to. But he was keeping something from her. She knew how furious he'd been when Eva pushed her off the yacht. She knew that Abigail meant what she'd said about the message in Eva's bag. Regardless of whether she was right, Abigail truly believed it had been Toby. But perhaps most frighteningly of all, she knew he was almost certainly lying about where he'd been before the wedding; in the minutes before Eva's body was discovered.

'I'm going to find the museum,' she said quietly. 'There's something I need to see.'

He thought for a second, before giving a nod. 'OK. Well, shall we . . . I mean, can I come with you?'

She wanted to say no. To have him wait right there until she had decided exactly what her suspicions were.

But she didn't see that she had much choice. She had to go to the museum. If not to satisfy her curiosity then because, if she was right, it would help the police. But how could she insist to Toby that she go alone without also letting him know why the thought of him coming bothered her so much?

She didn't want to tiptoe around him. What she wanted was proof. Some piece of hard evidence that would irrefutably lay her fears to rest. That would convince her, without fail, that Toby couldn't possibly have killed Eva.

But in the absence of such a lifeline, she reluctantly agreed, and together they walked up the sloping staircase, passing through an archway at the top into a second, much smaller court-yard. The watchtower loomed overhead, with a small building at its base. A sign beside the door read *Museo del Castello*.

The temperature struck her the moment they stepped inside. It was clearly air conditioned, and she found herself breathing a sigh of relief as they left the heat of the midday sun behind.

There were no windows, the room lit by spotlights either mounted on the ceiling or illuminating exhibits inside a collection of around a dozen glass cases. It gave Robyn the sensation of stepping into some kind of neatly furnished cave. Some of the display cases hugged the walls, while others formed aisles in the centre of the room. Nearly all contained weapons. Swords, crossbows, spears . . . Robyn looked at a plaque in the nearest case, reading about a longbow which had belonged to one of the various generations of invaders and defenders to have occupied the castle over the centuries.

Toby followed her inside. 'You think the knife came from in here?'

'Dagger,' she said. 'It isn't a knife. It's a dagger.'

'Is that important?'

She didn't reply. Instead, she began to weave between the cases, inspecting their various contents. She ignored the plaques and labels. She didn't need them. She knew what she was looking for. And with the museum only being small, it didn't take long to find.

Stopping at a final case towards the back of the museum, Toby came to stand beside her.

'Doesn't look like there's anything missing. No cases broken into.' Seeing how intently she was staring at the final case, he paused. 'What is it?'

'This is it,' she said.

'It's what?'

She nodded towards the dagger in the centre of the case. 'This is the one. Look at it. Jeremy showed it to me yesterday, in a book. And I recognised it when we were down in the cove. The green jewel in the bronze hilt . . .'

'Jeremy?' Toby frowned. 'Why were you and Jeremy . . . ?' He stopped, seemingly remembering why they were there. 'This can't be it, Robyn. The knife—' He caught himself. 'The *dagger* that Eva's been stabbed with. It's still . . . I mean, it hasn't been . . .' He tailed off, struggling for the right words.

'I know,' said Robyn. 'It's still in the cove. I can't explain it, but I promise: this dagger here and the one that's been used to kill Eva . . . They're the same.'

26

Vito practically floated into the casermetta.

He was numb, his body moving forward entirely of its own accord. He saw his feet climbing the stairs to the first floor, but he had no recollection of instructing them to do so. He was aware of people all around him, talking and crying, but it was just white noise. All he could think of – all that mattered – was the waking nightmare in which they had found themselves.

This couldn't be happening. Surely those hadn't been Eva's eyes, wide and lifeless. That hadn't been her blood, staining the shale. Any moment, someone was going to tell him how the trick had been played. Or perhaps he would simply wake up. For so many months, he had been staving off nightmares of his debtors finally coming for his family. This was just another. All he had to do was wake up.

But as he looked around, he realised this was all too real. He saw Dina, weeping at the oak table that occupied the upper floor of the casermetta. He saw Paola, her face grave as her brother and his wife tried to comfort her. Even Beatrice and Giulia, both sheet-white.

Somehow, this was real.

As it dawned on him, he felt his knees go weak. His breathing became frantic. He tried to speak but no words came.

This couldn't have happened. He had done what they asked. He had swapped the daggers, placed the real one in the cove.

He stumbled towards the window, his feet suddenly made of lead, and closed his eyes. He took a deep breath, gripping the window frame, and felt the sun on his face. Letting the breath go, he tried to take another, but it caught in his throat.

He opened his eyes again, tears pricking at the corners of his vision.

Laurence's family was gathered in the courtyard below. Vito watched, seeing how they all fussed around the young man.

Then he saw them, loitering by the gates. The two strangers. The handsome one, with his dark hair hanging loose at his shoulders, and the older-looking one, with his beard and ponytail.

It must have been them. He knew it with complete and utter certainty. He had brought them to the island. He had done everything they'd asked. And yet, they had done this anyway.

The numbness faded, replaced instead by a burning fury. A desire to kill, just as Eva had been killed.

It was all he could do not to scream at them through the window. He felt his entire body tremble, his teeth clenching so hard they might break. Then he was moving, turning away from the window and barging back towards the stairs.

'Vito,' Paola called after him. 'Vito!'

He didn't answer her. He didn't even look back.

27

In the courtyard, Leo watched as Gabriel slipped the phone into his pocket, swore and then ran a hand across his beard.

'What's happening?'

Gabriel didn't reply, continuing simply to swear repeatedly.

'Gabriel. What's happening?'

'They aren't coming. That's what's happening. They aren't fucking coming.'

Leo tried to quell his panic. 'What do you mean, they aren't coming? How can they just not come?'

'Guys on the boat aren't risking it. Not now a body's turned up. They don't want to be here when the police arrive.'

'But the police aren't coming. She isn't calling them until we've gone.'

Gabriel rounded on him. 'You don't think I told them that? They say they still won't risk it.'

'They can't do that,' said Leo. 'They have to come for us!'

Gabriel scowled, letting down his ponytail. 'They don't have to do anything. Not now the dagger's lost and especially not while they think there are police on the way. If I was them, I'd leave us too.'

'But they can't be far away, can they? Even if the police *were* coming, surely they must be close enough that they could get here first?'

Gabriel's eyes flared. 'What exactly do you think's happening here? You think they've just been bobbing next to the island for half an hour, waiting for us to call? Wouldn't be subtle, would it? Wherever they've been waiting, they're a good distance away and out of sight. Now they say they won't come within a mile of this place.'

Leo didn't reply this time, the realisation sinking in. They were on their own.

'Does the dagger have to be lost?' he asked. 'What if you cause a distraction of some kind? Get them all away from the cove? I could run down there. We could still get it—'

'Shut up,' Gabriel hissed. 'Just shut up and think. The whole point was that no one would know it had been stolen. Bianchi puts the fake inside the museum, we collect the real one from the cove and no one's any the wiser. But that can't happen now, can it? It can hardly be sold when the whole world knows it's been taken.'

Leo tried to protest but he couldn't manage even that, despair beginning to take hold.

'Why did you follow them?' said Gabriel. 'Why did you go up to the wedding? It was the simplest plan in the world. We go to the cove. We pick up the dagger. We call for the boat and we're away before the ceremony's even over.'

'What was I supposed to do? You saw it, one of those kids in the polo shirts came over and started trying to usher me with the guests.'

'You should have told her to fuck off.'

'The mother of the groom was right there! How do you suppose telling one of the staff to fuck off would have looked while they're trying to direct me to her son's wedding?'

Gabriel paced, swearing some more.

'Will you stop looking at me like I've screwed this all up?' said Leo.

'You have screwed it all up. You've done *nothing but* screw it all up.'

Leo thought for a moment, trying to deduce what else he could have done wrong.

'You mean that girl on the boat?' he asked. 'What was I meant to do? Just let her fall?'

'Yes! Let her fucking fall. We're meant to *not draw attention* to ourselves. She'd taken a good look at your face before we'd even got to the fucking island.'

Leo took a breath, preparing to push back. But before the words could take form, he restrained himself.

Gabriel was right. They had failed and it was his fault. But the worst part, perhaps, was that he shouldn't even have been there. He had asked for this job. The new recruit, eager to prove himself, he'd asked for something important. Something that would help him stand out.

Fighting the urge to panic, he dropped his voice to little more than a whisper.

'There's still time to pull this back, isn't there? She hasn't yet called the police.'

'Not yet,' Gabriel muttered. 'But she's right. If no one turns up soon, the wedding party will start asking questions. It won't take long for one of them to lose their patience and just make the call themselves.'

'So what are we going to do?'

Gabriel didn't reply immediately, glaring instead in the direction of the casermetta. 'I know a guy,' he said. 'He has a boat. I'll give him a call.'

'You think he'll come?'

'He might. I'll owe him one hell of a favour. But yes. I think he might.'

Gabriel slipped the phone from his jacket again.

'He'll be here soon, right?' said Leo. 'This friend of yours. He won't keep us waiting? No one said anything in the harbour, but I don't suppose it'll take much longer for someone to realise we aren't actually Eva's cousins.'

Gabriel raised an eyebrow. 'He lives at the far end of the lake.'

In an instant, any hope that Leo had allowed himself to feel was snuffed out. The far end of the lake . . . Depending on how quick this boat was, it could take hours for Gabriel's friend to reach them. Whereas the police . . . As soon as they received the call, Leo struggled to imagine it would take them more than fifteen minutes.

He looked down at the cobbled ground, trying to distract himself from the likelihood of ending their day in custody.

'How much was that dagger going to sell for?' he asked.

'Nothing to do with us. We were only ever meant to collect it.'

'I know. But you must have had an idea.'

Gabriel grimaced. 'I heard Francesco saying the right buyer would pay a million euros. Maybe more.'

'A million euros . . .' Leo looked back towards the office. 'And do you really think she'll keep the police away?'

Gabriel sneered. 'If she doesn't, I'll kill that son of hers myself when we see him in prison.'

Turning away from the office, Leo looked across the court-yard, just in time to see Vito storming towards them from the casermetta.

28

'I don't understand,' said Toby. 'How can this dagger have been used to kill Eva?'

'It can't be *exactly* the same,' Robyn said, hearing the hint of irritation in her own voice. 'At least, it can't physically be the same object. Perhaps one's a replica. Or there's a twin.'

'But you think someone wanted to stab her with this dagger, specifically? Or, at least, one that looks like it?'

It certainly seemed that way. Robyn stared at it through the glass, her eyes narrowing.

There were half a million ways to kill someone. But stabbing them . . .

She'd never given any serious thought to how she might commit murder, but she could imagine that to stab someone wasn't like shooting or poisoning them. It was personal. Intimate. You couldn't do it from a distance or just set it up and let nature take its course. To go through with something like that, you had to really want someone dead. And to insist on doing it with a dagger that *looked* a certain way . . . That was another level of detail altogether.

She thought of Jeremy, eagerly flicking through his

guidebook. What had *he* been doing before the wedding? She pictured him taking his seat on the terrace, remembering the grim expression with which he had fixed Margot.

Could he have been to see Vito? Deliver a final warning before Laurence and Eva were married that he wouldn't receive a penny from HCM? Or had he been to visit the bride, dagger in hand, to ensure the wedding didn't go ahead?

'Which do you think's the original?' Toby asked.

Robyn chewed her lip, pleading for his ignorance to be genuine.

'I've no idea. As you say, there's nothing to suggest the case has been broken into. No way of telling if the original might somehow have been swapped out. And even if it *could* be done, imagine the risk. If someone caught you, you'd be screwed.'

She looked towards the ceiling, where a small security camera was mounted in the far corner. It looked embarrassingly out of place, a white plastic dome drilled into the ancient stonework. There would be footage, at least. If a swap had taken place, the police would soon know about it.

They were both silent for a minute, mulling over the severity of what was happening. The murdered bride, the identical daggers.

'Toby,' she said quietly. 'What were you doing before the wedding?'

He paused before replying. 'I told you. I was getting some water.'

Her heart sank. He was lying to her. She didn't know what the truth was, but she knew that this wasn't it.

He took her by the hand and led her from the museum. She felt a sudden rush as their skin touched, his fingers slipping between hers. She wanted desperately to shake off her suspicions – her fears – that he could be involved. But no matter how hard she tried, so long as he was lying to her she knew she wouldn't entirely manage it.

Stepping back into the sun, they passed through the little archway and descended the stone staircase, returning to the courtyard just in time to see Vito emerge from the casermetta.

He stormed across the cobbled stones, his eyes bloodshot. He was muttering to himself, heading in the direction of the castle gates, and Robyn felt a sudden rush of panic as she became convinced that he was heading for Cam. The photographer was completely alone, standing on a patch of neatly tended lawn with her camera bag slung over her shoulder. Seeing Vito thundering towards her, Robyn watched as she reached the same conclusion, tensing and beginning quickly to retreat.

As Vito grew closer, though, Robyn realised it wasn't Cam that he was making for at all. Huddling only a few feet away were the two men from the boat – Eva's cousins – and as Cam scurried clear, it quickly became apparent that they were the ones in Vito's sights.

Apparently realising the same thing, they turned to face him, the younger-looking man putting up a hand as if to hold him at bay.

It didn't work. Now just a few feet away, Vito's murmuring rose until he was outright shouting at them in hurried, frantic Italian. He grasped the young man by the lapels and began to shake him violently, his fury becoming more apparent with every word.

'Vito!' Seeing the commotion, Laurence sprang up from his bench. 'Vito, stop!'

Vito paid no notice, and in the end it took a joint effort from

Laurence, Chadwick and Miles to pull him away. Only once they'd been forcibly separated did Vito stop shouting. For several seconds, his face was a picture of pure hatred. Then he turned away and stalked back in the direction of the casermetta, shoving his way past a handful of uncomfortable-looking Italians who had followed him helplessly into the courtyard.

As he left, Robyn studied the two men. The younger-looking one, who just moments earlier Vito had been shaking by the lapels, flashed an awkward smile to the small crowd of startled bystanders, taking a moment to straighten his jacket and run a hand through his hair. His companion's expression, meanwhile, was grave. Robyn watched as his dark eyes followed Vito across the courtyard and into the casermetta.

But there was something else. She hadn't seen it happen, but while Vito had been raging, the man with the beard and pony-tail had slipped a hand inside his jacket.

He kept it there a moment, resting, presumably, on whatever was inside. Only once Vito had disappeared from view did he quickly slide it free. Whatever was inside his jacket, he'd left it there, his hand now hanging empty by his side.

'Ladies and gentlemen!' Sofia appeared at the door to the casermetta, calling out across the courtyard. 'Ladies and gentlemen! Can I please have your attention?'

Her voice was trembling slightly. With the way Laurence was glaring at her, Robyn couldn't blame her.

'I have called the police,' she said. 'They're coming but they will be some time.'

'How long?' Margot asked.

'I can't say.'

Nobody replied, although Margot's expression said enough.

184

'Please understand,' Sofia continued. 'This is not London. It isn't even Rome or Milan. The police operation here is small. They don't have the same resources—'

'Someone has died,' Margot snapped. 'Do they not realise that? They should be here now!'

Sofia paled. For a brief moment, she looked past the crowd. Following her gaze, Robyn saw Eva's cousins lingering at the back of the group. They were watching her intently, the bearded man with a face like stone.

'They'll be here as soon as they can,' she said, returning her attention to Margot. 'For now, I must ask everyone to please remain calm. It's very hot today, so please stay in the shade. If you need water, our staff will bring some for you. There is a bathroom inside the casermetta—'

'This is ridiculous,' said Miles. 'We aren't going to just wait here. Let's call a boat and wait for the police in Malcesine.'

'The police have asked that nobody leaves the island until they have arrived.'

An uncomfortable silence fell on the group, Sofia visibly struggling to maintain her confidence.

'What is it that's stopping the police from coming?' Jeremy asked. 'Do they have far to travel? Are there no available officers? Whatever else they're dealing with, what's happened here should surely be treated as the highest priority.'

Sofia cleared her throat. 'They are coming,' she said, forcing a note of authority into her voice. 'They'll be here as soon as they can. If I hear anything else, I will tell you. For now, please stay calm and stay in the shade.'

Before anyone from the group could protest any further, she began to stride in the direction of the gatehouse.

29

Closing the office door behind her, Sofia swore. She swore over and over again, teeth gritted as she tried to release some of the nervous energy that was burning inside her veins.

The group inside the casermetta — the guests on the bride's side — had been exactly the same. When were the police coming? How long would they be? What was keeping them? The worst part, perhaps, was that she couldn't blame them. If she were in their shoes she would be asking exactly the same questions.

Had they believed her? It seemed as if they might. But for how long? Tempers were already wearing thin. How long would it take for someone to take matters into their own hands and call the police themselves?

She looked at the phone on the desk. This was insane. Utterly insane. But what could she do?

She closed her eyes, the image of her son burned into her mind.

Hearing the door open, she turned to see the two men entering the office. She put on the bravest face she could muster. They terrified her. But she didn't want them to see it. 'Well?'

'Someone's coming.'

'When?'

She noticed it was always the man with the beard and pony-tail who spoke. The younger, more fresh-faced of the two seemed to constantly linger behind him, his expression somewhere between avid curiosity and profound discomfort.

The bearded man's eyes narrowed. 'There's a boat coming from the southern shore.'

'The southern shore?' Sofia's eyes flew wide. 'That'll take at least an hour!'

'Two.'

'*Two hours?*' She glanced at the clock on the wall, suddenly so terrified she thought she might be sick. 'What am I meant to tell these people for *two hours*? How do I explain that the police won't come until after *three o'clock*? No one will believe it!'

The bearded man didn't reply. Instead, those dark eyes twitched to the desk. Sofia's heart leapt into her throat. The picture of her son . . . She hadn't yet put it back inside the drawer. It sat on the surface of the desk, clear for them all to see.

She and the bearded man locked eyes. Nothing was said. Nothing needed to be. For a split second she wondered if he had been the one on the phone. The one who had recited her instructions. Maybe even the one who had taken the photo. She doubted it. But it didn't matter. All that mattered was that he knew what had been promised to her if she failed to do what they asked.

Finally, after what felt like a painstakingly long time, he broke the silence.

'Two hours,' he said. 'No police.'

One o'clock

30

The mood among the guests had become so bleak that Robyn struggled to believe only an hour had passed since she had been seated on the terrace, waiting for the ceremony to begin.

Laurence had once again sunk onto one of the stone benches that occupied the courtyard, staring into space as Chadwick and Miles fussed over him. Margot, Jeremy, Stephen and Abigail all looked on, their expressions grim. Harper took a vape out of her bag and made for the gates, apparently planning to smoke it on the jetty. Eva's cousins, meanwhile, congregated near the gatehouse.

Robyn lingered on them for a moment, wishing she'd understood what Vito had been saying. They were his nephews, supposedly. At least, that was what they had told Laurence in the harbour. But the way he had just come at them . . . The fury in his voice. Even the way they were loitering in the courtyard, rather than joining the other Italians inside the casermetta . . .

The truth was that they just didn't seem right. Robyn understood that families could strain. She'd seen that clearly enough these past two days, with Toby and the Heywoods. But this was different. And with every passing moment, she couldn't help but feel a growing sense that something about these two men just wasn't being said.

Looking away, she tried to quell her unease, searching instead for Cam.

The photographer had moved to the opposite side of the courtyard, standing now on a different patch of lawn. She was still completely alone, and while Robyn couldn't quite make out the expression behind her sunglasses, she seemed to be chewing her lip, her arms tightly folded.

Returning in her mind to the moment she'd been fished out of the lake, Robyn remembered how Cam had come over on the upper deck. She pictured the bottle of water and the glass of champagne, the kindness written plainly across her face . . .

'I'm going to check Cam's all right.'

'The photographer?' Toby made no effort to keep the surprise out of his voice. 'Won't Harper look after her?'

'She's on her own, Toby. And this is hardly what she signed up for. I'm just going to make sure she's OK.'

He recoiled slightly and, once again, Robyn realised she had spoken to him more sharply than she had meant.

'OK,' he said quietly. 'Sure.'

She crossed the courtyard quickly, silently relieved to be putting some distance between them, even if only for a few minutes. Seeing her approach, Cam gave a small smile. As Robyn grew closer, though, she could see that the photographer's cheeks were puffy. She had clearly been crying.

'Wanted to check you're all right,' she said. 'I bet you'd give anything right now for that cold studio and a crap coffee.'

Cam gave a short laugh, looking down at her hands. They

were trembling. 'You're not wrong. For a minute there, I really thought Eva's dad was coming for me.' She breathed out a sigh. 'Do you know what he was saying?'

'No idea. I don't speak a word of Italian.'

Cam nodded. Seeing how badly shaken she was, Robyn attempted a sympathetic smile.

'I'm sorry about your feature.'

'Thanks. I've had a few messages from my editor, asking how it's all going. Haven't had the heart to tell her yet. She's going to be so pissed off.'

'Would she really give you a hard time? You can't exactly help it if the bride doesn't make it down the aisle.'

'True. But she was desperate to cover this, and the flights and hotel won't have been cheap. All money down the drain now.'

Robyn watched her, thinking about the photos she must have taken before the rest of the wedding party had arrived on the island. The bridal party getting ready inside the casermetta. The guests mingling in the courtyard. The terrace, decorated for the ceremony. None of them would ever see the light of day.

But as she thought of Cam's ruined feature, picturing her scurrying around the castle with her camera, another thought crept into Robyn's mind. A way to perhaps ease her concerns about Toby.

'Cam,' she said, in as level a voice as she could manage. 'When did you last see Eva?'

Cam tensed. 'Why?'

'I'm not trying to suggest anything.' Robyn threw up her hands. 'I promise, I'm not. I only thought . . . You must have been sticking pretty close to her this morning. I wondered if you might have seen . . .'

She tailed off, Cam beginning to glare at her.

'Listen,' she tried, carefully weighing each word. 'I'm worried someone might have been . . .' She swallowed. 'Involved. You were here all morning. You've been taking pictures all around the castle. I only wondered if you'd seen something – anything – that might put my mind at ease. That might help to prove I'm wrong.'

Cam didn't reply at first. She just stood, sizing Robyn up from behind her sunglasses. After a few moments, though, she seemed to relax. Not completely. But enough, at least, to talk.

'The last I saw of Eva was just as you guys were arriving. We were taking some pictures up on the terrace with the bridal party, while the castle was empty and their make-up was fresh. We took a few shots, then Eva spotted that the boats were coming. She didn't want anyone to see her dress before she walked up the aisle, so she went back inside the casermetta.'

'She went by herself?'

'She went inside by herself, but we all left the terrace together. When we reached the courtyard, the bridesmaids went straight to the jetty to meet you all, and Eva went into the casermetta.'

'Where were you?'

'I went with the bridesmaids. I wanted some shots of everyone arriving.'

'I didn't see you.'

Cam gave a little shrug. 'That's kind of the idea, isn't it? A

194

good wedding photographer should capture everything without ever really being seen.'

She lifted her camera and began flicking through her pictures. There were dozens of the wedding party in the courtyard. She stopped for a moment on a beautiful shot of Robyn and Toby. Robyn looked at the two of them, smiling together, and for a moment her heart ached.

She lowered the camera again. 'Who is it that you're worried about?'

Robyn floundered, caught off guard. 'I . . . I don't know if I should say.'

'Robyn, come on. You think someone in here might be a killer and you really aren't going to tell me who? I'm on my own!' She was pleading now, a hint of desperation in her voice. 'Is it Vito?'

Robyn started. 'You think he would kill his own daughter? Why? Because of the way he came at those two?'

'It isn't just that. He was acting strangely all morning. Even before . . .' She hesitated, then grimaced and breathed a sigh. 'He and Eva had a massive bust-up before the rest of you arrived.'

'Over what?'

'No idea, it was all in Italian. But it just . . . I don't know. It seemed odd. He and Eva's mum caught the boat over with us first thing. I thought it was meant to be just the bridal party, the hairdressers, the make-up artists and me. Then suddenly the pair of them are there, getting on the boats with us. I didn't question it. I guessed they just wanted to get some nice family pictures before everyone else arrived. But about an hour after we'd got here, Eva blew up at him.'

Robyn thought of the last time she'd seen Eva. She'd been furious then, too, storming from the restaurant after finding the message in her bag.

'Could it have been to do with that note?' Then, remembering that Cam hadn't been allowed in the restaurant, she added, 'Did you hear about that? Has someone told you what happened?'

Cam nodded. 'Harper filled me in. She tiptoed around Eva all morning, trying not to set her off again – sounds like she must have really lost it. I couldn't tell you, though, if that had anything to do with this fight with her dad. As I say, they spoke in Italian.'

'Could none of the others have translated? One of the bridesmaids, maybe? Everyone was getting ready in the casermetta, right? They must have heard it too.'

Cam shook her head. 'This didn't happen in the casermetta. It was up there.'

Robyn's stomach dropped as she pointed towards the top of the narrower staircase. Towards the archway she and Toby had passed through a few minutes ago on their way to the museum.

'It was Eva's turn to have her make-up done,' Cam explained, 'and she wanted a shot of her adoring father looking on, doughy-eyed. But there was no sign of him. She went looking and she must have found him up there. I don't know what he'd been doing, but whatever it was, she seemed livid.'

'Didn't it bother them that you were there?'

'They didn't even realise. I had plenty of pictures of the bridesmaids having their hair and make-up done, so I'd been taking advantage of the opportunity to get some of the castle while it was empty. One of the bridesmaids had told me that

Eva was about to start getting ready, so I was on my way back to the casermetta when I heard them. They probably thought they were completely alone.'

Robyn's mind raced. It had to be a coincidence. Surely. Vito wouldn't murder his own daughter. But then, what had he been doing outside the museum? Why had he come early to the island? And what could he have done to upset Eva?

'So?' Cam demanded. 'Is it him? Is he the one you're worried about?'

'I . . .' Robyn tailed off, her mind doing backflips. 'I really don't think I should say. I might be wrong. I *hope* I'm wrong. I don't want to go putting anyone in the firing line.'

Cam grimaced, but she didn't push any further. 'Fine. But for what it's worth, I'd steer clear of him. He'd have to be a real piece of work to kill her. But until the police get here and I've told them what I saw . . .'

Robyn nodded. 'I'll watch out for him. Thank you.'

'I should find Harper. She looked pretty shaken up down in the cove.' Cam's expression softened slightly. 'Thanks, though. For coming over. It was kind of you.'

Robyn nodded again, and for a little while after she'd gone, thought over what Cam had shared.

She had to find something that would help explain where Toby had been. She was going to go mad if she didn't. And while she had hoped Cam might offer that, the photographer had unwittingly made it worse.

If Eva had gone back into the casermetta as the boats were arriving, that would have placed it at half past eleven. And if she had failed to walk down the aisle at twelve, that suggested a half-hour window in which . . .

Robyn stopped herself, trying hard to keep the scene in the cove from flashing into her mind's eye.

A half-hour window in which *it* must have happened.

So when had she gone from the casermetta to the cove? They'd all been in the courtyard for a good fifteen minutes after getting off the boats. And while Cam might have moved among the crowd with relative anonymity, there was no chance of Eva doing the same in her wedding dress.

She must have moved after the staff and bridesmaids had cleared the courtyard, ushering everyone up to the terrace at quarter to twelve. That would cut the half-hour window in which she had gone to the cove down from thirty minutes to just fifteen. Specifically, the fifteen minutes in which Toby had gone looking for a glass of water. And where had he gone for it? The casermetta.

Robyn dug her nails into her palms, trying to fight off a sense of steadily rising dread.

It could be a coincidence. While she didn't believe he had spent fifteen minutes looking for a glass of water, Robyn was reluctant to assume Toby had instead spent that time murdering Eva.

What about the argument Cam had witnessed between Eva and Vito?

When they had sailed to the island, it hadn't seemed strange that Vito and Paola weren't there. In all honesty, Robyn had been so distracted by her discomfort at being back out on the lake that the question of why Vito might choose to go to the island with the bridal party hadn't crossed her mind.

But thinking about it now . . .

Cam was right. Vito would have to be a real piece of work to murder his own daughter. And whatever Eva had been berating him for, it could be pure coincidence that she'd done so near the museum. The castle wasn't huge, after all.

All the same, she cast another glance at the two men from the boat, her sense of unease continuing to grow as they lingered outside the gatehouse. She watched them for a moment, wishing again that she had understood what Vito had said to them. She thought of the fury in his voice as he'd stormed across the courtyard. The way the bearded man had reached inside his jacket . . .

She shuddered and tried to think of something less distressing. Her mind, however, settled on something equally puzzling. Just a few metres away stood Abigail. She was completely still, her mouth set in a thin line. And she was staring, without question, at Robyn.

Robyn met her gaze, wondering if perhaps she was imagining it. Waiting for Abigail at any moment to look away or flash her a half-hearted smile.

She did neither.

Robyn began to walk, moving as casually as she could across the cobblestones. After a few yards, she stopped and looked back. She had hoped to see Abigail watching the spot where she had just been, or to have been distracted by something else. Instead, she had followed her, the same venomous stare fixed firmly in place.

There was no denying that she was the object of Abigail's attention. The way she was glaring, though . . . In her entire life, Robyn didn't think she had ever been looked at with such unbridled resentment.

31

After nearly twenty years by his side, Stephen finally knew what it took to faze Laurence.

The thought of the police coming any day to arrest them for murder hadn't done it. The minutes before his wedding, his family watching as he stood at the top of the aisle hadn't even done it. In the end, it had taken the sight of his fiancée, splayed upon the floor with a dagger in her chest.

Of course, he, too, was shaken by what they had seen in the cove. How could he not be? But something had happened to Laurence. Within the space of a few minutes he had become a different man, staring into space as he sat on the bench outside the casermetta. His jacket had been discarded onto the floor, his shoulders slumped. Stephen felt as if he should say something – do something – but he had no idea what. This wasn't the Laurence he knew.

There was a part of him that wanted to feel vindicated. After everything Laurence and Eva had put him and Abigail through – all the sleepless nights – he wanted to feel glad someone had finally shown them, once and for all, that they were not in fact untouchable.

But he couldn't manage it. No matter how badly he wanted to tell himself she'd had it coming, no one deserved what had happened to Eva.

Abigail interrupted his thoughts, taking him by the elbow and leading him silently away. Stephen looked back at Laurence. If he had even noticed that they were leaving, he didn't show it.

She led him to the far corner of the courtyard, where she swept a quick glance around. Apparently satisfied no one could hear them, she looked him straight in the eye, dropping her voice low.

'Where were they during the wedding?'

Stephen peered at her.

'Who?'

'Who do you think?'

One by one, he ran through the guests in his head, until it dawned on him exactly what Abigail was suggesting. 'Oh, come on . . .'

'I didn't see Toby up on the terrace,' she said. 'Did you see Robyn?'

'You can't seriously think they would do this.'

'Don't you? After that warning in Eva's bag, how can you not?'

He forced calm into his voice, his mouth suddenly dry. 'Abi. You can't accuse them of murder just because you think they slipped a bit of paper into Eva's bag.'

'You *know* it wasn't just a bit of paper—'

'Think about it, Abi.' He spoke over her, his voice urgent. 'Just think. If Robyn or Toby were planning to kill Eva, why would they give her that message? I've never planned a murder before, but I would imagine that giving your victim a day's warning probably isn't a great way to go about it.'

Abigail's expression softened, and as Stephen realised what he'd just said, his own words catching up with him, he felt his knees go weak.

He looked down at the ground. 'I thought you'd be pleased. You wanted her gone, didn't you?'

Abigail's fury snapped immediately back into place. 'All I wanted was for her to be out of our lives. I didn't want her dead! We have to do something, Stephen. We have to talk to Laurence. Maybe even Jeremy.'

Stephen grasped her hands. 'Please, Abi. I know it looks bad. But you can't say anything to Laurence. Especially not before the police have even arrived. Just look at him. If you tell him that Toby and his girlfriend murdered Eva, she won't be the only one leaving this island in a body bag.'

Abigail thought for a moment, looking over at Laurence. Finally, she relented, shrugging him roughly away.

'The moment the police arrive,' she said. 'The second they get here I'm telling them about the note. But if they do anything else in the meantime – *anything* – I'm going straight to Laurence.'

Stephen said nothing. He looked into her eyes, seeing without doubt just how serious she was, and hoped beyond hope that the police would arrive soon.

32

Harper stood on the jetty, staring out across the lake.

When she'd first set foot on those boards that morning, she had been fizzing with optimism. So hopeful for what the day would mean for Eva's career. Now, as she watched the light shimmer on the water, feeling the warmth on her face, she was thinking instead about what she could salvage from the soon-to-be wreckage of her own.

With a quivering hand, she lifted the vape and took a deep breath. She wished she'd taken the advice of her colleagues and brought a hipflask. She was working, she had insisted. There would be plenty of time to find a glass of fizz after Cam had what she needed. If only she had known how the day would go. A swig of Bacardi would take the edge off much more effectively than the sweet-scented vapour.

What had she been thinking?

She asked herself over and over again, as if an answer might somehow present itself, when really, deep down, she knew.

She hadn't been thinking. As she'd stormed to confront Eva in the casermetta, there had scarcely been a conscious thought in her head. Instead, she had been fuelled by pure, unfiltered rage. Rage for all of her wasted work. All of the weekends and the late nights, trying anything she could think of to repair the damage that had been done with Rachel Carlisle. Rage for Eva's obliviousness.

No. She hadn't been thinking. She had simply wanted to hurt Eva. Hurt her as deeply as she could, with whatever means were available to her.

But she would never have wanted her to die.

The sight of her in the cove . . . Splayed upon the shale with that dagger buried in her chest. It was, without exception, the most horrific thing Harper had ever seen.

Inside her bag, she heard her phone buzz. Her manager, presumably, trying a third time to call. Just as with the first two attempts, she ignored it. A few seconds later there came another buzz, sharper than before. A WhatsApp message.

This time, Harper did take out her phone. The message hovered in the middle of the screen, taunting her.

WTF is happening? Call me!

It was all she could do not to throw the phone into the lake.

The second she'd done it, she'd known there was no taking it back. She hadn't felt a morsel of regret, though. She had given Eva no less than she deserved.

But the moment Dina's scream rang out through the castle, the thought took root in Harper's mind that she might have made a mistake. And when Eva's body was found, she knew without a doubt.

Now the police were coming, and a murder investigation was about to begin. She would be questioned, presumably. Like everyone else in the castle. Her movements would be assessed and any motives for wanting Eva dead would be brought into the light.

Perhaps no one would suspect her. No one in the castle had asked her any questions. If anything, the two families barely seemed to have noticed she was there. And while the news of what she'd done had evidently reached the agency, her manager's message at least indicated that she didn't seem to suspect Harper of having played a role.

She took another pull on the vape.

It wasn't fair. It was a futile thought, and it irritated her to find it creeping into her mind. But she couldn't help it.

All she had ever wanted was to please her clients. Impress her team. Forge a career that others would one day look on with envy. She wondered if there had ever been hope for her, or if she had been doomed to fail the moment Eva came into her life.

A pair of brightly coloured jet-skis hummed past, kicking up plumes of water in their wake. Harper watched them go, and for a split second felt a sob rise into her throat, the hole she had dug for herself threatening to overwhelm her.

She fought the tears back down.

It didn't matter what she had done. It had been a mistake, yes. A stupid one, at that. But it didn't have to be the end of her. If she was smart – kept her head down and played dumb until they could leave – she would be fine. Her phone could be ignored. She would have a considerable amount of explaining to do when she did finally respond to the office, but with Eva lying dead on a beach, she could hardly be questioned for being somewhat distracted.

She would plead ignorance where she could and offer deflections where she had to. For better or worse, Eva was gone now. And Harper wasn't going to go down with her.

33

No matter how she tried, Robyn couldn't stop thinking about the daggers.

Would the police find fingerprints? She doubted it. If Eva's killer had the foresight to bring a perfect replica of the Vincenzi dagger – potentially even the means to swap it for the real one without leaving a trace – they would surely have thought to bring a pair of gloves.

There might be other DNA, she supposed. Skin. Hair. But how long would that take to analyse? And how conclusive would it be? She had absolutely no idea.

Before she could ponder it further, Laurence rose abruptly from his bench.

'I'm not doing this. I'm not sitting here, waiting for the bloody police. Someone get them here. Get them here now!' He wheeled around, eyes bulging. 'Don't they understand what's happening? Don't they know that my fiancée is *dead*?'

As if in answer to his question, there was movement at the door of the casermetta. Following it, Robyn saw Dina emerge from the yellow-stone building, dabbing at her eyes.

'Dina!' Laurence strode to intercept her. 'Please, Dina. How did you find her? What made you look in the cove?'

She didn't reply, looking up at him with fear written plainly across her face.

Toby stepped forward. 'That's enough, Laurence. Come away. Give her some room.'

Laurence ignored him. He towered over Eva's younger sister, his hands on her shoulders as if to hold her in place.

'I don't know,' she managed, her voice quivering. 'Giulia looked for her inside the casermetta. Beatrice went to the museum. I went to the beach.'

'But what was she doing down there?' Laurence pressed. 'When did you last see her? Why did she leave you?'

'I don't know! She went inside when we met the boats. When we went to find her, after we'd sent you all to the terrace, she was gone.' Her voice was shaking badly now, her terror becoming clearer for all to see.

Toby put a hand on Laurence's shoulder. '*That's enough.* Leave her alone.'

At Toby's touch, Laurence seemed to completely forget Dina. He turned and with both hands shoved his brother roughly away.

'My fiancée is dead! Why does nobody know what she was doing in that cove? Why does nobody *care*?'

Before anyone could respond, Vito emerged from the casermetta, his bloodshot eyes flitting from Laurence to Dina.

'What's happening?'

'Nothing is happening.' Margot stepped forward, her voice cold with unquestionable authority.

They stood there for a moment, the father of the bride and the mother of the groom, staring at each other so intently that Robyn thought one of them might shatter.

She remembered the last time she had heard them speak, in the restaurant. Was Vito now asking the same question that she, herself, had asked of Jeremy in the museum? Was he wondering if they might somehow have arranged Eva's death?

If he was, he didn't say as much. Without a word, he put his arm around the still quivering Dina and guided her back inside. Laurence, meanwhile, sank again onto his bench, his shoulders heaving with quiet sobs as he pressed his hands to his face.

Robyn supposed she should feel some kind of sympathy for him. Instead, as she saw how he'd left Dina, shaking like a daisy in a gale, she was momentarily repulsed.

Still, as begrudging as she was to admit it, his outburst had yielded something useful. Dina, in her terror, had more or less confirmed Cam's timeline. Eva and the bridesmaids had left the terrace together. She had gone inside and they had set off to meet the boats, only to find that she was missing when they themselves returned to the casermetta. Why she had gone to the cove, though, and quite how she had managed it without being seen, Robyn was still none the wiser.

She wanted to speak to someone. To share her theory that Eva must have left the casermetta sometime between quarter to and twelve o'clock, after the guests had moved to the terrace. She wanted Toby . . .

She watched him for a little while, standing by Laurence with a pained expression. Then, over his shoulder, she saw movement. If she'd looked just a moment later, she'd have missed it.

Instead, she was just in time to see Jeremy Lambourne disappear through the archway at the top of the narrow staircase.

She frowned, so confused that her fears momentarily evaporated. Because there was only one place he could be going. The museum.

She flicked a quick glance at the group, to see if anyone else had noticed. Toby was still fixed on Laurence, his back to the staircase. Even Margot was deep in conversation with Abigail and Stephen. Robyn, it seemed, had been the only one.

She looked towards the archway. As she did, she heard Jeremy's conversation with Vito in the restaurant. She saw his curious exchange with Margot on the terrace, just minutes before Dina's scream rang out. She saw the dagger in his guidebook – the book he had bought personally before travelling to Italy.

Why, now, was he quietly slipping away to the museum?

She should tell someone. Pursuing a potential murderer hardly seemed an advisable course of action. Even less so, when considering doing it alone.

But what if this helped? What if following Jeremy would prove, somehow, that Toby couldn't be the culprit?

She checked one last time that no one was watching. Confident she wouldn't be seen, she hurried up the stone staircase before she could change her mind and passed once again through the archway.

Heart pounding, she slipped quietly into the museum. Jeremy had gone straight to the far end, his back to her as he inspected the case containing the dagger. Lingering by the doorway in case she needed to retreat, she took out her phone and began to film him. Evidence, she told herself. Although evidence of what, she had no idea.

She peered at him, transfixed. What was he doing? They must have stood there for an entire minute, Robyn's mind racing as Jeremy hovered before the cabinet.

She should turn back. Nobody knew that she'd followed him. That she was *alone* with him. She could leave right then, without him realising she'd ever been there. And yet she stayed rooted in place. There were several metres between them, and she could outrun him if she had to.

The thought didn't fill her with as much confidence as she would have liked.

'Are you going to come inside?' Jeremy asked, raising his voice so that it echoed from the stone walls.

The fear gripped her so suddenly it was all she could do not to turn and run.

'I can see you in the glass,' he explained. 'You can stay there if you like. But you don't need to worry. I didn't kill her.'

Robyn screwed her eyes shut, cursing her own carelessness. Opening them again, she called back across the museum. 'What are you doing then?'

'The same thing you are, I'd imagine. Seeing it for myself.'

He turned, weighing her up from behind his thick-rimmed glasses. She looked back into the little courtyard. She should leave. Right now.

'It's the same,' she said, fighting to keep the fear from her voice. 'Isn't it? I recognised it in the cove. It was in the guide-book you showed me yesterday, the green jewel in the hilt. It looked quite distinctive.'

Jeremy returned his attention to the dagger. 'It most certainly is,' he said, speaking to the glass. 'The Vincenzi dagger.

Awarded by the Republic of Venice to the general who reclaimed this castle from the French in the sixteenth century.'

His voice gave no indication whatsoever that they might be speaking about a potential murder weapon. If anything, there was something wistful in his tone. Robyn couldn't help but give a shiver.

'Does it have a twin?' she asked. 'Was it . . . I don't know. Was it made as a pair, perhaps?'

'Never. As I understand it, it was intended as one of a kind.'

'So one's a fake.'

'It would seem so.'

'Can you tell which?'

Jeremy took a deep breath, the sound hissing in the stillness of the museum. 'The jewel is Murano glass. It's an artform that's been practised for over a thousand years, originating on the island of Murano, in Venice. Every piece is unique, hand-crafted by a master artisan. So yes, if someone with knowledge of this particular piece were given the chance, it's entirely possible they would be able to pick out the original. I'd very much like to try it myself, but I'm no expert. Even if I were, I would need to take a closer look at the other dagger, and given where it's currently residing, that wouldn't be at all appropriate. And of course, once the police arrive, it'll be taken away as evidence. What I will say, though, is that if this one's the fake, it seems to me that it's remarkably convincing.'

Ignoring her instincts, Robyn took a step closer. He clearly wasn't interested in her. He was there for the dagger.

'It's valuable,' she said. 'Isn't it?'

'It's priceless.'

'And why would someone want to kill Eva specifically with this dagger? Or if it's the replica that's been used, one that looks like it? It seems to me that whoever it was has gone to some serious effort in order to do it.'

'No reason at all. At least, none that I'm aware of.'

'She isn't some long-lost descendant of the Venetian general?'

Jeremy snorted. 'There isn't anything remotely interesting about the Bianchi line.'

Robyn thought back to the conversation she'd overheard in the restaurant. Jeremy told Vito that he and Margot had made an investigation into his business affairs. It sounded now as though he'd looked into much more than that. He'd been digging into Eva's ancestry, too.

'So why do you think it's been used? Why would it be so important for someone to kill Eva with this dagger?'

'I haven't the faintest idea.'

Robyn chewed her lip, wondering if she was brave enough to ask. 'Could all of this be to do with Vito's business?'

Immediately, she regretted it. Jeremy looked away from the dagger, his eyes narrowing as he abruptly turned his gaze on her.

'You heard us in the restaurant.'

'Do you think it could be connected?'

She held his gaze, determined not to look away. After what felt like an eternity but must have only been a few seconds, his features shifted into a stern expression.

'We've spoken enough. The police are bound to be here soon, and when they arrive I'll make sure they're aware of the daggers. For the time being, I suggest you do all you can not to be involved. Now. Shall we?'

He motioned towards the door, his tone making it clear that this was very much a rhetorical question.

She didn't protest. Nor did she think about trying to press him any further on Vito's financial troubles. He'd shared all that he was going to.

She nodded and allowed him to usher her back into the sunlight.

34

Following Jeremy through the stone archway, Robyn looked down into the courtyard.

Toby was speaking to Margot, concern on his face. She saw him shake his head, shrug and cast a look around. Immediately she knew what was happening. He was looking for her.

Panic took hold, and before she could think about where her feet might be taking her, she hurried down the narrow staircase and darted across the courtyard towards the only cover she could see. The casermetta.

The moment she was inside, she swore under her breath. It would have been difficult enough explaining to Toby why she'd followed Jeremy to the museum. But outright hiding from him would be something else entirely.

She felt a sudden flush of frustration at the idea of having to explain anything to him at all. He was the one acting so suspiciously. The one who was so clearly lying. Why should she be the one explaining her actions?

Surveying her surroundings, she saw thick wooden beams adorning the roof like railway sleepers. At the far end of the hallway, daylight poured through a pair of French windows, a small balcony on the other side of the glass offering an elevated view of the lake. The place was cool, too, much like the museum. She wasn't sure if it was just the air conditioning or the traditional Italian architecture, but she was intensely grateful for how effectively these old buildings managed to keep the heat at bay.

A staff member appeared, apparently startling herself with the sudden sight of a guest. She looked to be the youngest of the four waiters Robyn had seen; barely much older, at a guess, than eighteen. Was this a summer job for her? Perhaps she was a student somewhere. Robyn wondered what was running through her mind. She must be terrified.

'Can I help with anything?' she asked.

Robyn shook her head. 'No, thank you. Just getting out of the sun for a minute.'

She nodded, attempting an unconvincing smile, before continuing out into the courtyard.

With her flat shoes padding softly on the tiled floor, Robyn walked the length of the hallway. Passing the archway through which the young woman had appeared, she looked into an ornate dining room. Inside was a long table with several chairs on either side, each place laid with gleaming cutlery and sparkling glassware. Four enormous buckets, filled with champagne and ice, waited on the top. Robyn supposed they would have been popped open towards the end of the ceremony, and served as the guests descended from the terrace into the courtyard. She wondered what they would have eaten, had they made it to the wedding breakfast. Noticing the sheer number of utensils that had been laid for each place setting, it looked as if whatever was planned might have been served over as many as five or six different courses.

Reaching the glass doors at the end of the hallway, she stood and looked towards the shore, picking out buildings the size of thumbnails, cars tracing along the shoreline like a marching procession of steadily moving ants. She had never felt so stranded in all her life. She was desperate to be off this island. Desperate to climb into a taxi and go to the airport. Seeing it all there, just a fifteen-minute boat ride away, made it worse. Not even the fear of being out on the water again could have stopped her from seizing an opportunity to leave.

A speedboat drifted past, bringing her thoughts back to the little vessel she had seen circling the island before Eva's body had been found.

As she pictured the skipper, turning away and heading back to shore, a sudden thought occurred to her. He'd broken his loop just moments before Dina's scream rang out. She tried to remember where, exactly, he had been when he turned away. Would he have been able to see into the cove? Had he been watching – waiting – for Eva's body to be found?

She felt a quiet rush of excitement at the possibility of a tangible theory. But as quickly as it had appeared, it then dwindled.

What would be the point? And why had Eva been in the cove at all? Would it really be possible for the skipper to sail in, sneak up to the casermetta and somehow lure her back down with him, only to then watch the island until her body was dis-covered before making his escape?

Possible, yes. But plausible? Robyn doubted it.

She heard the Italians moving around upstairs. Realising she couldn't simply linger in the hallway, she approached a door directly to her left. Opening it gently, she found it led to a kitchen.

It was a bizarre sight, the gleaming catering equipment

painfully out of place against the classic Italian architecture. The two chefs she had seen in the courtyard were now back inside. Still dressed in their whites and aprons, they were talking quietly, grim expressions on their faces as they leaned against a steel-topped counter. At the sight of Robyn, however, they paused.

'Sorry,' she said, a sudden thought occurring to her. 'I was looking for some water.'

The male chef waved her inside and opened a cupboard, revealing several rows of polished glasses. Taking one, he approached an enormous American-style fridge, opened the door and fetched out a bottle of spring water. Over his shoulder, Robyn saw that the fridge was even larger than she had expected, trays of delicate-looking canapés and intricately decorated desserts filling the shelves.

'Very hot,' the chef said, pressing the glass into Robyn's hand.

'Yes,' she agreed. 'Yes, it's hot out there.'

She sipped at the water, realising it was the first drink she'd had since they left the villa two and a half hours ago.

Two and a half hours . . . Was that really all it had been? It felt like days.

Relishing the ice-cold water, her sips quickly turned to glugs, the chef watching her with a raised eyebrow.

'More?' he asked.

Robyn held out the glass. 'Please.'

After he'd refilled it, she wondered if they were going to send her back out. Under ordinary circumstances, she doubted she would even have been allowed in. If he did want to send her away, though, he didn't show it. Instead, he returned to the conversation with his colleague.

Watching them, Robyn leaned against a counter of her own,

moving cautiously as if they might scold her or shoot her a dirty look. Still, they didn't protest. She noticed now that they had fetched beers from somewhere, the female chef saying something in Italian that made her colleague wince and shake his head.

Confident that they weren't going to send her away, Robyn allowed herself to relax a little, taking her time with this second glass of water.

Fifteen minutes it had apparently taken Toby to fetch a drink before the wedding. The chef had just done it in less than fifteen seconds. Admittedly, Toby wouldn't have known which cupboard to look in for the glasses. But fifteen minutes to find them? Absolutely not. And wouldn't the chefs have been there to help him, just as they had her?

Before she could stop herself, she thought of something an old lecturer used to tell her. A mantra on which he had apparently leaned every day as an investigative reporter.

People lie. Facts don't.

She closed her eyes, trying to organise her thoughts. Toby was lying to her. There was no questioning it. So what had he actually been doing just before Eva had died? She had to work it out. She didn't think she could face him again without knowing.

Taking her phone from her bag, she caught sight of the time. Half-past one. Sofia hadn't been wrong when she addressed the group. With more than an hour having now passed since she disappeared into the gatehouse to call them, the police really were taking their time.

Robyn shook the thought from her mind, trying hard not to let it rattle her. There was nothing she could do about the police. Instead, she unlocked the phone, opened a new note and typed out a timeline:

11:30 – We arrive on the island. Sofia ushers us from the jetty to the castle. Eva goes into the casermetta.

11:45 – Bridesmaids send us from the courtyard to the terrace. Toby goes into the casermetta.

12:00 – Ceremony is due to begin. Toby comes to the terrace.

12:10 – Dina finds Eva in the cove.

She stared at the words, willing an answer to present itself. Some perfectly innocent explanation, so obvious that she couldn't believe she had missed it, which would lay all of her fears to rest.

Nothing came.

With a growing sense of dread, she focused on the time between quarter to and twelve o'clock. The window in which Toby had been gone and Eva must have moved from the casermetta to the cove.

Who else had been there during those fifteen minutes?

Robyn hadn't seen Vito and Paola in the courtyard, but she knew that Vito was going to walk Eva up the aisle. They must have been inside, keeping her company while the bridesmaids helped shepherd everyone up to the terrace.

As for the bridesmaids themselves . . . Robyn had seen the three of them on the terrace at quarter to, making sure everyone was settled. She knew they must have left at some point to rejoin Eva, but she hadn't been paying them enough attention to remember when, exactly, they had gone.

Sofia might have gone inside. Again, Robyn hadn't been paying her much attention, but she supposed Sofia would have spent those fifteen minutes drifting between the terrace and the casermetta, making sure all was ready before the ceremony began.

Then there was the possibility of an intruder. Someone who wasn't part of the wedding party, and who had been hiding inside the castle, waiting for their opportunity. Much as Robyn would like to believe it, though, that particular theory felt like a luxury she couldn't afford. She struggled to see how someone could sneak onto the island, remain hidden until a few minutes before the ceremony and then either escape unnoticed or have continued since to avoid detection.

There it was. Eva's parents. The bridesmaids. Sofia. All had been inside the casermetta at some point between quarter to and twelve o'clock. One of them must, surely, have seen Toby. One of them must know what he had been doing.

But then, this was the same group that had somehow failed to notice Eva – the bride, of all people – get up and leave, just minutes before she was due to walk up the aisle.

A new theory began, unbidden, to take shape in Robyn's mind. The bridal party had been getting ready upstairs. After all, there seemed to be nothing downstairs except the kitchen and the dining room. Say that Toby really had been in the kitchen, and for some reason Eva had come downstairs. They could have walked straight out of the front door without anyone else inside the casermetta being any the wiser.

She scowled, shaking the thought away.

Eager to try a different approach, she considered the other questions surrounding Eva's death, wondering if one of them might hold the answer.

Why had Eva been in the cove? And why kill her with the Vincenzi dagger?

The question of the dagger had her well and truly stumped. Casting a quick glance around the kitchen, it struck her with a shiver that there was a veritable array of equally deadly knives within much easier reach. Someone had clearly felt the need to use the dagger, but she had no idea why.

She thought about how little Jeremy had said in the museum. No theory on why the dagger had been used. Nothing to suggest which was even real. All he'd been able to tell her was that the dagger was priceless and that it was one of a kind, both of which she had more or less already guessed herself.

She began to think of other reasons that might exist for members of the wedding party to kill Eva. There was Jeremy and Margot, of course, protecting HCM from Vito's debt. Likewise, there was the curious argument Cam had witnessed between Eva and Vito, although Robyn could still think of no reason why Eva's parents would murder their own daughter.

There was Dina, she supposed. Eva's sister had, after all, been the one to find the body. To reduce suspicion, perhaps? Or maybe even to cover some crucial piece of evidence before Eva was inevitably found. Robyn pictured her in her sage green dress, remembering Toby's story about her own ruined wedding plans.

And what about Harper? It was clear how badly unappreciated she was, and it was she who had been looking after Eva's bag when the note was found. Robyn had wondered how the message could have been slipped inside while Harper was watching it. What if the truth was that it had been Harper herself who put it there? Perhaps, after trying so desperately to keep Eva's career going in the wake of Rachel Carlisle's hospitalisation, she had finally snapped.

Struggling for other motives, she turned her mind to the two men who had shared their boat.

At first, they'd struck her as something of an oddity. But now . . . Their insistence on keeping so staunchly to themselves, the way Vito had confronted them so furiously after Eva's body had been found, and Robyn's suspicion that the man with the beard and ponytail had a weapon inside his jacket . . .

They were no longer just an oddity. And Robyn was quite certain they weren't simply Eva's cousins. She thought back to the previous evening, to the conversation she'd overheard between Vito, Margot and Jeremy.

So what if there are loans? Vito had demanded. *Is it not acceptable for a business to take out a loan?*

From a bank, Margot had replied. *Not from the sort of organisations* you *have been dealing with.*

Thinking once more of the two men from the boat, Robyn opened Google and typed two words into the search bar: *Bologna mafia.*

Bologna seemed like a sensible place to start. Laurence had said it was where the Bianchis lived. Presumably it was also where Vito had his dealership. But even as she typed the second word, she felt ridiculous. She was vaguely aware that the Italian mafia existed, but she had absolutely no idea how they operated. She didn't even know how widespread they might be. A part of her was quietly confident that if she hit 'search' she would only find trivia about *The Sopranos*.

All the same, she knew it was an idea that would scratch at her brain until she tested it.

When in Rome, she supposed. She took a deep breath and hit 'search'.

As expected, the first few results were less than enlightening. She saw a one-star TripAdvisor review for a restaurant that a customer suspected had been a money-laundering front. Then an Amazon link to a series of novels about Italian gangsters. It wasn't until around halfway down the page that she spotted it.

Her mouth suddenly feeling very dry, Robyn opened the article and began to read.

THE HIDDEN CRIMINALS POISONING NORTHERN ITALY

Local politicians have often claimed that there is no mafia presence in northern Italy. This is a familiar tune, with similar claims made about Sicily and Naples during the 1960s, before the Cosa Nostra, the Camorra and the 'Ndrangheta were revealed to in fact have considerable local influence. In towns and cities alike, criminal gangs penetrated the socio-economic fabric, destabilising much of Italy's south through violence, harassment and extortion.

Today, these groups take a different approach, although one that is no less insidious. They focus on infiltrating businesses through subsidies, protection and even funding schemes, in many cases effectively taking over the company. The gang then expands, destabilising the market, threatening competitors and bribing its way into public administrations.

A recent report published by the national anti-mafia agency has investigated the alarming extent of these unseen criminal activities in northern Italy, revealing that . . .

Robyn stopped reading and put the phone back in her bag.

Could this be it? Margot and Jeremy sounded certain that Vito was in the pocket of some more-than-questionable people.

But could he really be in debt to the mafia? And if so, how likely was it that they would send two enforcers to his daughter's wedding?

If this was indeed what had happened, Robyn could easily imagine why Vito would want to confront them after Eva's body had been found. She could even imagine that murdering Eva with a priceless, bronze-hilted dagger was the sort of dramatic action a vast criminal network with an international reputation might take. It had certainly left an impression on the wedding party.

Was this it, then? Was Eva's death a mafia hit, in response to Vito failing to pay his debt?

She couldn't say. For the time being, it seemed all she *could* do was speak with someone who had been in the casermetta. Someone who could have seen what Toby had actually been doing and perhaps even know why Eva might have gone to the cove. It wasn't an extensive list, and it was made even shorter by the fact that Paola, Beatrice and Giulia seemed only to speak Italian. Her best options were Vito, Dina and perhaps Sofia. Cam might be worth trying too, although she'd been clear in the courtyard that she hadn't seen anything useful.

Robyn knew she had to speak with them. The question was how. She couldn't imagine Vito letting anyone near Dina after the way Laurence had just approached her. Nor could she see him being eager to speak with her himself.

She would have to start with Sofia.

35

It seemed to Stephen that, somehow, the heat had become even more intense. He had long since abandoned his jacket, rolling up his sleeves and clinging wherever possible to the shade of the castle walls. None of it seemed to help.

To make matters worse, the mood among the group in the courtyard was becoming unbearable.

It wasn't just the horror of the scene in the cove that was putting everyone on edge. Nor the painfully long time the police were taking to arrive. It was Laurence. Since he'd accosted Dina outside the casermetta, all but Chadwick, Miles, Margot and Jeremy seemed to be staying away from him. Everyone else was keeping a safe distance, as if he were a landmine that might go off if they stepped too close.

Stephen stood a little way off with Abigail, although not quite together. She seemed to be insisting on keeping at least a few metres between them, making no attempt to hide her fury at his reluctance to immediately name Robyn or Toby as Eva's murderer.

Looking up, he saw Toby approaching, his brow creased with concern.

'Have you seen Robyn?'

From the corner of his eye, Stephen saw Abigail suddenly step a little closer.

'She was right next to me,' Toby continued. 'When Dina came outside, she was right there. I turned around a minute later and she was gone.'

'No,' Stephen replied. 'We haven't seen her.'

Toby shook his head. 'I don't know where she could be. I looked inside the casermetta. Then by the jetty. Jeremy's just said he saw her up by the museum, but she isn't there now.'

Stephen made a conscious effort not to look at Abigail. 'Maybe she's gone to the bathroom,' he said. 'It's hot out here. Everyone's pretty shaken up. She might have just wanted to splash some water on her face.'

Toby nodded, although he didn't look convinced. 'I'll check inside again.'

He moved along, Abigail fixing Stephen with a glare.

'It doesn't mean anything,' he insisted. 'She could be any-where.'

Abigail said nothing.

'*It doesn't mean anything*,' he repeated.

This time, it looked as though she might reply. But before she could, Stephen saw Robyn, standing in the doorway of the casermetta.

He looked back at Abigail, doing all he could not to adopt an 'I told you so' expression. He couldn't tell if he'd been success-ful. Either way, she scowled at him and stalked off in the opposite direction.

Where were the police? Fifteen minutes . . . That was all it had taken for the boats to ferry them to the castle. Checking his watch, he saw that over an hour and a half had passed since Eva had been found.

An hour – nearly two – to respond to a murder? He understood that they were hardly in the middle of a bustling city, but even so.

He hoped they would arrive soon. More than that, he hoped that they would be quick about identifying Eva's killer. Because much as he tried to ignore it, an infinitely more uncomfortable thought had crept into his mind. One that he was finding impossible to shake loose.

They had all been in the restaurant. They had all seen the message, and if they were clever about it, any one of them could have sneaked it into Eva's bag. And yet, Abigail, after months of pleading for him to get Eva out of their lives, was the only person trying so adamantly to convince him that Robyn or Toby must be Eva's killer.

He tried desperately to remember where, exactly, Abigail had been before Eva was found. After they had left the boats, the entire wedding party spent fifteen minutes or so congregating in the courtyard. She'd been by his side the entire time; he was sure of that. But what then?

He and Laurence had been sent to speak with the celebrant about how the ceremony would run. That was around the same time the rest of the guests had been ushered up to the terrace.

Had Abigail gone with them? It occurred to him that he had absolutely no idea. He remembered looking back at the congregation and seeing her in the second row as he'd wondered what could be delaying Eva. But what had she been doing before then?

He tried to force the thought from his mind. Abigail had desperately wanted Eva gone. They both had. But he couldn't seriously suspect her of murder.

Could he . . . ?

36

Standing in the doorway of the casermetta, Robyn could just about see Sofia. She was on the terrace, at the top of the staircase, and looked deep in conversation with the celebrant.

Robyn wanted to make a beeline straight for her, but there was no chance. Toby had spotted her.

'Where were you? I've been looking everywhere.'

'Just inside.'

'Doing what?'

'Jesus, Toby, I was in the loo. Leave it alone.'

'Leave it alone? Robyn, I was worried.' He looked pleadingly into her eyes. 'What's going on? What's *actually* going on? I know you're upset by what we saw down in the cove. We all are. But . . . Well, even by those standards, you don't seem quite right.'

She looked at him for a little while, trying to decide if she was going to call him out again. Before she could, she saw movement over his shoulder. Margot, stalking in their direction.

Following her line of sight, Toby turned and locked eyes with his mother.

'Come with me.' Margot's voice was cold, inviting no argument. Still, it didn't stop Toby from trying.

'What's going on?'

'Don't argue. Just come inside.'

'I'm not going anywhere until you tell me what's happening.'

Margot glowered, evidently unhappy at being questioned, and gave Robyn one of the dirtiest looks she had ever received. 'We need to talk.'

'Why can't we talk here?'

'It's a family discussion.'

Toby's nostrils flared, and for a moment Robyn expected him to push back. But to her surprise, he relented, his shoulders slumping.

'Stay here,' he told her. 'Please. I'm coming right back.'

Robyn watched them go, wondering what Margot could want to discuss as they disappeared inside the casermetta.

She didn't wait around to theorise. Realising her opportunity, she practically jogged up to the terrace. Upon reaching the top of the stairs, though, she paused, so struck by the sight before her that she couldn't help but give a little gasp.

The seats in which they had waited for the ceremony to begin were abandoned, a few even knocked over, presumably in the rush to identify the source of Dina's scream. Many of the white rose petals that had been spread upon the aisle now looked dirty and tattered, trampled underfoot. Discarded orders of service littered the ground. Even the string quartet looked less regal. Having abandoned their formal wear, they huddled in the corner, smoking cigarettes.

It was a stark transformation from the picture-perfect scene that had greeted them barely a couple of hours earlier.

Catching sight of her, Sofia frowned, and Robyn took a second to shake herself back into focus. She had to be quick. Whatever Toby and Margot were discussing, she couldn't afford to assume they would be long.

'Sorry,' she said gingerly. 'It was Sofia, wasn't it?'

Sofia peered at her, evidently suspicious.

'Please . . . I only have a minute, but I was hoping you could help me.'

Sofia said something in Italian to the celebrant, who nodded in return and moved along. Then she returned her attention to Robyn. 'Is there something you need?'

Robyn took a breath. 'I wanted to ask you a question. It might sound strange, but . . . After we had all moved up to the terrace, before the ceremony was due to begin . . . Did you go inside the casermetta?'

Sofia thought for a moment. 'I was everywhere. I was up here, seeing that you were all seated and the celebrant was ready. I was in the courtyard, making sure no one was left behind.'

'But did you go inside?'

Sofia's eyes narrowed. 'Why are you asking me this?'

Robyn took a breath. 'Inside the casermetta . . . Between quarter to and twelve o'clock, did you see Toby?'

'Who is Toby?'

Robyn looked back down the staircase into the courtyard, wondering if she could point him out, but it was no good. He and Margot must still be inside. She took out her phone, aware of how quizzically Sofia was watching, and showed her the lock screen photo.

Sofia studied the photo for a moment before nodding. 'Yes, I think I saw him.'

'What was he doing?'

'I don't know. I remember seeing him, but I didn't pay him any attention. The ceremony was about to begin and we had just realised no one knew where the bride was.'

Robyn felt her herself begin to flounder. 'Please. Is there nothing you can tell me? Was he doing anything? Was he with anyone?'

'I'm telling you, I don't know. I remember walking past him in the corridor, but that's all.'

Noticing that a hint of irritation had crept into Sofia's voice, Robyn restrained herself from pressing further. It clearly wasn't going to help. She flicked a look back into the court-yard, and with still no sign of Toby, decided instead to try a different question.

'How did you realise that Eva was missing?'

Sofia hesitated, her expression softening slightly. 'It was a few minutes before the ceremony was due to begin. You were all settled on the terrace, so I asked the bridesmaids if Eva was ready. They said that she was inside, with her parents, but when I went to find her there was no sign. Her parents thought she was with the photographer. I had just seen the photographer, though. She was up here, ready to take Eva's picture as she walked up the aisle.'

Robyn felt her heart beat a little quicker, imagining the panic that must have gripped them.

'When did you last see her?'

'Before you arrived on the boats. She'd come up here with the bridesmaids to take some pictures, and I went to the office.' Sofia's expression hardened again. 'He's your boyfriend, right?

The man you showed me. Why do you want to know if he was inside?'

Robyn felt a momentary flicker of panic, her mind racing as she scrambled for an excuse.

She took a breath, bracing to deliver a hurried deflection that would almost certainly sound a good deal less convincing than she needed it to. But before the words could pass her lips, a raised voice drifted up to them from the courtyard.

Two o'clock

37

'What's this?'

Laurence rose slowly from the bench, holding his phone out in front of him.

Arriving at the foot of the staircase with Sofia, Robyn swept a hurried glance around the courtyard. With Margot and Toby still inside the casermetta, only a few were there. Those who were, however, started to gather round.

'What the fuck is this?' His voice cracking, Laurence held up the phone.

Squinting at the little screen, Robyn saw that it was an Instagram post. An image containing a few lines of text.

Taking out her own phone, she found the offending post right at the top of her feed. It was a screenshot, posted from Eva's account and containing the first two paragraphs of a news article.

Robyn felt her breath catch in her throat. Immediately she understood why it had affected Laurence so deeply. Because she had seen this article before. And while she already knew exactly what it contained, she couldn't stop herself now from reading it again.

INFLUENCER BLAMED AFTER TEENAGER FOUND UNCONSCIOUS

Owen Lock, Lifestyle Correspondent

An ambulance has been called to a home in Reading after a teenager who had been sustaining herself on meal replacement supplements advertised on social media was found unconscious by her parents.

Rachel Carlisle, 15, was treated by paramedics after fainting in the family home. They reported her blood pressure as being dangerously low, while her friends revealed that for several days she had sustained herself solely on a line of ultra-low-calorie meal replacement shakes. Rachel had seen the shakes advertised on social media and been feigning sickness, as well as claiming to have eaten elsewhere, in order to avoid meals at home.

Robyn noticed that the post contained a second image. With a trembling thumb, she swiped it into view. Sure enough, it was another screenshot, containing the next part of the article. The following paragraphs explained how Rachel's parents held Eva responsible for her condition, with the quote from her mother describing Eva as 'obscenely irresponsible'.

Robyn began to scroll through the comments that the post was already accumulating. Some told Eva how ashamed she should be. Others were speculating whether her account had been hacked. Several declared their intention to unfollow her immediately.

'Who's done this?' Laurence wheeled around on the spot. 'Who's done it?' He tried to raise his voice but it didn't quite work. It seemed to be taking all of the effort he could muster not to burst into tears.

Robyn looked around the courtyard. No one answered him. Instead, they all stared at their phones. Stephen had gone sheet-white. Harper looked like she might be sick, scrolling, presumably, through the comments that Robyn had just seen. Sofia looked to be reading the article itself, a hand over her mouth.

Hearing movement above them, Robyn looked up, towards the top floor of the casermetta. Dina was in the window, her usual fearful expression fixed firmly in place as she watched the commotion. Vito and Paola were just visible behind her.

Stephen broke the silence, his voice trembling. 'It says it was posted two hours ago. It's two o'clock now. So whoever posted this did it at twelve.' He looked up from his screen, his gaze settling on Harper. 'Could this have been posted from any phone other than Eva's? Was she signed in anywhere else?'

Harper shook her head, visibly despairing. 'I've never had access. If someone really knew what they were doing, I guess it's possible they could hack her account. Otherwise, no. Only Eva knew her login details and she would change her password every month.'

Stephen nodded, taking a deep breath. 'So where was her phone at twelve?'

He looked around at the group. No one came forward.

'It might not have been twelve,' said Robyn. 'Saying two hours doesn't mean it was posted two hours ago exactly. It means more than two hours ago but less than three.'

Stephen considered this for a moment. 'So all we know is that it was posted at some point *before* twelve.'

'But after eleven. If we want to know exactly when, we'll need to watch and wait for the minute it rolls over to three hours.'

There was no enthusiasm in Robyn's voice. It wasn't lost on her that this hour-long window perfectly accommodated the fifteen minutes in which Toby had been gone.

'I'll watch it,' said Harper. 'See when it changes.'

Stephen nodded again. He was doing a good job of holding it together, Robyn thought. But she could see clearly enough just how much this new development bothered him. She supposed the thought of Laurence blowing up again wasn't an appealing one.

'Where was the phone during that hour?' he asked. 'I think we can safely assume Eva didn't post this herself. Did anyone see it?'

No one answered.

'Where is it now, then?' he tried, his voice beginning to strain slightly. 'Can we even be sure Eva doesn't have it?'

'She's wearing a bloody wedding dress,' Abigail muttered.

'So where is it?' Stephen rounded on her, his voice rising as the composure that he had been forcing began to slip.

'Eva changed into her dress inside the casermetta,' said Sofia. 'Perhaps it's in there.'

She hurried inside, just as Toby and Margot appeared in the doorway. They each looked around, confusion on Toby's face as he took in the crowd that now nervously occupied the courtyard.

'What's happening?' he asked.

For the past minute or two, Laurence seemed to have been in a trance. But at the sound of Toby's voice, he immediately snapped back into life.

'You.' He sprang forward, gripped by a sudden fury, and grabbed Toby by the shirt. 'Did you do it? Did you kill her?'

Toby protested, trying to wrestle Laurence off. Margot, too, tried to shout Laurence down. In the end it took Chadwick and Miles to step in and help before Laurence finally released him. The moment he was torn away, Laurence threw up his phone, holding it in Toby's face. Robyn watched as he read it, eyes wide.

'You think *I* did this?' he asked.

'Did you?'

Robyn felt as if her heart had momentarily stopped. She could have hugged Laurence for saying this, watching Toby intently as his defiance evaporated. He shot her a look, panic twitching in his eyes.

Please, she willed him. Say something. Anything.

Before he could answer, though, Sofia returned, emerging from the casermetta with an iPhone in her hand. She held it in a napkin, presumably to avoid leaving her fingerprints on it.

'It was on the dining table,' she said. 'Just sitting there.'

Laurence snatched it off her, no concern apparently for his own fingerprints.

'Is that it?' Stephen asked him.

Laurence didn't reply, the trance settling again.

'Laurence,' Stephen pressed. 'Is that it?'

Laurence nodded. He didn't seem capable of much else.

'We need to be smart about this,' Stephen announced to the courtyard. 'We can't just assume that whoever posted this also killed Eva.'

'Of course we can,' said Abigail. 'Why else would they do it?'

'Why *would* they? Think about it. If you'd just killed someone, and you were planning to get away with it, would you tell five hundred thousand people on Instagram why you'd done it?'

'Is it a distraction?' Robyn suggested. 'Make us all think that this was the reason, when in fact it was something else?'

'If so, it isn't a particularly good one. It's taken us two hours to see it.'

'How *has* it taken two hours?' Abigail asked. 'How have we not noticed it until now?'

'Speak for yourself, Abi,' said Stephen. 'But I haven't been eagerly scrolling through my feed since Eva was found. Anyone else?'

He swept a look around the group. No one came forward. Not even Abigail seemed to have a reply, her eyes dropping to the ground.

'What if it's a reputational thing?' said Robyn. 'Maybe it wasn't enough to kill Eva. Maybe whoever did it wanted to kill her image too. Just look at the comments. If that's what they wanted to do, I'd say they've succeeded.'

Laurence grimaced, his face contorting as if in physical pain.

'This isn't helping,' Margot snapped.

Stephen nodded, turning once more to Harper. 'We have to be smart,' he said again. 'We wait and see exactly when it was posted. Once we have a time, we need to pin down who had access to Eva's phone in that moment.'

'How would someone even get into it?' asked Toby. 'Isn't it password protected?'

Robyn watched him. Why was he suggesting this? To cover himself?

Stephen turned to Laurence, who was still staring at the phone. He nodded, clearing his throat.

'It needs a pin.'

'Is there anyone who would have known it?' asked Stephen.

Laurence closed his eyes, pressing a hand to his face. 'I don't know. I can't . . .'

'Did *you* know it?' Toby asked.

Laurence's eyes snapped open again. 'Why are you asking *me*?'

'I'm just asking—'

'I can't do this,' said Laurence. 'I'm *not* doing it. I'm calling the police.'

He raised his own phone, but before he could dial, Sofia hurried over to him.

'No! Mr Heywood, the police are coming.'

He shrugged her off.

'Mr Heywood,' she insisted. 'Please, I've told you already. The police are coming.'

'Then where the fuck are they? It's been two hours. Do you understand? Two hours!'

Robyn had been sure this explosion was coming, brimming just below the surface. But to see it happen so violently still took her by surprise. Sofia recoiled, fear in her eyes as Laurence advanced on her. Again, Chadwick and Miles leapt forward, each seizing an arm as they held him at bay.

Robyn watched it all play out. She saw the rage in Laurence's bloodshot eyes, heard the pain in his voice as it rose and then cracked.

Then she felt a hand grip her tightly by the arm.

It was Abigail. With the others distracted by Laurence's outburst, she began to pull, fingers digging like talons into Robyn's skin as she dragged her roughly towards the casermetta.

38

From the top floor of the casermetta, Vito heard footsteps on the stairs. Seeing the two strangers emerge on the landing, he rushed towards them, his blood searing.

'Haven't you done enough?' he hissed. 'You stay away from my family!'

Before he could say another word, the bearded man shot out a hand and gripped Vito's so tightly it made him gasp. He leaned in close, his breath warm as he spoke softly in Vito's ear.

'We're leaving shortly, Vito. But before we go, we need to speak about your debt. Perhaps you'd prefer it if we chatted away from your family.'

Vito could feel himself turning red, his hand being squeezed so tightly it felt as if the bones might break. Looking over his shoulder, he saw Paola and Dina, both watching nervously.

This was happening, he realised. But he couldn't do it in front of them. He had managed for an entire year to keep them in the dark. If there was any way he could continue to do so a little longer, he would take it.

Turning back to the strangers, he gave a begrudging nod.

Immediately his hand was released and they motioned for him to cross the landing.

'Vito . . . ?' Paola followed him to the doorway.

'Stay there, Paola.'

'But what's happening?'

'Just stay there!'

He snapped at her before he could summon the willpower to restrain himself, self-loathing immediately seizing him. All at once, he was both terrified and furious.

With her brother stepping forward to put an arm around her shoulder, a look of severe disapproval on his face, Vito left Paola behind and crossed the landing with the two strangers, finding himself in an ornate lounge.

'Now listen to me,' he said, rounding on them with all of the courage he could summon. 'If either of you come near another member of my family—'

He didn't get any further. The bearded man silenced him with a short, sharp slap, the sound of his hand connecting with Vito's cheek filling the stone-floored room like a branch cracking underfoot.

'We aren't interested in your family,' he said, his voice perfectly level. 'As I said, we need to speak about your debt.'

Vito was silent, gingerly touching his face. He felt his cheek begin to throb, imagining a hand-shaped patch of red skin fading into view. 'My debt? You've murdered my daughter!'

'We didn't kill Eva.'

'You expect me to believe that?'

'You should. We were sent here for money, Vito. The money that *you* owe. What would killing Eva achieve?'

'It was a message . . . You were showing me that—'

'You aren't listening,' the bearded man told him. 'We didn't provide you with a fake dagger to send a message. We didn't arrange for the cameras in the museum to be off, or for the case to be unlocked, to send a message. We can send you a message any time we like. We can come to your dealership. We can come to your house. We came *here* for the dagger.'

Vito looked at him pleadingly. 'I did what you asked. I did everything you wanted . . .'

'And now the dagger is worthless. You were provided with a fake so that no one would know the real one was missing. We can hardly take it now that it's a murder weapon.'

Vito's mind raced, and he attempted one last show of defiance. 'I don't believe you. This is a trick. A lie.'

'It isn't a lie, Vito. We'll be leaving this island shortly. And we want you to know that when we do, the message we'll be taking with us is that your debt remains unsettled. Someone's going to be punished for what's happened here today, and I sure as shit am not prepared for it to be me.'

'Punished?' Vito repeated. 'What do you mean . . . punished?'

The bearded man shrugged. 'Perhaps there'll be an increase to what you owe. Perhaps it'll be something more colourful. But you can be sure there'll be something. Losing that dagger won't be easily forgiven.'

The stranger stepped closer, towering over Vito. 'Remember, Vito. Your business. Your house. Your wife. Your remaining daughter. We don't need a special dagger to deliver a message. We can do it at any time and in any way we like. Something for you to think on, as you consider how you'll pay off your outstanding balance.'

They left without another word, and Vito collapsed onto the sofa. This couldn't be happening, he told himself. This was supposed to be the day he fixed things. The day he made everything better.

He thought of his argument with Eva outside the museum. The last conversation the two of them had shared.

You use my day for this? she had demanded. *My day?*

It had broken his heart that she caught him. Doubly so, to hear how much he had shamed her. But when she stormed back to the casermetta, he had consoled himself with the promise that she would understand. That she was hurt now – understandably so – but once the wedding was over, and the debt was cleared, they would talk properly. She would come around.

That would never happen now. Instead, the last memory he had of speaking with his eldest daughter would be the moment in which she'd told him how much she hated him.

He pressed his hands to his face, tears filling his eyes.

Did he believe them? Could it be true that they hadn't killed Eva?

He didn't know. In that moment, he could scarcely hold a coherent thought, let alone comb through the lies of two career criminals.

He heard footsteps as someone else entered the room. It wasn't the strangers, though. These footsteps were softer. Lighter.

Removing his hands from his face, he saw Paola settling onto the opposite sofa. He knew immediately that the farce was over. She looked at him in a way that, in their thirty years of marriage, he had never before seen, bloodshot eyes burning in a face of stone.

'You need to tell me what's happening,' she said. 'And you need to tell me right now.'

39

Dragging Robyn inside, Abigail pushed her into the dining room.

She thought about making a run for it. But Abigail had planted herself squarely in the middle of the archway, and while Robyn was confident she could outrun her if she could just get away, she wasn't about to go barging past a woman who was four months pregnant.

For a few seconds, neither of them spoke. Then, just as Robyn was beginning to think that perhaps they weren't going to, Abigail took a deep breath.

'Let's do this properly,' she said. 'No bullshit. Let's just talk. Because I think I've worked it out. I think I know who you are.'

Robyn said nothing. She had no idea what she *could* say.

'First there's the message in Eva's bag,' said Abigail. 'Subtle, by the way. The secret Eva's *locked away*. Very fucking subtle. And now here we are again, with Eva posting about it all from beyond the grave. For a second I thought you must be after money. You clearly know what happened. Maybe you saw an opportunity to cash in. But you can hardly blackmail Eva after you've killed her, so this must be about something else.'

Robyn's stomach sank. 'You think I killed Eva?'

'Didn't you?'

Robyn took a deep breath, weighing every word with the utmost precision. 'You're right,' she said. 'I do know about Rachel. After you came to our room last night, I found the article describing what had happened. But I don't want to blackmail anyone and I certainly didn't plant that message in Eva's bag. And as for this post . . . How would I even do that? How would I know Eva's pin? Get hold of her phone?'

Abigail turned away. 'You worked with him,' she said quietly. 'Owen. Laurence said that you studied to be a journalist. So what was it? Were you his protégée? A junior reporter he took under his wing?'

Robyn didn't reply. She had no idea who Abigail was even talking about, let alone what she could say.

'It's the only theory that makes sense,' Abigail continued. 'He had a wife. Millie. I remember hearing that they worked together. That she was a reporter, too, or something like that. But you're too young to be her and I doubt you'd go to all this effort if you were just a fling or a bit on the side. You could be his sister, I suppose. But I don't remember there ever being any mention of him having one. So I think he must have been some kind of mentor to you.'

Robyn stared at her, mind racing as she tried to keep up.

'Here's what happened,' said Abigail. 'You got with Toby so that you could be close to Eva. He's the weakest link the Heywoods have, so it makes all the sense in the world that he would be your way in. And when the wedding came around, you saw your opportunity. The best day of Eva's life. And on an island, of all places, in a completely different country. But you didn't want it to be over quickly. You wanted her to be afraid, like *he* must have been afraid. So you put that message in her bag. And it absolutely worked. We all saw how she freaked out when she found it. Went running from the fucking restaurant.'

Robyn shook her head, completely lost for words.

'And now that she's dead,' Abigail continued, 'you want the whole world to know what a terrible person she was. As you said yourself, just outside, it wasn't enough to kill Eva. You wanted to kill her reputation too. So you steal her phone and you make sure all of her followers know what she did.'

Robyn gawped at her, completely dumbstruck. She believed this. She truly believed it.

'Please, Abigail,' she said. 'I have no idea what you're talking about. Literally none. Who's Owen?'

Abigail brought a fist down on the dining table. 'Stop it,' she snapped. 'Just stop it!' She took another deep breath.

'I'm sorry about what happened. I really, really am. No one wanted him to die. Stephen didn't even want to be there. Chadwick and Miles just did what Laurence asked, and he only asked them because he didn't have the nerve to do it himself when Eva asked *him*. But Stephen was trying to stop them. Do you understand? If they'd just listened to him, it wouldn't have happened at all. Owen would still be alive.'

She shook her head. 'I thought we could at least talk about this. But I can see now. You aren't here to talk. So here's what's going to happen instead. My priority – my only priority – is protecting my family. Making sure that when my baby is born, my husband isn't serving a prison sentence for Laurence Heywood and *Eva fucking Bianchi*. So when the police get here – when they *finally* get here – I'm going to make sure they

251

know who you are. I don't feel good about it. But as I say, I need to protect my family. You might have come for Eva, but I can't have you coming for anyone else.'

Before Robyn could reply – before she could even move – Abigail turned on the spot. She didn't barge straight out, though. Instead she hovered for a moment in the archway.

'For what it's worth,' she said, genuine sadness lacing her voice, 'I meant what I told you last night. I really did hope it would be Toby.'

And with that she was gone.

40

Stephen was doing all he could not to panic.

He had left Laurence in the courtyard, weeping on his bench but at the very least leaving Sofia alone. Once Chadwick and Miles had pulled Laurence away, Stephen turned to her and suggested that if there was anything she could do to get the police there quicker – anything at all – she should do it now. She had nodded enthusiastically, before hurrying to her office.

But now Abigail was gone. And perhaps even more worryingly, Robyn was too.

He stepped inside the casermetta, just in time to see his wife emerging from an archway on the right-hand side of the hallway.

'Where were you?' he whispered, failing entirely to keep the frustration from his voice.

She didn't reply, brushing past him as she went out into the courtyard. He went to the archway and looked through into a dining room. As expected, Robyn stood by the table, her face pale.

Swearing to himself, Stephen retreated before she had a chance to notice him and hurried after Abigail into the courtyard.

'Jesus, Abi!' he hissed. 'What have you done?'

'Exactly what we should have done before.'

'What does that mean?' He grabbed her by the wrist. '*What does that mean?*'

'I've told her that I'm on to her. That I know it was her.'

'But we don't!'

'Of course we do. First there's the note in Eva's bag. Now this post on Instagram. And to cap it all off she's a journalist!'

He shook his head, pleading with her. 'It isn't enough. You can't just go telling people you think they're murderers, Abi. You need proof!'

'Who else is it going to be?' She glared at him, eyes burning as she waited for an answer.

But he didn't answer. He couldn't. Because the answer he wanted to give was too terrible to speak out loud.

Apparently realising he wasn't going to reply, Abigail wrenched herself free and began to stalk away. Stephen watched her go, swearing again under his breath.

It can't be Abigail, he told himself. It just can't be.

And yet, he couldn't shake his suspicions loose. Couldn't ignore all the times Abigail had told him that she wanted Eva gone.

He felt despair take him. He wanted to be away from this castle. From these people. He wanted never to have met Laurence Heywood.

Before his despair could drag him too far under, though, the stillness was broken by Margot, asking a question to the entire courtyard.

'Has anyone seen Jeremy?'

41

For a good couple of minutes after Abigail had left, Robyn was so shaken she couldn't move. She just stood in the dining room, her knees going weak.

Abigail thought she had killed Eva.

For Robyn to have killed anyone sounded too far-fetched to even consider, and yet, Abigail seemed adamant. She thought Robyn had put the message about Rachel Carlisle in Eva's bag. Even thought she had somehow posted from Eva's Instagram. But to have killed her? Really?

Robyn took a deep breath, trying as calmly as she could to assess the worst Abigail could do with this theory.

Her first port of call would presumably be Stephen. If she could convince him, he in turn might convince Laurence. Perhaps even Margot and Jeremy. By the time the police arrived, the entire Heywood clan might think Robyn had planted a dagger in Eva's heart.

Her dread turned to fear, the walls seeming to close in around her, and she had to force herself to take several long, deep breaths. When, at last, she was able to order her thoughts, she turned her mind to the other question raised by her conversation with Abigail.

Who, exactly, did Abigail think she was?

She had spoken about a man. A journalist, seemingly, called Owen, who Robyn somehow knew and who, at Eva's request, Laurence's groomsmen had played a role in killing. She had spoken about her fear that Stephen could go to prison. About how Robyn now wanted to kill Eva for some kind of revenge.

Could she really think that? Could she *actually* believe it? Eva had clearly had a vicious streak. But could she really have convinced Laurence and his friends to kill someone for her? Even the idea that Robyn would date Toby for an opportunity to get close to her was almost too ridiculous to consider. Toby did all he could to stay away from Eva.

No. Abigail's theory was absurd. And yet, there must at least be a grain of truth. For her to believe Robyn had killed Eva out of revenge, a journalist must have been killed.

It took Robyn seconds to make the connection. Abigail hadn't shot her down when she mentioned Rachel Carlisle. She hadn't even seemed confused. Which could only mean . . .

Taking out her phone, Robyn went straight to Instagram. Even in the few minutes she had been with Abigail, Eva's post had racked up nearly fifty additional comments. But she wasn't interested in them. She wasn't even interested in the body of the article. Instead, she wanted the name of the reporter who had written it.

Owen Lock.

Robyn's mind raced.

This had to be who Abigail meant. What had she said?

Subtle, by the way. The secret Eva's locked away. Very fucking subtle.

But what had happened to him? Robyn could certainly imagine Eva being angry with Owen for writing this article, but could Abigail really be right? Could Chadwick and Miles really have killed him for it?

Turning to Google, Robyn keyed in Owen's name. It wasn't long before she found something. A news headline which caused her heart to pound against her ribs.

She swore quietly under her breath, hoping that this wasn't it. That the headline before her had nothing to do with Eva and the Heywoods. Already, though, she knew on some instinctive level that her search was over.

With her hand beginning to tremble, she opened the report and began to read.

42

Vito told Paola everything. He told her how the dealership had been failing. He told her about the loans, and who had given them to him. He even recounted his conversation with Jeremy and Margot in the restaurant.

'You brought these people here,' she said. 'You brought them *here*? To our daughter's wedding?'

'I didn't have a choice. I could never have paid back the interest they were demanding. But when they learned where Eva was getting married they decided they wanted some dagger instead. Said that if I helped them get it, the debt would be paid. I'd never hear from them again.'

'And you believed them?'

Vito didn't reply. He didn't think he could.

'Do you believe them now?' Paola asked. 'That they didn't . . . That Eva . . .'

She couldn't finish, tears beading in her eyes.

'I don't know,' said Vito. 'When she was found, I was certain it had been them. They're killers, after all. It must have been. But now . . . Perhaps they're right. Perhaps it doesn't make sense. They wanted money, and with that dagger they would have walked out of here with a fortune. They can hardly do that now.'

Paola was silent.

'Paola . . .' said Vito. '*Amore—*'

'Don't.' She snapped at him so sharply he was immediately silenced. 'If they're telling the truth . . . If they weren't the ones who . . .' She tailed off again, taking a deep breath to steady herself. 'Then who did?'

Vito didn't answer.

'You said that Laurence's mother knows about them,' Paola pressed. 'About the debt. Jeremy Lambourne too. Could it have been them?'

'I don't know.'

'So think!'

Vito flinched. 'When we spoke in the restaurant,' he said slowly, 'they thought I was planning to ask Laurence for money after he and Eva were married.'

'And were you?'

Defiance flashed in Vito's eyes. 'I'm not asking my daughter's husband for money. I got us into this. I will get us out.'

'So do you think it was them? That they wanted to protect their assets by stopping the wedding?'

'I don't know.'

Paola grimaced. 'What did they mean? You said they're leaving soon. How can they just leave?'

'I don't know.'

'What *do* you know?'

'That I'm sorry. And I love you. And I only ever wanted to do what's right for our family.'

Paola closed her eyes, fighting back tears again. Vito wanted to say something that might comfort her. That might somehow make their situation seem less desperate. But if there were any words that would achieve such a feat, he didn't possess them. So instead he sat, hating himself a little more with each trembling breath his wife drew.

They remained together in silence for a good few minutes. In the neighbouring room he could just about hear his brother-in-law trying to quietly soothe the still-shaken Dina. It was Paola who eventually broke the stalemate, eyes widening as a realisation seemed to dawn on her.

'The police . . .' she murmured.

Vito looked at her.

'The police are coming. If we speak to them when they arrive, tell them who these people are, they'll be able to—'

'No.' Vito's voice was like stone. 'We can't say anything to the police.'

'But if they—'

'Think, Paola. These are just two people in a vast organisation. If we have the police take them away, think of the response. They'll come after Dina. Come after *you*. I can't give them any more reason to threaten us than they already have.'

Paola swore, taking several deep breaths in an effort to remain calm.

'Who called them?' she asked. 'The police. Who was it?'

'The wedding planner. But you can't think . . .'

'It's been two hours. Someone should be here. They should have been here straight away. What if Sofia never called? Or what if they have people in the police? People who are stopping anyone from coming?'

She took out her phone.

'What are you doing?' Vito asked.

'I'm calling the police myself.'

'Stop,' he said, panic in his voice. 'Paola, stop!' He shot out a hand, seizing her wrist. 'The police are coming. They have to be; they can't just leave us here. But if these men find out that we've called them – that we've done *anything* to get the police here before they've left . . .' He looked into Paola's eyes, pleading with her. 'They said that they're leaving soon. Please . . . Just wait until they've gone. Then we'll call.'

Reluctantly, she set down her phone.

'I'm sorry,' he said. 'I'm so sorry. I never meant to—'

'Enough,' said Paola. 'We'll do this later. Properly. Right now, our priority is Dina. Making sure these people stay away from her, and making sure she never knows any of this is happening. Whether it's these criminals or the Heywoods, someone is coming for our family. So we keep her close and we keep her safe.'

43

Sofia barged into the office, slammed the door behind her and once again fetched the brandy from the desk. Her entire body trembled as she took two large swigs, cursing between shuddering breaths.

Laurence Heywood had been seconds away from calling the police. Seconds from unwittingly signing her son's death sentence. What if she hadn't been there? What if she hadn't stopped him? It could so easily have happened. After all, she couldn't be everywhere at once.

Screwing her eyes shut, she forced the image of her son, lying dead on the floor of his cell, from her mind. She thought about looking at the photo again, just to remind herself that he was still alive. But she didn't want to see him that way, thin and fierce behind the bars of a prison cell. In the sanctuary of her imagination, she pictured him instead as he'd been before. Her boy. Her everything.

Opening her eyes again, she looked at the clock, mounted on the wall above her desk.

It was half past two. If the two strangers were right, then in just half an hour, their boat would come and they would be gone. The minute they were clear – the second, even – she would be on the phone to the police. Get here now, she would tell them. As quickly as you can.

She had to get back into the courtyard. She was so close . . . She couldn't afford to leave Laurence Heywood unattended for this final stretch.

Taking one more swig of brandy, she tucked the bottle back into the desk. Then, as she rose to her feet, she flicked a quick habitual glance at the computer monitor on her desk. There was the museum, just as she had left it.

Or was it? She leaned forward, both hands on the desk, and squinted at the screen.

Was it a trick of the light? No. She looked so often at this image that she could have drawn it from memory. She knew every inch of that museum, and she was all too aware that the dark shape on the floor, poking out from behind one of the display cases, did not belong.

She leaned a little closer, her face now inches from the screen. Was that . . . ?

All at once, the dark patch on the floor took shape. As it did, and Sofia realised just what she was seeing, her blood ran cold.

'*Porca puttana*,' she murmured. 'Oh, God, no . . .'

44

Robyn stalked across the courtyard, moving with such intensity that as she left the casermetta she almost barged straight into Cam.

'Robyn . . .' The photographer called after her. 'Robyn, what's wrong?'

She didn't answer. She had Toby in her sights, fury coursing through her veins. Hearing her footsteps on the cobbled ground, he turned to face her. As he saw how she was thundering towards him – saw the anger that she could feel manifesting on her face – his eyes narrowed slightly, his brow creasing with concern.

He tried, as she grew closer, to ask what was wrong. She was so angry she could barely speak. Taking him by the arm, she led him to a quiet corner of the courtyard. A note of fear flashed across his face, but before he could speak, Robyn took out her phone, holding it up for him to see.

'Journalist dies after assault outside home.'

She knew that he could read the headline perfectly well. But she had wanted to say it anyway. To drive it home. As he stared at the screen, she had hoped that she would see surprise in his expression. That he would simply frown and ask why she was showing it to him. Instead, she saw terror.

She felt her anger rise even further. This wasn't the first time he'd read this headline. He had known.

'Last night,' she said, 'after we'd gone back to the villa, I wondered if the warning in Eva's bag – if the secret she'd locked away – might be to do with Rachel Carlisle. Eva touts a meal replacement shake on Instagram and a teenage girl turns up unconscious. A news report then appears in a national broad-sheet, in which Eva's described as dangerously irresponsible.

'That's pretty bad, right? Disastrous, I'd imagine, for her ambition to work with brands dealing in nutrition. That didn't add up, though. What happened to Rachel wasn't a secret; it had been reported on by a national paper. But now I see that she was only the first part of an even more terrible story. Two weeks after that article was published, Owen Lock, the reporter who wrote it, was killed. Jumped outside his house by three men in dark hoodies. He goes to hospital and after three days he dies from his injuries.'

Toby stared at the phone, utterly blindsided. 'I don't under-stand,' he said, almost whispering. 'You can't have arrived at this by yourself. Who told you?'

Robyn glowered at him, so angry she almost didn't want to tell him. 'I found Rachel myself. Abigail put me on to Owen.' She raised her voice as much as she dared, speaking through gritted teeth. 'Laurence made this happen, didn't he? On Friday evening, when you told him at the villa that Eva was a bad influence. That she made him do something . . .'

'He didn't do it.' Toby spoke without hesitating, a hint of defiance in his voice.

'I know he didn't. At least, he didn't do it himself.'

Robyn returned her attention briefly to the phone, before presenting Toby with something else. This time, it was a picture. Laurence and Eva, posing in a restaurant with a group of smiling friends.

'This is the only picture on Eva's entire feed that features Laurence. Can you guess *when* she posted it? I'll tell you. It was the same night Owen was jumped. Now, I might be reading too much into it. But it looks very much to me like she's planted this for the benefit of anyone who knew what Owen had been writing and might try to point in her direction when they hear he's been beaten up. She's saying, look at us! We weren't there!

'So no. Laurence didn't kill Owen Lock himself. But you think Eva made him organise it. She's a nasty piece of work and she's seriously pissed off with this journalist, so she asks Laurence to teach him a lesson. He sends some of his boys round to rough Owen up outside his house, and to reduce the risk of anyone accusing her of being involved, Eva broadcasts to her five hundred thousand followers that the two of them are having dinner on the other side of London while it happened.'

Robyn glared at Toby. 'How could you not tell me about this?'

'How *could* I have told you? How are you supposed to tell anyone that you think your brother had someone killed? You're complaining because you didn't know. I wish I'd never known!'

For a moment, Robyn was caught completely off guard. She had expected resistance. Denial, even. But she hadn't been prepared to hear such pain in his voice.

'It was the groomsmen,' she said quietly. 'Wasn't it? Chadwick and Miles. Stephen, too.'

Toby didn't reply.

'You might as well say so,' she said. 'Abigail more or less told me anyway.'

'I don't know.'

'But you've suspected.'

He sighed. 'I don't think Owen was meant to die. Laurence and I haven't ever spoken about it. I've had to piece it all together myself, just like you. But I can only imagine that they just meant to beat him up. Frighten him a little. A real-life fist fight isn't like the ones you see on TV, though. It isn't a case of two guys beating the crap out of each other for fifteen minutes. If you hit someone too hard, in the wrong place, you're going to kill them.'

'Did Jeremy help?' Robyn pressed. 'Eva's Instagram post is all well and good. But you told me on Friday night that whenever Laurence makes a mess, no matter how serious, it's Jeremy who steps in, pulls the right strings and makes everything go away. There's nothing in this piece – or in any other coverage – to suggest that the police knew who the three guys might be. So did he do something to help cover it all up? Pay them off? Interfere with the investigation?'

Again, Toby said nothing. But the look in his eyes told Robyn all she needed to know.

'Did you know he was married?' she demanded. 'Abigail said her name was Millie. Did you know that they *widowed* someone when they went to Owen's house that night?'

Toby looked like he might be sick. 'Why would Abigail tell you that?'

'Because she thought for a moment that *I* might be her. She said Millie was a reporter too – that she and Owen worked together – and she knows I studied to be a journalist.'

'That's ridiculous. She can't honestly think—'

'No. She's ditched that particular theory, apparently. Now she thinks I was Owen's understudy. Maybe even had a fling with him.' Something changed in Robyn's voice, the anger suddenly slipping away. 'She thinks I killed Eva, Toby. She thinks I'm only with you to get close to her. To frighten her with the message in her bag and then kill her for what happened to Owen.'

'She can't seriously believe that.'

'She does! She really, really does.'

They were silent for a moment, Toby visibly despairing.

'Toby,' Robyn said quietly. 'Please just tell me. Did you put that message in her bag?'

His eyes flew wide. 'How can you ask me that?'

'Because Abigail spoke to me last night, too. Before it occurred to her that I might somehow have known Owen. She said no one else at that table would have brought all of this back up. I couldn't understand why she would think that – I didn't even know what the message was referring to – but now it makes sense. Laurence, your mum, Jeremy, the groomsmen . . . If they really did manage to get away with killing Owen, there's no way any of them would ever want to bring it up again.'

'So you think it was me?'

'Was it?'

'No! Robyn, why would I do that?'

She looked down at the ground, suddenly feeling foolish. 'I thought you might be standing up for me. After what happened on the yacht . . . I thought you were trying to scare Eva off. Get her to leave me alone.'

Toby's expression softened. 'I was angry on the yacht. Of

course I was. After the stunt Eva pulled I wanted never to let her near you again. But I swear I didn't put that message in her bag.'

They were quiet for a moment, a painfully uncomfortable silence settling between them.

'Do you really think this is all to do with Owen?' Toby asked.

'It has to be. Think about the message; the way it's worded. "The secret you've locked away." Unless you know what happened to Owen, that second part doesn't add anything. "I know what you did" would surely have been enough on its own. Whoever gave Eva that message wanted to make sure she knew exactly what they were talking about, but in a way that someone who didn't know – someone like me, for example – couldn't possibly understand from those words alone. The secret that Eva's "locked away". Owen Lock.'

Toby's face paled. 'But why would they do that? Did they want her to know they were coming? Want her to be . . . I don't know. Afraid, or something?'

'Your guess is as good as mine.' Robyn looked around the courtyard, taking in each of the others in turn. 'Is there anyone here who doesn't know about Owen?'

Toby grimaced. 'I can't speak for the Italians. And I don't know about Harper, either. But I think everyone else on our side must know.'

'So Abigail's going to convince them too. She's going to tell them all that I knew Owen and I came here to kill Eva.'

'Let her. We'll stay out of the way, and when the police arrive, they'll investigate. They'll look for DNA, or something. Work out who actually did it.'

Toby stepped forward, his arms outstretched as if to draw her into a hug. But she pulled away.

'Robyn . . .' He looked pained. 'You can't really think I would plant that note. I mean . . . I hated Eva. I can't deny that. But you can't actually think I would kill her.'

Robyn glared at him. 'I don't know what to think. She pushes me off the yacht and this warning turns up in her bag. You know all of this and yet you keep it from me. And then today, you disappear for fifteen minutes right before she turns up dead.'

She fixed him with a pleading expression. 'Please, Toby. *Please*. Tell me what you were doing before the ceremony. Tell me what you were *actually* doing.'

Suddenly nervous again, he took a breath. But before he could answer her there came another sound.

Someone, somewhere in the castle, was calling out for help.

45

Robyn and Toby bolted towards the upper courtyard, taking the steps two at a time. When they reached the archway, everyone else seemed already to be there, gathering outside the museum. Not just the guests, but two of the waiters in their white polo shirts and the chefs as well. Even the celebrant and the musicians had come across from the terrace. They had all turned out to see what had caused such commotion.

'What is it?' Toby called out. 'What's happened?'

At first, nobody answered him. They were all crowding around the door, trying to look inside. Eventually, however, Stephen turned, his face pale.

'It's Jeremy.'

He didn't say anything more. There was no need. Robyn could see it in his eyes.

She felt her stomach drop. 'How?'

'Shot,' Stephen said quietly. 'Looks like he might have been shot.'

Toby jostled his way through the crowd, pushing past Vito and the bridesmaids to reach the front. Robyn followed, peering over his shoulder. She saw Jeremy's feet protruding from behind a glass display case. It would almost have been comical, had Margot and Laurence not both been on their knees, trying in vain to help him. Sofia paced round the museum, her hands pressed to her face.

Robyn watched it all. She hadn't known Jeremy Lambourne well, and from what she had known, she hadn't particularly liked him. But for him to be dead . . . It just didn't seem possible. Not when they had been speaking only an hour earlier. She pictured him, standing in front of the case, inspecting the dagger through the glass. Heard the slight mocking tone in his voice.

Suddenly feeling nauseous, she made her way back through the little crowd. Standing in the archway, she put a steadying hand against the rough stone and closed her eyes.

There was still a killer on the island. Perhaps even two. She couldn't, after all, think of any immediate reason why someone would want both Eva and Jeremy dead. If anything, Jeremy had been one of her prime suspects. But someone, standing presumably just a few metres away, was undoubtedly capable of committing murder.

Feeling a presence behind her, she tensed.

'Robyn . . .'

A hand settled on her shoulder, and at the sound of Toby's voice, she shrugged him roughly away, her eyes snapping open.

'Robyn,' he said. 'Please . . .'

She ignored him entirely. Partly because she had no desire whatsoever to speak to him further after learning about Owen Lock. But also because as she looked through the archway, into the courtyard, a thought was occurring to her.

Everyone was now gathered behind them, outside the museum. Her eyes settled on the gatehouse, and as they did, she thought of the little plastic dome, mounted onto the ceiling of the museum.

Before she could think about it long enough to stop herself, she began to hurry back down into the courtyard.

46

Vito stared at the body.

He hated Jeremy Lambourne. With his threats and investigations, in the near twenty-four hours they had known each other, Vito had despised him almost as much as the criminals holding his family to ransom. And since telling Paola the truth of their situation, he had been giving serious thought to her suggestion that it might be Jeremy or Margot who had killed Eva.

Now that he was dead, there was a part of Vito that wanted to be pleased. He looked through the door of the museum — saw the body splayed on the tiles and the grief on Margot Heywood's face — and tried to tell himself that Jeremy had deserved it. That justice had been done.

But he couldn't manage it. In part, he was held back by his fear of the danger they were undeniably still in. But he also couldn't shake the feeling that this latest murder might somehow be his fault.

Jeremy, it seemed, had been well aware of who Vito's debtors were. If they had, in fact, killed Eva, and they had somehow discovered that Jeremy was aware of them, was it not entirely possible they would kill him too? They would need to protect themselves, after all.

He looked towards the case, in which the fake dagger still stood.

He could vividly remember the day it had come to the dealership, handed to him in a brown envelope with a set of instructions. It had been arranged for the display case to be unlocked and the CCTV camera to be disabled. All Vito had to do was swap the daggers and place the real one in the cove. After that, his debt would be cleared.

It had been so simple that Vito wondered at first why they hadn't just taken it themselves. If they'd sourced the fake dagger, arranged for the case to be unlocked and the cameras to be off, why couldn't they also make the swap?

But the more he thought on it, the more he'd understood. He was to be their scapegoat. If something went wrong – if the camera hadn't been disabled or if someone caught him – it would be Vito going straight to prison.

It was a valid concern. Because of course Vito *had* been caught . . .

He thought again of the look on Eva's face, as he emerged from the museum with the dagger wrapped in a cloth. Thought of the fury in her voice after he explained what was happening – why he'd *had* to do it.

For that to have been their last conversation would haunt him until his own dying day. She hated him, she had said. For the rest of her life, she would never forgive him. The rest of her life . . . He had assumed he would have years to beg her forgiveness. Decades, even. How could either of them have known that she was actually speaking about a matter of hours?

But it raised the question: who could have known the dagger was in the cove? Had he been seen by the cameras? Had Eva told someone? And who would have had reason to kill both her and Jeremy?

He looked at Paola, standing beside him as Laurence's sobs filled the museum. She must be feeling it too. The fear. The doubt. If it hadn't been the two strangers, and it hadn't been Jeremy, then who had killed Eva?

He turned to Dina, who had gone deathly pale at the sight of Jeremy's body. She had always been so much more gentle than Eva. Even as children, the two sisters couldn't have been more different.

He put his arm around her shoulder and looked to Paola. '*Amore*. Come back to the courtyard. There's no need for us to see this.'

Paola shook her head, her eyes fixed on the grisly scene. 'Someone should stay with them.'

'But does it need to be you?'

She glared at him in response, and he quickly decided not to argue. He could see that she wasn't going to be moved. Without a word, he steered Dina towards the door and ushered her away.

47

The office was a small space, with a desk and chair taking up most of the available room. Not that the top of the desk could really be seen. A computer, a telephone, a fan and a messy pile of papers all meant that barely an inch of it was visible.

Toby followed Robyn inside, having scurried after her down the staircase and, apparently recognising the urgency, shut the door quickly behind them. It was dim inside the little room, the only daylight seeping through the cracks in a pair of wooden shutters that had been closed over a single window.

'Jesus, Robyn,' he whispered, as if someone outside the museum might somehow hear. 'What are we doing?'

She didn't reply. Instead, she went straight to the computer. As she'd hoped, it displayed an image of the museum. Specifically, a CCTV link from the security camera.

Toby's eyes widened a little as he realised why they were there. The feed was live, Jeremy's feet sticking out from behind a display case. There was no sound, but Robyn could see Laurence's shoulders heaving up down as he sobbed beside Jeremy's body. Chadwick and Miles stood behind him, both at a loss for what to do. At the back of the museum, she could see the dagger in its case.

She thought about the conversation she and Jeremy had shared in the villa. Neither he nor Laurence had ever said as much, and she imagined that if she were to press them on it, neither of them would. But she felt certain that in the absence of Laurence's own father, Jeremy filled something of a surrogate role. For a split second she wondered which of the afternoon's deaths would hit him hardest: his fiancée's or Jeremy's.

Sitting down at the desk, Robyn laid a hand on the mouse. 'The footage must be saved somewhere,' she said, more to herself than to Toby. 'We can see who he was with. Perhaps even if someone really did swap the daggers.'

'Isn't that for the police to do?'

Robyn ignored him, waving the cursor aimlessly across the screen, as if the computer would helpfully point her in the right direction.

'Let me.' Grimacing, Toby nudged her out of the seat, reaching for the mouse. 'If we're going to do this, let's do it quickly.'

'You know how to use it?'

'It looks a little like the system we have at work. I've had to pull up footage once or twice for the police when we've had the odd fight break out.' He squinted at the screen. 'I can't read these commands, though. They're all in Italian.'

Taking her phone from her bag, Robyn used Google Translate to call out English equivalents of the on-screen labels. With each one, the cursor began to fly around the monitor with increasing speed, as Toby got to grips with the system.

After a minute or two, he leaned back in his seat, shaking his head. 'I don't think this is recording. It's just a live feed.'

Robyn began to despair, her hopes of unmasking Jeremy's killer immediately dashed. Before she could speak, though, Toby frowned, leaning forward again over the keyboard.

'What is it?' she asked.

He didn't reply at first, instead waving the mouse a little more and clicking on a few nondescript labels. 'It isn't recording right now,' he said. 'But I think it should have been. Look. These are video files from the past two weeks. Each one's a new day.'

'Perhaps a recording's only saved once the session's completed. It might save to the system at midnight, and the next one automatically begins.'

'I mean . . . maybe. But if there's anything here to suggest this is being recorded, I can't see it.'

Robyn took a breath. If – *if* – that day's feed from the museum wasn't being recorded, what did that suggest?

'It isn't exactly the same as the system I'm used to,' said Toby. 'And it's all still in Italian. I might just be missing something.'

Robyn shook her head. 'It's too much of a coincidence. Files saved every day except for today – the day someone's murdered in there and an antique dagger is presumably stolen.' She glared at the screen. 'Two questions. First, who would have known about the camera in order to come here and stop the recording? Second, was it stopped for the daggers to be swapped? Or for Jeremy to be murdered?'

'It could have been both,' Toby suggested. 'What if Jeremy worked out who had swapped the daggers, and they killed him in the museum because they knew that nothing was being recorded?'

'Maybe,' Robyn agreed. 'It's pretty secluded. If you knew the camera wasn't recording it would be a good place to do it.' She looked down at the ground. 'It just doesn't make sense. Whoever killed Eva went to so much trouble to use that dagger. Bringing a fake to the island. Making sure the camera wasn't recording . . . But there's no reason for it. Jeremy told me himself that Eva had no familial connection to it. Nothing sentimental either. So why go to all the trouble?'

She leaned closer to the screen, peering at Jeremy's feet as they poked from behind the case. 'What was he even doing in there? Was he there already and the killer found him? Or was he lured up there?'

They were silent, the only sounds being the gentle whirring of the computer and the distant call of birds on the lake. Then, with his eyes glued firmly to the surface of the desk, Toby spoke.

'I was with him.'

Robyn stared at him, so taken aback that for a moment she was sure she must have misheard.

'Before the wedding,' he explained. 'You asked where I'd been. I was with Jeremy.'

'In the casermetta?'

Toby nodded. 'He wanted to speak about this job at HCM. The position Laurence is insisting I take. He suggested we do it after the ceremony, but I didn't want to wait. So I sent him a text this morning, saying let's speak before.'

'Why?'

'Because I've had my loan approved.'

He said it so matter-of-factly that it took Robyn a few seconds to process.

280

'The business loan,' he said. 'For my bar. It's been approved.'

'When?'

'The day we flew out here, although I didn't know until yesterday evening. When we were in the restaurant, with Eva's family, and you went to the loo. I checked my emails and there it was. A note from the bank, confirming it all.'

For a few minutes, as he helped her with the security footage, Robyn had forgotten just how furious she was with Toby for keeping her in the dark over Owen Lock. But now, as it turned out he'd kept yet another life-altering piece of information from her, all of that frustration came rushing back.

She remembered the moment she had returned to the table. Remembered how quickly he had hidden his phone when he saw her approaching. How he'd tried to hurry the conversation along and how his hand had trembled when he'd poured her another drink.

'Congratulations,' she muttered, making no effort to hide the disdain in her voice.

'Robyn . . .'

'So, what? You told Jeremy about this?'

Toby sighed. 'I told him to meet me before the wedding. Said let's just get it out of the way. I went inside. We spoke for a few minutes; I told him about the bar and about the loan. Said that I wouldn't ever be coming to HCM.'

'And how did he take it?'

'Not well.'

Robyn thought of the interaction she'd seen between Margot and Jeremy before the wedding had been due to begin. The way Jeremy had turned to Margot, shaking his head as he took his seat. And the way she, in turn, had looked out across the water, her own expression grim.

'Is that what your mum came to speak to you about?' Robyn asked. 'Before Laurence found that post on Eva's Instagram?'

Toby nodded. 'Jeremy had just told her. She's livid. As you can imagine.'

Robyn could indeed imagine, although that didn't make it any less repulsive. Her eldest son's fiancée was lying dead on a beach. And yet Margot was apparently more offended by the notion of Toby opening a cocktail bar.

'Why didn't you tell me this?'

'Because I didn't want them to accuse you of making me go through with it. And I was right not to. You heard Laurence on our first night here. He's convinced that I'm only pushing ahead with this because you want me to. For the life of him he can't understand that it's something *I want to do*. Eva said something similar on the yacht, didn't she?'

Robyn thought back to her conversation with Eva, just minutes before she was pushed into the lake. *Laurence called me last night*, she had said. *He thinks you're leading Toby astray. Telling him to open a bar when he should be working for HCM.*

Toby shook his head. 'Even Jeremy. The first thing he said when I gave him the news was that I shouldn't be letting you talk me into this. That it isn't what my dad would have wanted for me, and I shouldn't be doing it just to impress you.'

His voice shook a little, as if he were suddenly fighting back tears. 'They were giving you so much shit. I just thought that until we got home, and we were away from them all, the less you knew the better off you would be.'

Begrudgingly, Robyn supposed she understood. In his own

misguided way, he had thought that he was helping. Sparing her from the scorn of his family. But that didn't make being kept in the dark any less infuriating.

In the silence, Toby turned to the screen, staring, wide-eyed, at Jeremy's shoes. 'I've never liked him,' he said. 'I don't think he's ever liked me much, either. I was just the ungrateful kid squandering everything my dad had left for me. But he's always been there. I suppose he was family. Now he's gone.' He looked up at Robyn. 'Why would someone kill him? It's got to be connected to Eva, right? There can't be two different murderers on this island.'

Robyn stared into space. 'I think it might be more complicated than that.'

48

Inside the museum, Sofia paced back and forth.

Jeremy Lambourne lay on his back, his eyes wide and lips slightly parted, as if he couldn't quite believe that he was dead. But if the angry red mark in the centre of his chest didn't confirm it, neat as if it had been drawn on his shirt with a fine-tip pen, the small puddle of blood in which he lay cast no doubt.

Sofia tried to determine how long he had been there. A few minutes, at least. Some of the blood was already dry, his skin starting to pale.

Within seconds of her crying out for help, everyone inside the castle seemed to have come to the museum. Most stood just outside, peering through the door. Laurence Heywood, however, had come barging in, dropping to his knees at the sight of the body.

Sofia wondered exactly what their relationship had been. With their different surnames, it seemed unlikely that they would be father and son. And yet, with the way Laurence was now crying, huddled over Jeremy's chest, he certainly looked as if he'd lost a parent. A stepfather, perhaps? The bereft expression upon Margot Heywood's face, the woman who up until this moment seemed to have been made of steel, might suggest so.

'He's been shot. That's a bullet wound.' It was the best man who had spoken, having followed Laurence into the museum. He seemed to announce it to no one in particular, before turning away and pointing towards the top corner of the room. 'Where's the footage for that?'

Sofia's blood ran cold. The video camera.

Could she lie? Tell him it wasn't working? Too risky. They all knew where her office was. If one of them went to see, and found the camera to be very much in working order, there would be no explaining herself.

Looking towards the door, she saw the two strangers. They were standing at the back of the little crowd, glaring at her.

Had they done this? Perhaps their story of having to wait until three o'clock until they could be picked up had been a lie. Perhaps what they had actually needed was enough time to commit a second murder.

With one last look at the false dagger in its case, she turned back to the group, the best man still looking at her expectantly. She couldn't lie. At least, not here. Her only option was to take them to see the footage. If she could pretend she had no idea why it wasn't recording – plant the idea that whoever killed Eva and Jeremy must have seen to it that it wasn't – she might just save herself.

She looked the best man in the eye. Would he believe her? She had no choice. She would just have to make him.

'My office,' she said, her voice shaking. 'The footage is saved in my office.'

49

'The mafia,' Toby said after Robyn had finished. 'The actual Italian mafia?'

Quickly, she had told him about the conversation she'd overheard in the restaurant, between Vito, Margot and Jeremy. She told him about the article she'd found, describing mafia influence in northern Italy. And she told him about how, when Vito confronted them in the courtyard, she had seen the stranger with the beard and ponytail reaching for something inside his jacket, only to emerge empty-handed when Vito backed off.

Toby had listened to every word, wide-eyed.

'You really think the guy might have a gun?'

Robyn shrugged. 'He was reaching for something.'

'Should we tell someone?'

'We'll tell the police.'

'The police? Robyn, Jeremy's dead. We can't just wait for the police. What if they killed him?'

'Exactly. What if they did? We're stuck here with them, Toby. If I'm right, and one of them really is carrying some kind of weapon, how do you think they're going to respond to us announcing to the entire island that they're murderers?'

Toby sighed and ran a hand through his hair. 'So . . . you think, what? That Eva's dad is in debt to these guys, and Jeremy murdered her to keep them away from HCM? And now they've killed Jeremy as an act of revenge?'

'I was considering it. But that was before I knew you and Jeremy were in the casermetta while Eva was being murdered. He couldn't have been with you in there *and* with her in the cove.'

'Couldn't Eva have been killed before we all arrived on the island? The entire bridal party was here. One of them could have done it.'

Robyn shook her head. 'Cam told me that Eva went inside as our boats were arriving at half past eleven. So she was definitely still alive then.'

She paused, a sudden thought occurring to her. 'You went into the casermetta at quarter to twelve. I saw that. And you came up to the terrace just at twelve o'clock. Did you go anywhere else during those fifteen minutes? Anywhere at all?'

Toby shook his head. 'After Jeremy and I were done, I came straight back to you.'

'And where were you? When you were inside, where did the two of you speak?'

'In the dining room.'

Right by the door, Robyn thought.

'You must have seen Eva leaving,' she said. 'If she went inside at half past eleven, she couldn't have gone to the cove until at least quarter to twelve. If she had, everyone in the courtyard would have seen her. So if you were there between quarter to and twelve o'clock, she must have walked right past you.'

'I didn't see her.'

'You must have done.'

'I'm telling you, I didn't. In fairness, Jeremy and I were really getting into it. But I was facing the door. If she'd left while we were there, I'm sure I'd have seen her.'

Robyn didn't know what to say. He was wrong, she thought. He had to be. Maybe he and Jeremy had been arguing so fervently he just hadn't noticed Eva passing by in the background. Or if Jeremy had been standing in just the right place, perhaps he wouldn't even have seen.

She struggled to believe it, though. Her old lecturer's mantra echoed in her mind.

People lie. Facts don't.

It was a fact that Eva had gone into the casermetta at half past eleven. It was a fact that if she had left at any point before quarter to twelve, she would have been seen by everyone in the courtyard. And it was a fact that she had been found dead in the cove at ten past twelve.

But Sofia had said that she hadn't seen Eva while she was inside between quarter to and twelve o'clock. And now Toby was claiming that, despite standing by the front door for the entire fifteen-minute period, he hadn't seen her walk through it.

Could Robyn have it wrong? Could Eva have left *after* twelve o'clock? That would still allow a good ten minutes for her to be murdered, before Dina found her in the cove. But even that didn't add up. As Sofia had said, the bridal party had noticed before twelve o'clock that Eva was missing.

So how could it have been done? How could the bride have been smuggled out of the casermetta while the door was being watched? Or walked through a courtyard full of people, without anyone having seen? It simply wasn't possible.

People lie. Facts don't.

So who was lying?

Her thoughts were interrupted by the sound of movement outside. People were returning to the courtyard.

Springing from the chair, Toby crossed the little office in two short strides and peered through the window, squinting as he tried to look through the cracks in the shutters.

'Oh, God,' he murmured. 'Robyn . . . They're coming this way.'

Three o'clock

50

With the office too small for Robyn and Toby to be interrogated inside, Sofia promptly ushered them into the courtyard, where she, Stephen and Abigail gathered around. Harper and Cam were there too, as were the two men from the boat. Robyn also noticed a small group of the Italian guests, huddled protectively around Vito and Dina, watching from a bench outside the casermetta. It seemed they were eager to observe but from an apparently safe distance. Laurence and Margot had stayed inside the museum with Jeremy's body, watched over by Paola, Chadwick and Miles.

'So Jeremy's found inside the museum,' said Stephen. 'And while the rest of us are trying to work out what happened, you two go straight to the office. Now today's CCTV footage has been erased.' He spread his hands wide. 'You must see how that looks.'

'I'm telling you,' Robyn insisted. 'I swear. We didn't delete anything. We only wanted to see it.'

'Why? Why not wait for the rest of us?'

Robyn didn't answer. She couldn't. She just looked at him,

trying to stifle her fear while she scrambled frantically for an answer he might accept.

'Just tell us,' he said. 'What were you hoping to see that couldn't wait?'

Robyn took a deep breath, forcing as much confidence into her voice as she could manage. 'I wanted to see who had swapped the daggers this morning.' Seeing the confusion on Stephen's face, she frowned at him. 'Didn't you notice? Down in the cove? The dagger that Eva's been . . .' She tailed off, trying hard not to picture the murdered bride. 'The dagger . . . There's an identical one in the museum.'

Abigail tried to step in – to shoot Robyn down – but Stephen loudly shushed her, throwing up a hand as if to physically hold her back.

'What are you saying?' he asked. 'Why would that be important?'

'Because whoever killed Eva clearly wanted to do it specifically with *that dagger*. They brought a fake with them to the island, which they exchanged for the real one so that no one would notice it had gone before they could get to her. And to make sure they weren't caught making the swap, we now know that they've deleted today's CCTV footage.'

'What about Jeremy? Where does he factor into this theory?'

'He must have worked it out. I spoke to him an hour ago; he'd noticed the daggers too. Said he was going to tell the police about it when they arrived. The killer clearly needed to silence him somewhere, to protect their identity, and they obviously knew that the camera inside the museum wasn't recording. So they must have thought it would be a safe place to do it.'

Stephen turned to Sofia. 'Did you not notice any of this?'

She scowled at him. 'I was paying more attention to the dead bride.'

He looked back at Robyn, taking a moment to process. She could see that he wasn't yet fully convinced. But he did, at least, seem to be considering it. If nothing else, that gave her a glimmer of hope.

That hope was quickly stifled, however, by the realisation that Abigail was considerably less receptive.

'I'm not listening to this.' She jabbed a finger at Robyn. 'She's lying. Can't you see that? She's trying to distract us. This is about Owen Lock. She planted a message about him in Eva's bag. *She's* the one who posted his article on Eva's Instagram.'

Panic suddenly gripping her, Robyn tried desperately to protest. 'That isn't true,' she managed. 'None of that is true!'

But Abigail was too far gone. Her voice was rising, her accusations becoming more impassioned with each word. 'She killed Eva. Probably Jeremy, too. And *he* must have helped her.' She pointed now at Toby. 'There's no second dagger. No one sneaked into the museum to swap them over. It's ridiculous. A story she's making up just to throw us all off.'

'Abi.' Stephen took a step towards her, teeth gritted. 'You have to stop. We can't just assume—'

'I'm not *assuming* anything.' She motioned towards the office. 'Look at where we just caught them. And if that isn't enough, look at everything else. The warning in Eva's bag. Even the Instagram post. Just think about it. Who was it that told you how to check when it had been posted?'

Stephen looked as if he might argue. But his words seemed to die on his tongue, a frown appearing on his face.

'That's right,' Abigail continued. 'She must have posted it

just when she needed. To give herself some kind of alibi. If we hadn't—'

'All right, stop. Everyone, just stop.' Harper, who had so far said nothing, now stepped forward, raising her voice to be heard over Abigail. 'It wasn't Robyn,' she said. 'At least, the Instagram post wasn't. I can't speak for the rest of it. But that wasn't her.'

'And how would you know?'

'I just do.'

Abigail looked at her as if she'd tried to claim she'd been to the moon. 'You *just do*?'

'Yes.'

'Case closed, then. Robyn couldn't possibly have killed Eva, because you *just know* that the Instagram post wasn't her. Let's all sit on our hands and wait for the police to arrive, shall we?'

Stephen took a deep breath, trying hard, it seemed, to maintain his rapidly waning patience. 'Harper,' he said slowly. 'If you know who actually did this, you have to tell us.'

Harper grimaced. 'I don't know who killed her. All I know is that Robyn didn't post on her Instagram.'

She looked Stephen in the eye, apparently hoping that this would be enough to placate him. Seeming to recognise, however, that it wouldn't, she let out a breath that was halfway between a sigh and a growl.

'It was me. I did it.'

Robyn stared at Harper. Stephen's eyes widened. Even Abigail looked momentarily knocked off guard, although she quickly recovered.

'Why would you do that? Isn't it your job to make Eva look *good*?'

Harper gave a short laugh. 'Not any more.'

'Obviously, not any more. But you couldn't have known what was about to—'

'Eva was going to fire me.' Harper let this hang in the air a moment. As the seconds passed, though, the defiance in her expression eased, her gaze slipped to the floor and she said it again, as if to convince herself more than anyone else. 'She was going to fire me.'

'So . . . what?' Abigail demanded. 'You did it to get back at her?'

Harper gave a small shrug. 'I'd just found out. I was furious.'

Abigail shook her head. 'I don't buy it. You wouldn't leap straight to sabotaging her public image. You'd try to talk her out of it. Salvage the situation. If you were caught, you'd never work again.'

Harper shot her a look that could cut stone. 'You don't get it. You couldn't, if you hadn't ever worked for her yourself. After everything I've done – the late nights, the awful messages, the shitty pay . . .' She took a breath, trying to bring her sudden anger under control. 'I had to hear it from her. Had to know it was true. So I went to confront her.'

Robyn noticed Vito, who had risen from the bench, slowly approaching the group. She wondered how much more he could take, his heart visibly breaking as Harper described her betrayal. Dina came closer too, although she trailed a little way behind him, looking more nervous than ever.

'Where did this happen?' asked Stephen.

Harper nodded towards the casermetta. 'We'd been on the terrace; Cam was taking pictures of the bridal party. But when we saw the boats approaching, Eva went inside. At least, I thought she did. When I followed her, she wasn't there. But I was too angry to just let it go. It was too fresh. So I tried to think of some way to hurt her. To get back at her.'

Abigail scowled, apparently starting to believe. 'You had her phone.'

Harper nodded. 'As you said, she could hardly carry it herself while she was wearing her wedding dress. I'd been looking after it all morning.'

Stephen looked to Cam. 'Is this true?'

Cam opened her mouth to reply, but Harper stepped in first.

'She wasn't there. She left the terrace with Eva and the bridesmaids.'

'And how did you get into her phone? Had she told you her pin?'

Harper shrugged. 'I saw her type it in yesterday, when we were waiting for you all beside the yacht.'

Vito shook his head. 'Why? I understand that you were upset. But this . . . ? You would have ruined her entire career!'

Harper rounded on him, fury flaring in her eyes. 'She ruined her own career! The minute she started posting about meal replacements to an audience full of teenagers, she might as well have been done. I told her to take it down. Begged her, even. But she kept going. She'd convinced herself that if we were going to work with brands dealing in nutrition, she had to be showing she was already doing it. I tried to make her stop. I really, really tried. It didn't matter what I said, though. She only agreed after we'd heard about Rachel.'

'But why was she going to fire you?' asked Stephen. 'Did she blame you for not stopping her?'

'No. To her credit, she knew she'd screwed up. What she blamed me for was not making it go away. It's been a year, she would tell me. Why did she still not have a collaboration with Nutribullet? Or Whey Protein?

'She just didn't seem to understand. How was I supposed to convince a business that makes its name off health and well-being to work with her after what happened? She told me over and over that they wouldn't know. So much time has passed, she would say. But these people aren't idiots. They vet their influencers before agreeing to work with them, and it isn't exactly difficult to find out what happened.'

Harper drew a short breath before continuing, 'What did she think a different agent would do that I haven't? I'm the only reason *anyone* still works with her, and yet she blamed me for a mistake she made. A mistake I did everything I could to prevent.'

'So you wanted to hurt her.' It wasn't a question. Stephen said it completely matter-of-factly.

Harper nodded. 'As I say, she wasn't there for me to confront. And I'd reached the end of my tether. So I did the only thing I could. I barely thought about it. It couldn't have taken more than a minute.'

'And when you were done, you left the phone on the table.'

'Couldn't risk being caught with it. Not after what I'd done.'

The group was silent for a moment as Harper's confession sank in. Robyn stared at her, so full of sympathy that she'd all but forgotten the danger she and Toby had been in only minutes earlier.

'You say you'd only just found out that you were going to be fired,' said Abigail. 'That you had to hear it from Eva herself before you would believe it. Where *did* you hear it from?'

Harper faltered, chewing her lip as she seemed to decide

whether she was going to answer. She didn't speak. But she did eventually turn to another member of the group. Robyn followed as she looked over their shoulders, her gaze settling on Dina.

'Dina . . .' Vito stared at her. '*Tesoro* . . . You did this?'

For a few seconds, Dina looked as shocked as her father. Robyn wondered if she might be about to protest. To argue her innocence. Instead, with everyone in the courtyard now watching her, tears began to gather in her eyes.

'I wanted to hurt her, Papà. Being in this place, wearing this dress . . .' Her voice cracked and she had to pause for a moment, taking several deep breaths before she could continue. 'I thought I could make it through today. But it's too painful. I wanted *my* day. *My* wedding. *My* husband. I couldn't have any of those things, because Eva ruined them. So I ruined something too. Something that would mean as much to her as what she had taken from me.'

'Dina . . .' Vito took her hand. 'What happened with Nico was terrible. But it wasn't Eva's fault.'

'It was *all* Eva's fault!' Dina raised her voice almost to a shriek. 'She wasn't the perfect *topolina* you thought she was, *Papà*. She was heartless. *Crudele*. You and *Mamma* refused to see it, but everyone else knew exactly what she was.'

The group was completely silent as Vito, now seemingly broken, stared into space.

'Fine,' Abigail announced, rounding once again on Harper. 'The Instagram post was you. But that doesn't change anything else.' She turned to Stephen. 'Why are we wasting time talking about this? You said it yourself inside the museum. Jeremy's been shot. So who has a gun?'

Robyn felt her fear return as Abigail's gaze fell upon her.

'I don't have a gun,' she said.

'Prove it. Show us your bag.'

'I *don't* have a gun.'

'So show. Us. Your. Bag.'

Abigail advanced on Robyn, but her path was quickly blocked as Toby sprang between them, drawing himself to full height.

'That's enough!' Stephen threw up his hands, trying to calm the situation. 'Abi, stop! This isn't helping.'

'I'll stop when she proves she doesn't have a gun.'

Stephen sighed, before looking to Robyn, resignation in his eyes. 'Please.'

Recognising the impasse, she handed him her bag. Carefully, his discomfort clear, he clipped it open. After a moment spent delicately turning through the contents, he turned to Abigail.

'No gun.'

Robyn looked to Abigail, expecting for a few seconds that she would argue. She could feel Toby at her side, bristling. Abigail didn't say anything, though. Instead, she scowled, turned on her heel and stormed towards the casermetta.

51

Stephen followed Abigail inside, their footsteps echoing against the tiled floor.

'Abi,' he called after her. 'Abi, wait.'

She ignored him, striding ahead. At the sound of their approach, two of Eva's schoolfriends, who had been huddling by the glass doors, hurried upstairs.

'Abi, please!'

Reaching the end of the hallway, she turned and faced him, fixing him with a look so ferocious it stopped him dead in his tracks.

'What were you doing out there?' she hissed at him. 'Why weren't you siding with me?'

He took a step closer, dropping his voice. 'You can't just accuse people of murder, Abi. Not when the police aren't here and certainly not when we can't know for sure who it was.'

'You really don't think it was her?'

'It might not have been!'

'Who else, then? You tell me, Stephen. Who else could it have been?'

He didn't answer. He couldn't find the words.

Abigail's eyes narrowed. 'Why are you looking at me like that?'

He took a deep breath, bracing himself for what he was about to ask. 'Where were you before the ceremony?'

'Before the ceremony?'

He nodded, swallowing back a lump from his throat. 'When we got off the boats, we all gathered in the courtyard for a few minutes. Then I went with Laurence to speak with the celebrant—'

'What are you talking about? Why are you asking me this?'

Again, Stephen paused to find the right words. But before he could continue, Abigail's eyes widened.

'You think it was me?'

'I don't—'

'How could you possibly think it was me?'

Stephen took a breath, trying to still his thumping heart. 'Any one of us could have put that message in Eva's bag. And we have nothing to suggest that Robyn knew Owen Lock beyond the fact she studied journalism. But you're gunning for her like your life depends on it.'

'Because it might! Because it's so clearly her!' Abigail shook her head. 'I can't believe this. I'm trying to protect you. Protect *our family*. And here you are, refusing to believe me. Accusing me of murdering two people!'

'Look at it from where I'm standing, Abi. Just for a moment. How many times have you told me you want Eva out of our lives? How many times have you said that we'd be so much better off without her?'

'But I wouldn't *kill* her!'

Stephen saw the betrayal on his wife's face. Saw the tears threatening to form in the corners of her eyes.

'You bring them into our lives,' she said, her voice quivering. 'Into *my* life. You get yourself involved in what happened to Owen, and you trap me there with you. Right in the middle of this shitshow. And I've stayed there. Because we're a team. Because you've told me you'll get us out.'

Stephen could hardly speak, his resolve completely abandoning him. 'Abi, please . . .'

He took a step a closer, reaching out for her. But she shrugged him off.

'I'm not doing this any more,' she said quietly. 'I'm not bringing a child – *my child* – into this. You work everything out with Laurence. But you do it without me.'

'What are you saying?'

'I'm saying I'm done. I'm saying that when we get back to London, I'm not coming home with you. Until you've worked all of this out . . . Until you've shaken Laurence off and realised how ridiculous the accusation you've just made actually is, you're on your own.'

The tears finally began to fall, and with nowhere else to go, she climbed the steps to the top floor. Stephen, meanwhile, stared at the spot she had just occupied, too stunned to even call after her.

His mind rattled, swimming with thoughts of all that Laurence had put them through, and questions of how it had all gone so very wrong.

Except it wasn't Laurence. Not all of it. Abigail was right. Stephen was the one who had inflicted Laurence on her. Who dragged her down to the bottom of his pocket. And now he was accusing his own wife of murder. The wife who had stood by him through everything that had happened to Owen Lock.

Of course it couldn't be her. She was a victim. *His* victim.

The realisation now fully dawning on him, the grief in his stomach turned to rage.

52

By the time Robyn started hurrying after her, Harper was already climbing up to the terrace.

'Harper,' Robyn called out. 'Harper!'

For a few steps, she was plainly ignoring her. But at the top she stopped. She looked defeated, the defiance with which she had stood up to Stephen and Abigail now long gone.

'Hey,' said Robyn. 'Listen . . . Thanks for stepping in.'

Harper gave a small shrug. 'I couldn't just let you take the blame for that post. Don't expect me to help you with the rest of it, though. The note in Eva's bag . . . You're on your own there.'

Robyn grimaced, trying hard not to dwell on the similar discussion that Abigail and Stephen must surely be having in the casermetta. 'Look,' she said. 'I wanted to ask . . . When did you say you went inside?'

Harper frowned at her.

'Please,' Robyn pressed. 'It's important. You said you followed Eva inside, but she wasn't there. How far behind her were you?'

Harper gave another shrug. 'Only a minute or two. When she saw that the boats were coming she went straight down there, while Cam and the bridesmaids went to the jetty. I was set to go too, but Dina asked me to stay for a minute. That's when she told me. Eva thought I wasn't delivering, and once the *London Living* feature was done with, she was planning to let me go.'

'And then?' Robyn tried to shimmy her along, noticing how the resentment was building in her voice again.

Harper sighed. 'Dina and I went into the courtyard together. She broke off to join the other bridesmaids and I headed inside to look for Eva.'

'But she wasn't there?'

Harper shook her head. 'I could hear her parents upstairs. But there was no sign of her.' Her eyes narrowed slightly. 'Why do you want to know?'

Before she could reply, Robyn heard a faint buzzing sound. Opening her bag, Harper took out her phone.

'My boss,' she said.

'She must be pretty worried.'

'She's freaking out. She's seen the Instagram post. Wants to know what's going on.'

'You haven't told her?'

'I've been trying to think of a way to dig myself out. See if I can save my job.' She sighed. 'I suppose there's no point holding out on her now, though.'

Robyn forced the most reassuring expression she could manage, trying hard to quell a sudden stab of guilt. 'She's waited this long. I'm sure you could keep her on the hook a little longer while you work something out.'

Harper shook her head, her eyes wide as she looked at the phone. 'Not when I've just confessed to half a dozen people.

I can be fired now or I can be fired when I get home. Might as well get it over with.'

She turned away, but as she made to leave, Robyn called after her.

'Harper . . . About Eva's bag. You were looking after it for the whole dinner, right? So how did the message even get there? Did you put it down for a minute? Leave it at the table to go to the loo or . . . ?'

Now it was Harper's turn to grimace. 'No way. Eva would have killed me. Whoever put that message in there . . . God knows how, but they did it right under my nose.'

She excused herself and went to the end of the terrace, where she took a seat in the front row and raised her phone to her ear.

Robyn didn't envy her. If anything, she felt sorry for her. But she didn't have time to dwell. Her mind was racing.

Cam had seen Eva go inside at half past eleven. But if Harper was to be believed, it now seemed that only a minute or two later she had gone.

Why go so suddenly from the casermetta to the cove? Could someone have been waiting for her? Hiding just inside the door, so that they could ambush her the moment she stepped inside? It would explain why Toby hadn't seen her leave between quarter to and twelve o'clock, as well as why Sofia hadn't seen her when visiting the casermetta herself in the minutes before the ceremony. But if that was what had happened – if Eva had gone to the cove in the sliver of time *before* the guests filled the courtyard, rather than *after* – who could have taken her?

Cam, Sofia and the bridesmaids had apparently gone to meet the boats. Vito and Paola had been inside, although Robyn could still think of no reason for them to murder their own daughter.

She paused. Perhaps, even, rather than waiting right in front of Eva, the killer had been following right behind her, catching her just as she stepped through the door.

Robyn looked again at Harper.

People lie. Facts don't.

Admitting to one transgression, in the hope of earning enough trust that you could convincingly deny being guilty of another, was a common interview strategy that journalists had to be wary of. More than that, it was a shockingly reliable one. Harper had freely admitted to posting Owen's article on Eva's Instagram. She had offered herself up for judgement and, in the process, seemingly convinced the group she wasn't also Eva's killer. But what if this hadn't simply been a confession? What if Harper had played them, shifting their attention elsewhere in order to make a clean getaway?

Robyn sat on the top step and cast a look around the terrace, a slight, merciful breeze tugging at the canopy under which Laurence and Eva would have sat during the ceremony. Taking out her phone, she went back to the article on Owen Lock's death. With a deep breath to steady herself, she read it the whole way through.

JOURNALIST DIES AFTER ASSAULT OUTSIDE HOME

Owen Lock, an investigative reporter for the *Guardian*, has died from a wound sustained during an assault outside his home in North London.

During the assault, which was witnessed by a neighbour, three men reportedly approached Mr Lock in the street and hit him multiple times before fleeing. Mr Lock died in hospital, three days later, as the result of a severed artery in his brain. Doctors believe the injury may have been sustained when he fell and struck his head on the pavement.

The attackers, all three of whom wore dark hoodies, have not been identified. However, an investigation is ongoing. Police have so far not confirmed whether Mr Lock's death is being treated as murder or manslaughter.

Mr Lock was a respected investigative reporter, having published powerful exposés on the dark web, international trafficking and drug rings. Most recently, he covered the rise of influencer culture, reporting on the near death of a teenager who undertook an extreme fasting diet that had been endorsed on Instagram.

Robyn set the phone down and took a deep breath.

So much about what had happened filled her with rage. The fact that Toby had kept it from her. The picture of Eva and Laurence, drinking prosecco in a swanky restaurant while Owen lay wounded in the street on the other side of London. The thought of Stephen, Chadwick and Miles donning black hoodies to beat him up at Laurence's request.

It occurred to her as well that Owen being a journalist made it worse. More than that, the kind of journalist that Robyn herself had once hoped to be. He had reported on people traffickers. Drug cartels. Even delved into the murky depths of the dark web. He'd crossed paths with people considerably more dangerous than Eva Bianchi. It made it all the more depressing that she had been the one to bring him down.

Robyn had already decided that when they were home, she would be taking this revelation to the police. But she wondered, briefly, what Millie Lock might be doing. Had she found him, on the pavement outside their home? Had she been the one to call for an ambulance? Could she even have seen it happen?

Returning her attention to the phone, Robyn went to the *Guardian*'s homepage and searched for *Millie Lock*. Expecting to find an extensive backlog of editorials, she was surprised instead to find nothing. Only a list of articles written by Owen, a handful about the State Pension triple-lock and another about hackers developing cunning new ways to unlock smartphones.

Robyn flicked through a few more pages of useless lock-themed results, combing for articles written by Millie. But it was no good. What had Abigail said? *I heard that they worked together. That she was a reporter, too, or something like that.*

Several different theories sprang into Robyn's mind. Millie could have written under a different name. Perhaps Millie Lock wasn't her name at all – she might easily have kept her maiden name when she and Owen married. Or maybe Abigail had simply got it wrong, and the truth was that Millie wrote for a different paper. It would explain why Robyn had found nothing on the *Guardian*, but it would be a strange detail to misremember.

Turning to Google, Robyn searched for *Millie Lock reporter*. Again, nothing presented itself. No articles published on other news sites. Nothing, if she was honest, to suggest that a reporter called Millie Lock even existed.

Admitting defeat, she slipped her phone back into her bag, set it down beside her and looked out across the water. A sailing boat passed by, and as it did, she thought again of the boat she had seen circling the island before the ceremony. Whoever the skipper had been, she wished more than ever that she had been with him. Wished she had been speeding towards the safety of the shore as Dina's scream rang throughout the castle.

She didn't have long to fantasise about her escape. Hearing movement beside her, she turned to see Cam settling on the step.

'You came to check on me earlier,' she announced, heaving the bulky camera bag off her shoulder as she lowered herself onto the stone. 'After the way they just grilled you in the courtyard, it seemed right that I return the favour. How are you holding up?'

Robyn gave a weak smile. 'I'll be better once I'm off this island.'

'God, yes.' Cam looked at her, adopting a quizzical expression. 'Can I ask you something? You don't have to answer if you'd rather not. But I can't help wondering. You said you studied to be a journalist.'

'That's right.'

'So why aren't you one?'

Just as it had when Laurence asked it in the villa, the question caught Robyn so off guard that she wasn't sure quite how to respond. 'I don't really know,' she said after a long pause. 'I guess . . . By the time I was done with studying, I just didn't see the point.'

'And what was the point meant to be? Why did you want to do it in the first place?'

Robyn thought for a little while, like exploring a house in

which she'd once lived but was struggling to remember. 'I guess I wanted to do all the stuff you see journalists doing in the movies. Chasing down leads. Reporting on the injustices of the world. But it sounds ridiculous now.'

Cam shook her head. 'Doesn't sound ridiculous at all.'

'Yeah, well. By the time I'd finished my degree, and I realised what I would actually end up doing if I went into modern journalism . . . Clickbait. Ad revenue. It was just too depressing.' She looked Cam in the eye, feeling a twinge of sadness for her abandoned ambitions. 'I think when all was said and done I just wanted to help people.'

'And you don't still want to do that?'

For a little while, Robyn said nothing, the silence finally broken by the sound of footsteps on the staircase. Seeing that Toby was climbing up to them, Cam rose to her feet again and began to gather up her things. Swinging the camera equipment onto her shoulder, she knocked over Robyn's bag. She stooped to pick it up, handed it back and descended into the courtyard, exchanging nods with Toby as she went.

Just as Robyn had done a few minutes earlier, he looked around at the terrace, his hands in his pockets, and blew a long sigh.

'You OK?' he asked.

She nodded, and he sat down beside her, pressing his head into his hands.

'The dream wedding. Who'd have thought it could all go so wrong?'

Robyn didn't answer. As the words left his mouth something seemed to click, like an orchestra suddenly finding its rhythm after several minutes of playing out of time.

Toby frowned at her. 'Robyn?'

Still, she didn't reply, her mind moving at a hundred miles per hour.

'Everything's going wrong,' she murmured. 'It's all going wrong.'

Toby watched her, knowing better this time than to interrupt.

She looked down into the courtyard, taking in the gatehouse, the casermetta, the door leading to the cove and the second staircase that went up to the museum. She breathed it all in, as if each had been physically moved into a more pleasing arrangement.

'What if we've been thinking about this all wrong?' she said, speaking more to herself than to Toby. 'I've been asking why Eva's killer would go to so much effort to use the dagger. Why they've swapped it for the replica. Made sure the CCTV footage wasn't being recorded. Jeremy told me that Eva had no connection to the dagger. No familial links. No sentimental value. So why would they go to all that trouble to use it?'

'But now I'm thinking . . . what if they didn't? What if the killer never meant to use the dagger? What if their plan *went wrong*?'

She stared into space, eyes wide as she tried frantically to connect the dots.

'Why take it, if not to murder Eva?' She turned to Toby. 'It must have been Vito. He must have stolen it to pay off his debt. That's why he came to the island with the bridal party – so that he could make the swap before the castle was full of guests. And it's why he was arguing outside the museum with Eva. She must have caught him.'

Robyn paused for a moment. 'But Eva didn't stop him.

314

Maybe she tried. Or maybe he just convinced her of how much trouble they were in. Either way, he plants the replica in the museum, takes the dagger to the cove and hides it. That's why two men from the mafia came with the guests. They must have been planning to collect it.

'That even explains why they swapped it for a fake in the first place. I assumed it was so that nobody would notice the real one had gone before it could be used to kill Eva. But that wasn't it at all. No one was supposed to know a swap had even taken place. Vito places the real dagger in the cove, the mafia collect it and with the replica in place inside the museum no one would ever have known.'

She paused again, catching up with her own theory. 'But the killer didn't know any of that had happened. When they took Eva down to the cove, they had no idea the dagger was there. All they knew was that it was a secluded place. Probably the one place on the island where they were unlikely to be interrupted. But Eva knew. Because she caught Vito stealing it. So when they're down in the cove, she pulls it out to defend herself and is killed in the struggle.'

'You think the killer meant to shoot her instead?' said Toby. 'Like Jeremy?'

Robyn looked across the water. 'Maybe they didn't mean to kill her at all. Just a few minutes before Eva was found, I saw a guy circling the island on a speedboat. He did three loops before turning away and going back to shore. He was looking for something. I couldn't think what, but I was sure of it.'

She turned back to Toby. 'The killer clearly had a gun, as you say. But what if they didn't want to kill Eva? What if they wanted something else from her, which they were planning to take at gunpoint? And the moment they had it, they were going to escape on the boat I saw? The cove would be perfect for that. Once the killer had what they needed, the boat could sail right inside and pick them up.'

'But what would they want?'

'Who knows? Information of some kind? Maybe it was Eva herself. Maybe they planned to kidnap her.'

'OK,' said Toby. 'So the plan goes wrong. Eva pulls the dagger out of nowhere, the two of them fight and she ends up killed. If the murderer has a boat there, circling the island as it waits to take them away, why didn't they leave? Why didn't they run for the hills?'

Robyn thought, scrambling for an answer. 'They must have thought it was safer inside the castle. Think about it. If someone had been missing after Eva was found, wouldn't we have immediately assumed they had done just that – killed her and fled? They must have thought it was safer to stay on the island and play dumb than give themselves away and try to outrun the police.'

'You don't think they might have stayed behind to kill Jeremy?'

'No. If I'm right – and I might not be, but if I am – Jeremy was never part of the plan. He couldn't have been. They were supposed to have left that cove on the boat, and be speeding back to shore with whatever it is they wanted from Eva.'

'So . . . what? They killed Jeremy because he worked out who they were?'

'I don't know. Maybe. If the only reason they decided not to run was that they thought they stood a better chance of staying hidden, then yes. Maybe they would kill again, if someone had managed to work them out.'

Toby sighed. 'All right. So who is it?'

Robyn didn't reply.

'Come on, Robyn. You've worked all of this out. You must have an idea.'

'I do,' she said. 'But I really, really want to be wrong.' She hesitated, taking a deep breath. 'It would have to be someone capable of leading both Eva and Jeremy away to secluded locations without arousing suspicion. Someone who could carry a gun without it being seen. Someone who could walk unseen among the guests. And someone who's been lying to cover their tracks.'

She looked into the courtyard. Margot was on the bench outside the casermetta, Chadwick and Miles standing over her.

'Where's Laurence?' she asked.

'Still inside the museum,' said Toby. 'Mum said he wouldn't leave Jeremy.'

'And why aren't Chadwick and Miles still with him? What are they doing in the courtyard?'

'They said he wanted a moment alone.' Toby looked suddenly concerned. 'What is it, Robyn? What's wrong?'

She didn't reply. Instead, she did a quick mental headcount of everyone in the courtyard. As she realised who was still there – and, crucially, who was missing – the last piece fitted into place, the answer presented itself and her heart sank.

53

Sofia stormed in the direction of the gatehouse, where the two strangers were loitering just outside the door.

'What's happening?' she hissed. 'Why did you kill him? Was it not enough to take Eva?'

'We haven't killed anyone.' Just as before, it was the man with the beard and ponytail who spoke, his voice perfectly level.

'Then what was it all for? The dagger. The camera. Why are you here? Why are people dying if not for you?'

'We haven't killed—'

'Stop it!' Sofia snapped at him. 'Just stop it!' She fell silent, taking a breath as she tried to collect herself. 'It doesn't matter any more. I just want you gone. Where's your boat? You said you were leaving at three.'

'It's late.'

'What do you mean, it's late? How can it be *late*?' She motioned towards the group, fighting to keep the panic from her voice. 'You've seen how they're all reacting. They're scared, terrified that they're going to be next. Even if you didn't kill those people, how am I supposed to keep the police away now someone else has turned up dead?'

The bearded man took a single step forward. It was a movement so small that anyone watching would barely have noticed it. And yet, in an instant he was looming over Sofia, silencing her completely.

'We haven't killed anyone,' he told her again, something dark straining in his voice. 'But there's still time. The boat will come when it comes. And if the police do arrive first . . .'

Sofia didn't speak. She couldn't. All she could think of was her son, sitting in his cell, staring into her eyes through the photograph she had been provided.

The fear rose inside her again. But she barely had time to register it. From the corner of her eye, she saw the best man marching furiously towards her.

'Where are the police?' he demanded.

Sofia stared at him, her fears being realised right in front of her.

'You must have called them again,' he insisted. 'Where are they?'

'Of course,' she managed, switching to English. 'Of course I've called them.'

'*So where the fuck are they?*'

She flinched as he raised his voice, painfully aware of how the two strangers were observing them. Did they speak English? She had no idea. They had only ever spoken to her in Italian. But even if they didn't, she was certain they would understand what was being asked. If nothing else, they must at least recognise the word 'police'.

She looked at the best man – Stephen, was it? – and forced as much authority into her voice as she could find. 'They're coming. They'll be here soon. Very soon.'

Stephen didn't reply. Instead, he swore, seemingly to himself, and began to stride in the direction of the office.

'What are you doing?'

'I'm going to call them myself.'

She stumbled after him, panic immediately gripping her. 'No! Please. I've told you already, there's no need. I've called them.'

'I don't care. I'm not standing here waiting any more. If you can't get them here for the sake of two dead bodies, I'll do it myself.'

'All right! All right. I'll do it now.'

Immediately, she realised her mistake. And as Stephen halted, just outside the office door, she saw that he had noticed it too.

'What do you mean, do it now? You just said you've done it already.'

'Of course. I meant I'll call them again.'

Stephen raised his wrist, inspecting his watch. Then he looked back at Sofia. She saw his fury turn to suspicion. Saw the thought process that was leading him to the one conclusion she had been trying so desperately to avoid.

'Three hours,' he said slowly. 'Two people murdered. And absolutely nothing but your word to suggest that the police are coming.' He paused. 'Have you called them at all?'

There it was. Sofia tried to scoff. To feign offence. But she couldn't manage it. Between the watchful eyes of the two strangers and the glare under which Stephen now held her, she was paralysed.

'Of course I have,' she said, her voice little more than a whisper. 'I told you—'

She was interrupted by the sound of shoes pounding against the cobbled ground. Looking up, she saw Laurence Heywood's brother sprinting towards them.

'Quick!' he cried out. 'All of you, please. Come with me. We need—'

Stephen put up a hand, holding him at bay. He didn't turn away though, his gaze still very much fixed on Sofia.

'You haven't,' he said. 'Have you? They aren't coming.'

'Stephen,' the new arrival urged. 'You don't understand. It's—'

'Shut up, Toby!' Stephen snarled at him, before returning his attention to Sofia, his shoulders heaving.

'I've told you . . .' said Sofia, struggling to force back tears. 'The police operation here is limited—'

'Right. So if I went into this office and looked at the phone log, I would see that at least two calls have been made to the police.'

She didn't answer. There was nothing to say. He had her trapped.

'What's happening?' Toby looked around the group.

Stephen took a breath, the air hissing between pursed lips. 'The police aren't coming. She hasn't called them.'

Toby didn't speak. He stared at Sofia, incredulous.

'Was it you?' Stephen advanced on her. 'Did you kill Eva? And Jeremy?'

Toby grabbed his arm. 'Look, I don't know what's happening here, but it isn't her. Please, we all need—'

Stephen shrugged him off, turning once again towards the office. 'I'm calling the police. I'm *actually* calling them.'

He got no further. Sofia watched in despair as Stephen turned on the spot, expecting to find the office door but instead finding himself face to face with the bearded man. The stranger barred his way, denying any access to the office, and smoothly withdrew a gun from inside his jacket.

54

Robyn flew up the stairs, passed through the archway and barged into the museum.

'Stop!' she cried out. 'Cam, don't!'

From the scene that greeted her, it was immediately clear that if she had arrived a moment later, there would more than likely have been a second corpse sprawled upon the museum floor. Beside Jeremy's body, Laurence was on his knees. Cam stood in front of him, a small silver item clutched in one hand and a gun in the other, pointed directly at his brow.

'Robyn!' Laurence shot her a look of pure terror. 'Jesus, Robyn, do something!'

He was taking deep, shuddering breaths, no longer crying but his eyes still bloodshot, his face streaked with tears. As for Cam . . . She and the woman Robyn had spoken with only moments earlier could have been completely different people. She gripped the gun tightly, looking down on Laurence with an expression so venomous it threatened to do the bullet's job for her.

At Robyn's sudden arrival, though, that venom turned to panic.

'Please,' said Robyn. 'Put it down, Cam. This has already gone too far.'

Cam shook her head. 'You can't be here. You can't be part of this.' Her eyes suddenly widened. 'Where's your bag?'

Robyn was so taken aback that for a moment she thought she'd misheard.

'Your bag,' Cam repeated. 'Where's your bag?'

Robyn's mind raced. She had been in such a hurry to reach the museum that she must have left her bag on the terrace. Although quite why Cam was so distressed to see her without it, she couldn't imagine.

She took a breath, returning her focus to the scene in front of her. Laurence on his knees. The gun in Cam's hand.

'Cam . . . It's OK. I know that Eva's death was an accident. You didn't mean for it to happen.'

Cam frowned at her. It wasn't confusion in her expression, though. It wasn't even disbelief. It looked like hope.

'You really think that?'

'I know it.' Robyn nodded towards the display case behind her, where the false dagger proudly stood watch. 'It's that. I've been trying to work out why someone would go to so much trouble to use it. The CCTV. The replica. Why did Eva *have* to be murdered with that dagger? Why was it so important? And the answer is that it wasn't. Eva was never meant to be murdered, and certainly not with the dagger. When you took her to the cove, you didn't even know it was there.'

Cam watched, chewing her lip as she listened to Robyn's assessment.

'It was an accident, Cam. If you let Laurence go, we can explain that to the others. Make them understand.'

She shook her head. 'No one will care. You really think anyone will forgive me, just because what happened in that cove didn't pan out as it should have?' She nudged the gun in Laurence's direction, causing him to whimper. 'Does everyone know? Or is it just you?'

Robyn scrambled for an answer. Toby had been right behind her, rounding up the others from the courtyard while she ran on ahead. He would be there any second, and between them all, they would apprehend Cam. For now, she just had to keep her talking.

'Just me,' she lied. 'I only worked it out a moment ago.'

'Then you have to leave. Go back to the others, pretend you never saw this. I'm going to prison, Robyn. My fingerprints will be all over Eva, all over the dagger. Sooner or later, the police will catch me, and I'm making my peace with that. But I can't have you mixed up in this too.' She gave Robyn a pleading look. 'Come on. If you've really worked out what this is about then you know Laurence deserves this.'

Robyn saw the fear intensify in Laurence's eyes. Saw the gun trembling in Cam's hand. Perhaps she was right. Perhaps he did deserve it. But Robyn couldn't bring herself to turn away. Not for Laurence's sake, but for Cam's.

She just had to keep talking.

'I don't know what happened with Jeremy. But I do think I know how you got Eva into the cove. There was something one of my lecturers used to say. People lie. Facts don't.'

Laurence's eyes bulged. '*What are you doing?*'

'You told me,' Robyn continued, raising her voice, 'that Eva went into the casermetta at half past eleven. But Harper says that when she went looking for her, just a couple of minutes

325

later, she wasn't there. I thought someone might have been inside, waiting to jump her. But unless there was someone else on the island, who's since managed to either escape or stay hidden, only her parents could have managed that. And I think we can safely say that neither of them would murder their own daughter. So it's much more likely someone was lying. Either you or Harper.

'I guess it could have been Harper. We all saw how upset she was at the thought of Eva firing her. But she'd already got her own back by posting Owen's article to half a million people. She wouldn't *need* to kill Eva. Once it occurred to me that whoever did never actually meant to, it became much more likely that you were the one who'd lied.

'The truth is that Eva didn't go into the casermetta at all. Up on the terrace, Dina was telling Harper about how Eva planned to fire her. In the courtyard, Sofia and the other bridesmaids went to meet the boats, having seen her turn away to go inside. But before she could, you must have called her back. Suggested going to the cove.

'How did you convince her to go, though? Was it the shot you told me about on the yacht? The one shot that she was so desperate for? It's beautiful in the cove. I can see how she would believe it might be the place. A few quick pictures before the guests arrived, and while her make-up was fresh.'

Cam forced a weak smile, tears appearing in her eyes. 'You know . . . You're really very clever.'

For a moment, Robyn couldn't speak. She couldn't even move. Why Cam? Of all the terrible people on this island, why did it have to be her?

Summoning enough courage to speak, albeit not quite

enough to keep his voice from quivering, Laurence broke the silence. 'Why didn't the bridesmaids notice? If you were supposed to meet the boats with them, why didn't they realise that you hadn't?'

'That's perhaps the cleverest part,' Robyn leapt in. 'You told me yourself, Cam. No one at a wedding pays the photographer any attention. You're almost *supposed* to be invisible. Everywhere and nowhere at the same time. So long as your camera's in your hand, you can more or less do whatever you want. You even convinced me that *I* must have seen you when we all got off the boats. In reality you were still down in the cove.'

Cam nodded, not even trying to deny it.

'Tell us,' said Robyn. 'Please. What happened down there?'

Cam took a deep breath. 'It was all over so quickly. Eva went on ahead and I told her to go to the shoreline. Look out at the water, so that I could . . .'

She tailed off, looking at the gun in her hand and almost laughing at the irony of what she was about to say.

'So that I could get *the shot*. I took out the gun. Not to use it, though. I never planned to use it. I just needed her to see that I was serious. I couldn't risk her making a run for it and I didn't have time for her to put up a fight. I told her to turn around, she saw the gun and we talked. She said exactly what I wanted to hear. What I *needed* to hear. Then she dived for something. She reached behind a rock and suddenly she was coming at me with a dagger.

'I panicked. I dropped the gun, and the next thing I knew I was trying to wrestle her off.' She fixed Robyn with a desperate, pleading look. 'I never meant to kill anyone.'

'I know. You wanted that.'

Robyn nodded towards the silver object in her spare hand. Cam turned it over. A tape recorder.

For a moment, Robyn was taken aback by the little machine. She had expected to see a phone, its screen displaying a voice recorder app. She recovered quickly, though. The device Cam had chosen didn't matter. Her intention was undoubtedly the same.

'A confession,' said Robyn. 'On tape. That's what this was all about. And once you had it, you were going to escape. I saw a speedboat circling the island, just before Dina found Eva's body. For the life of me, I couldn't work out what it was doing. But now I realise, it was waiting for you. You were going to signal it, somehow, when you were done. It would then pick you up from the cove and sail away.'

'Confession?' Laurence repeated, his confidence growing. 'A confession to what?'

Cam looked down at him, her lips peeling back into a snarl as she tightened her grip again on the gun.

'A confession to murder,' said Robyn. 'Cam is Owen Lock's widow.'

55

Stephen was first into the gatehouse, followed by Toby, Sofia and the bearded man, his gun still held out before him. The second stranger stayed outside to stand watch. Even if he had wanted to come inside, Stephen was certain there wouldn't have been room for him.

'Please,' said Toby, as the door closed behind them. 'Just listen to me. We aren't interested in you. You have to let us go.' He turned to Sofia, fear filling his voice. 'Do they understand? Can you translate?'

Stephen, meanwhile, stared at the gun. 'What is this? Who are they?'

'They're mafia.'

Immediately, the man jabbed his gun in Toby's direction, prompting Sofia to shriek at him.

'Stop. Don't hurt them!'

Stephen knew he should be frightened. Even without the fear that he could feel radiating from Toby and Sofia, this was the first time he had ever looked down the barrel of a gun. Aside from the morning Laurence had once taken him shooting during the Christmas holidays, he thought it might be the first time he had ever even seen one.

And yet he wasn't frightened. If anything, he was angry. He had accused Abigail of being involved in Eva's death. By even allowing the thought to enter his mind, he had betrayed her. Sabotaged his own marriage, perhaps irreparably. And now, the truth presented itself. Eva's killer stood before him, plain as day. Nothing more than a common criminal with a gun.

'We didn't kill anyone,' the stranger said.

'Is that right?' Stephen shot back at him. 'You'll have to excuse me if I struggle to believe that while you're pointing a fucking gun at us.'

'Shut up,' Toby hissed beside him. 'Look. He's telling the truth.'

Toby pointed towards the desk, where a monitor showed a live feed of the museum. Stephen peered at it, struggling to process the image on the screen. Laurence was on his knees, beside Jeremy's body. Robyn was a few metres away from him, her back to the camera. And standing almost completely motionless, holding something to Laurence's head . . .

'The photographer . . .'

Toby nodded solemnly. 'If Robyn's right, she's Owen Lock's widow.'

At the sound of Owen Lock's name, Stephen's anger evaporated, replaced by a fear more pressing than anything the stranger's gun could have achieved.

He stared at the screen, unable to tear his eyes from the photographer. He had always suspected that what had happened that night would come back to haunt them, but he'd never once thought there would be more death on the cards. Perhaps he should have. A life for a life.

330

Except that wasn't what had happened. She had taken two lives. Eva and Jeremy. And now . . . Yes, he could see it now. That was most definitely a gun in her hand. Any moment, it seemed, she was going to take Laurence too.

His heart pounded in his ears. How many of them was she planning to kill? How much did she even know? Would Laurence be the last or was she coming for him next? And what about Chadwick and Miles? Were they all on her list?

Managing at last to look away, he was brought abruptly back to the room by the sight of the gun.

'So what is this? If you didn't kill Eva, why are you here?'

'They came for the dagger,' Toby replied. 'They wanted to steal it.'

Stephen turned on Sofia, his mind beginning to spin. 'And you . . . You're in on this? You made sure the camera wasn't recording anything. Told us all that you'd called the police. All so they could take a dagger?'

Tears beaded in Sofia's eyes. 'I'm sorry. I'm so sorry. They were going to kill my son.'

Stephen turned back to the stranger, his anger returning. 'You say you didn't kill anyone. You might as well have killed Jeremy. Do you think he'd be dead if the police had actually been called? If they'd come the moment Eva was found?'

'It doesn't matter!' Toby raised his voice. 'None of that matters right now. Look. Just look at what's happening.' He jabbed a finger at the screen, meeting the stranger's eye. 'We know you didn't kill Eva. Or Jeremy. But Robyn's up there with the person who did. Laurence too. If you don't let us go and help them, right now, you *will* have deaths on your hands.'

The stranger thought for a moment, eyes burning as he held

331

the gun steady. Stephen could see how furious he was at having had to reveal himself. He breathed through his nose, nudged his head towards the door and answered in a thick Italian accent, the words slurring slightly.

'If you go out there, you'll tell everyone who we are. Someone calls the police.' He shook his head, scowling. 'No. When we are gone, you can leave.'

'What are you talking about?' Toby spat back at him. 'What do you mean, *when you're gone*?'

'They have a boat coming,' said Sofia. 'Any minute now.'

'We can't stand here waiting for a boat. Look. Look at what's happening!'

Stephen watched as the stranger jabbed the barrel of the gun against Toby's chest, silencing him in an instant. When he spoke again, it was through gritted teeth.

'No one leaves.'

56

There had already been fear in Laurence's eyes, but at the realisation of Cam's identity, it immediately grew a hundredfold. Even after several minutes with a gun pressed to his head, it was as if he had only just realised quite how much trouble he was actually in.

Robyn, meanwhile, was starting to panic. Toby should have been just seconds behind her with everyone he could gather from the courtyard. There was no reason for him to have taken this long.

But she didn't have time to consider what could be keeping him. Laurence was speaking again, terror causing him to jabber uncontrollably.

'Look. If you want to talk . . . If that's really all you want to do, we can talk. We can work this out. Just don't—'

Cam pressed the gun against his forehead and he fell silent, screwing his eyes shut as the metal touched his skin.

'Come on, Cam,' said Robyn, hearing the desperation in her own voice. 'You aren't really going to shoot him on tape, are you?'

Cam almost laughed. 'I'm not recording this. I was going to

show him what Eva had said in the cove. Make sure he knew exactly where we stood.' She looked Robyn in the eye. 'How did you know? About me. Have you known it all along?'

Robyn took a deep breath, trying hard to stay calm. Cam was still talking. And as long as she was talking, there was a chance of convincing her to stop.

'It was Abigail. She told me that Owen was married; for a minute she even thought he'd been married to *me*. But she threw me off. She said that Owen and his wife had worked together at the *Guardian*. That she was a reporter too. But when I ran a search for anything you might have written, nothing came up. I'm willing to bet there are two reasons for that. The first is that I ran a search for "Millie Lock". If I'd searched instead for "Camilla" I reckon I might actually have found something.'

Cam didn't speak, but the way the corners of her mouth twitched into something almost resembling a sad smile told Robyn she was right.

Cam, she remembered saying, when they first met on the yacht. *Short for anything?*

Nope. Just Cam.

She took a breath, bolstered slightly. 'But even if I had searched for Camilla, I wouldn't have found an editorial, would I? No articles written under your name. Because Abigail had got that part wrong. You might have worked for the *Guardian*, but not as a reporter. You're a photographer.'

Tears appeared in Cam's eyes. 'They killed him. This spoilt boy and his spoilt girlfriend. *They killed him.*'

'We never meant to—'

'Shut up! You shut the fuck up!'

Cam raised her voice, and for a split second Robyn was so

certain Laurence was finally about to be shot that she almost cried out in terror.

She slowed her breathing, trying to stay as calm as she could feasibly manage. If Toby wasn't coming it seemed she would have to subdue Cam alone. Quite how she would do it, she had no idea. But at the very least she could try to keep her talking.

'What about Jeremy?' she blurted out. 'I'm not going anywhere, so you might as well tell me. Did you mean to kill him or was he an accident too?'

Cam scowled, shaking her head. 'Before Eva pulled the dagger on me, she spoke about Jeremy covering up what had happened to Owen. Making sure the police investigation went away. I knew I'd be caught sooner or later. Knew I must have left so much evidence on Eva's body that the police would work it out eventually. So I decided to make the most of the time I had. To make sure that if I went down – *when* I went down – I'd gathered enough detail to take them all with me.'

'You tried to get a confession out of Jeremy, too.'

Cam nodded. 'I told him I'd seen something in a picture I'd taken earlier, something I thought might identify the killer. He immediately suggested we go to the museum; somewhere secluded where we could talk. Once we were alone I confronted him, told him I knew what he'd done. But it didn't work. He threatened me, said that if I didn't give him the recording he would make sure I went to prison for the rest of my life.'

From beneath the barrel of the gun, Laurence glared up at her. 'So you killed him too.'

There was hatred in his voice, swelling just enough to briefly overcome his fear. For a split second, Robyn could even understand it. First his fiancée. Then Jeremy, by all accounts the closest thing he'd had to a father for the best part of twenty years. By having Owen killed, he had taken everything from Cam. Now she'd returned the favour.

As Laurence's confidence grew, Robyn saw Cam's begin to slip. She looked down at Jeremy's body, as if noticing it for the first time.

'I tried to get out. When I realised I'd made a mistake – that I couldn't frighten Jeremy into giving me what I needed – I tried to escape. But he wouldn't let me leave. He stood in the way. Blocked me in. He wanted the recording I'd made of Eva, and when I refused to give it to him he came at me.'

Silence lingered in the air for a moment, and once again, Cam looked pleadingly at Robyn. 'You have to go,' she said. 'You can't be here for this. No one was meant to die, but I can live with it. I'm happy, even. It's still justice for Owen, even if it isn't the kind I wanted. But I can't have you involved. I won't take you with me.'

'And I won't leave you,' Robyn replied, hoping she sounded braver than she felt. 'If my being here is the only thing stopping you from killing someone else, I'm not moving an inch.'

Cam grimaced. Robyn's mind, meanwhile, was thundering. She had to keep speaking. With Toby clearly not coming, it was all she had. All she could do until she thought of a way to talk Cam down.

'Even the warning in Eva's bag makes sense now,' she said. 'I couldn't understand why someone would want her to see it. If they were going to kill her, and if they were doing it for what happened to Owen, why would they warn her that they were coming?

'I get it now, though. You were confident enough Eva was involved in what happened to Owen that you came out here, but you had to be sure. So you planted that message to see her reaction. "The secret you've locked away." A reference just subtle enough that if Eva wasn't guilty it would seem completely bizarre. But if she *was*, she would understand. And it worked, didn't it? Eva freaked out when she saw it. And there it was. You knew for sure. Now you could come for your confession.

'Even the way you put it there. We've all been assuming it was sneaked into the bag during dinner, because that's when Eva found it. But that couldn't have happened – Harper was looking after her bag all evening and she was watching it too closely. You must have put it there when we were all on the yacht. I remember seeing Harper tuck the bag away under a deckchair. You probably did it when Eva pushed me into the water and everyone was distracted.'

Cam said nothing.

'Please,' said Robyn. 'You've taken just as much from Laurence as he took from you. You don't have to kill him as well. You can give Eva's confession to the police. Make sure he serves jail time instead. You don't have to kill anyone else.'

Cam took a deep breath, and Robyn saw clearer than ever just how terrified she actually was.

'You really think that's what would happen? Jeremy told me himself. Right here. Eva's confession is worthless now that she's dead. The police won't care about *why* I did it. Only that I did. If you think that giving them this recording would ever result in Laurence seeing the inside of a prison cell, you're wrong.' She took one last breath, shaking badly now as fear threatened to overcome her. 'I wanted to do this properly. I really, really did. But I understand now – Jeremy, of all people, helped me understand. This is the only justice Owen's ever going to get.'

With Laurence quivering in front of her, she pressed the gun firmly against his head, her finger tightening on the trigger.

57

Inside the gatehouse, Stephen joined Toby in once again staring at the computer monitor. He saw Laurence on his knees, a gun against his head. He saw the photographer with the weapon in her hand. Robyn, still standing just a short distance away.

For several minutes now they had hardly moved. The footage was silent, but Stephen could see clearly enough that they were talking. Robyn, presumably, was trying to talk her down. More than that, he could feel the terror radiating from Toby. Stephen could hardly blame him. He imagined Abigail, alone in that room with the person who had killed both Eva and Jeremy.

He weighed the odds as best he could, trying to determine if Robyn might be successful. More than that, if he even wanted her to be. Of course, he didn't want to be next. A small part of him might even have been glad to be in the office, held instead by the criminals who had come for the dagger. But to see Laurence with his life in the balance left him about as conflicted as he had ever been in his life.

He thought of all they had braved together. Rushworth. HCM. All the trips Laurence had taken him on and the school holidays spent at the Heywoods' home, like a stray cat they'd decided to keep. He thought of all the doors Laurence had opened, and all the work Stephen had done in return.

Again, the question flitted into his mind. Were they friends?

Then he thought of Eva. He thought of Owen Lock and how, every time Abigail told him they needed Laurence out of their lives, he had unquestionably agreed.

He looked at the screen, saw the gun raised to Laurence's temple and for a brief, dark moment, supposed there were worse things that could happen than Robyn failing to prevent this woman from taking her shot.

The door opened and the second stranger — the younger looking man, who had been standing guard outside the office — peered inside.

'*La barca.*'

'What does that mean?' Toby demanded. 'What's *la barca*?'

'The boat,' said Sofia. 'They're leaving.'

Stephen watched what happened next as if in slow motion. The man with the gun stood for a moment, apparently deciding how he was going to move from the office to the jetty without letting his captives run free. Toby, meanwhile, turned from the now open door to the computer screen, taking one last look at the deadly stand-off in which his girlfriend and his brother were currently caught.

He took a deep breath, drawing himself to full height, and before anyone could react quickly enough to stop him, he threw himself towards the door.

58

In the courtyard, Vito jumped to his feet, listening as a slight humming noise drifted towards them on the air. It was faint at first. So faint that he wondered if he was imagining it. But with each passing second it grew steadily louder.

'What's that?' Dina looked up at him from the bench, panic straying across her face.

'A boat,' he said. 'There's a boat coming.'

'The police?'

Vito didn't answer. He knew better than to hope it might be the police. It was *them*. They were leaving, just as they'd said they would.

The wedding party began to gather in the courtyard, drawn by the sound. Vito saw Eva's agent come down from the terrace. Margot emerged from the casermetta, while the best man's wife appeared in the window. Even the celebrant and the musicians came to see if they were finally about to leave.

Without warning, the sound of the approaching engine was drowned by a crash in the far corner of the courtyard. Snapping round to face it, Vito saw Toby Heywood running from the gatehouse. He moved quickly, dashing into the courtyard.

He barely took three steps, however, before the younger of the two strangers flew after him.

Another sound came from the gatehouse, someone crying out. Vito realised it was his companion, calling frantically for him to stop. To let Toby go. But he was too late. Toby had been tackled heavily to the ground, drawing the attention of anyone who had now gathered.

For a few lingering seconds, nobody moved. Even the humming of the boat seemed to be forgotten. They all looked at Toby, his face twisted in pain as he clutched his arm. And inside the gatehouse, they saw Sofia, Stephen and the bearded stranger. He stood in the doorway, fury upon his face and a gun in his hand.

It was Dina who broke the silence, giving a cry of fright at the sight of the gun. Immediately, like runners signalled with a starting pistol, the others began to scramble, running for cover inside the casermetta or fleeing back up to the terrace.

Only Vito remained motionless, watching as the stranger strode from the gatehouse. He looked around the courtyard as they all fled, taking them in with disdain. The younger of the two men, who was now back on his feet, grabbed his jacket and tried to tug him towards the gate. Vito couldn't hear what he was saying, but he could guess. The boat was coming. They had to go.

But the bearded man shrugged his accomplice away, continuing instead towards Toby. Clutching his elbow, Toby climbed unsteadily to his feet, so that they were now face to face. Vito watched as the stranger raised the gun and glared at Toby with a look of hatred.

As he realised what was about to happen, Vito's breath

caught in his throat. They were indeed going to flee to the boat. But before they left, they were going to ensure that Toby Heywood – the one who had revealed them to the others, given them away after so many hours spent patiently hiding among the wedding party – never would.

Helpless, Vito watched as the stranger looked Toby in the eye and raised his gun.

59

In the museum, Robyn watched as Cam pressed the barrel of the gun against Laurence's forehead. She saw him shudder, flinching as the metal nuzzled against his skin. Saw Cam grimace, screwing up her face as she braced herself to pull the trigger.

Robyn thought about lunging for her. Only a few metres lingered between them. If she was quick, and if she managed to take her by surprise, she might be able to clear the distance in time and knock the gun from Cam's hand.

But it was too dangerous. If she startled Cam, she risked prompting her to shoot Laurence accidentally. If she *really* misjudged it, she could end up being shot herself. There was still only one way out. She had to calm Cam down, and as far as she could see, she had only one chance left.

'If you kill him, he can't tell you who killed Owen!'

She blurted out the words in such a frenzy that she ended up shouting them. Mercifully, however, it seemed to work. Even if only for a moment, Cam paused, confusion spreading across her face.

Breathing hard, Robyn willed herself to keep going. 'It

wasn't just three random thugs,' she said. 'He knows them. They're his friends.'

She could see the mental gymnastics taking place in Cam's head. See her trying to decide if Robyn might be lying.

'Let's make a deal,' she urged, before Cam could think too hard. 'You let him live and he'll confess. He'll tell the police.'

Uncertainty flickered in Laurence's eyes. He wanted to live. But he clearly wasn't on board with this particular bargaining chip.

'They're here,' said Robyn. 'Aren't they? All three of them?'

Laurence didn't reply. He didn't need to. From the fear in his expression, Cam seemed to realise that Robyn was telling the truth.

'The groomsmen . . .'

Robyn nodded. 'Do we have a deal? Let Laurence walk away and he'll go on the record. He'll give up the others. Owen will get his justice. Please, Cam. No one else has to die.'

Cam looked down at Laurence. In turn, he stared into the barrel of the gun.

'My friends,' he said, his voice shaking. 'I can't . . .' He grimaced, his face scrunching as if he'd been burned. 'All right,' he managed. 'All right, I'll do it. Let me go and I'll talk to the police. I'll tell them everything.'

For a few precious seconds, none of them moved. Robyn could hear her own breath rattling in the stillness, and allowed herself to feel a glimmer of hope as she watched Cam consider.

But that hope was quickly snuffed out.

'What are you waiting for?' Laurence snapped, some fire returning to his voice. 'I've said you can have them. Stephen,

Chadwick, Miles. I'll go on the record, see that they all go to prison. Now let me go. Put down that gun!'

Immediately, Robyn knew that any chance of an agreement was now gone. As Laurence rallied against her, Cam gritted her teeth, tightening her grip once again on the trigger.

'Listen to yourself,' she snarled. 'Willing to give up your friends if it means you can walk away. No. You aren't walking away from this. I'm not *letting you* walk away.' She turned to Robyn. 'Last chance. Please just leave.'

Robyn shook her head, no more words left to her. Cam nodded in response, her disappointment plain to see.

'I guess we're doing this together, then.'

She looked down on Laurence, her finger brushing the trigger. He closed his eyes, beginning once again to cry. Robyn, meanwhile, took a deep breath, tensing as she readied herself to dash across the museum. There was nothing else left. If she was quick – and if she wasn't shot in the process – she might just make it.

As if on cue, another sound filled the museum. Not a gunshot. Instead, it was heavy, hurried footsteps. Several pairs of boots hammering against stone, and a male voice, coming so suddenly that Robyn almost cried in fright.

'*Polizia! Metti giù la pistola!*' he bellowed. Then, in English, 'Police! Put down the gun!'

60

Robyn and Laurence made their way slowly down to the courtyard, escorted by men in dark uniforms and padded vests.
Guns glinted in their hands, the word *Polizia* emblazoned on
their shoulders.

Seeing them approach, Margot hurried forward, going
straight to Laurence. Toby, meanwhile, ran to meet Robyn.
She drew him into a hug, only to quickly release him as he let
out a short gasp.

'Sorry,' he said. 'My arm . . .'

'What happened?'

'Those bastards trapped us in the office. We were watching
you on the monitor but they wouldn't let us leave. I tried to
make a run for it and one of them tackled me.'

He massaged his elbow, wincing as he slowly flexed it back
and forth. Over his shoulder, Robyn saw the two strangers
being led, handcuffed, through the castle gates.

'Are you all right?'

'I don't think it's broken. Almost definitely sprained, though.
What about you?'

'I'm fine. But if these guys had arrived just a moment later, Laurence might not have been.'

Toby looked towards Laurence, who was doing an impressive job of convincing Margot that he was unfazed by his experience in the museum. His eyes were still bloodshot, but without Cam's gun against his head the Rushworth confidence seemed to be snapping back into place.

As for Toby . . . he wore an expression that Robyn couldn't quite decipher. There was anger, certainly. Resentment, even. But as he saw that his brother was unharmed, she thought that she might just be able to pick out a shade of relief.

'They almost didn't come at all,' he said. 'Sofia hadn't called them.'

For a second, Robyn was certain she must have misheard.

'They had her son,' Toby explained. 'Told her they'd kill him if she didn't help them escape before the police got here.'

'So how . . . ?'

'Eva's mum. Turns out she called them after Jeremy's body was found. While the others came down here, and caught us in the office, she stayed up by the museum. Sounds like she was on the phone to them the minute she was alone.'

An Italian police officer stepped forward, motioning towards the gates. 'This way, please. More boats are coming.'

As expected, not even the prospect of setting out onto the lake again could dull the intense relief Robyn felt to be leaving the island. She felt as if she could cry, though, at the sight of Cam being escorted towards a police boat. Again, she found herself wishing it could have been someone else. Anyone else.

With all of the other guests and staff having already hurried from the castle, Toby reached for Robyn's hand. But before he could lead her away, she pulled back.

'Just a minute,' she said. 'My bag.'

While the Italian police officer clearly disapproved, she didn't wait around long enough to let him stop her, turning away and running straight back up to the terrace. There it was, right where she had left it on the top step. Stooping to pick it up, she carefully opened it and looked inside. As she realised what Cam had done – why she had been so desperate for Robyn not to be caught up in Laurence's murder – her breath caught.

'Robyn!' Toby called up to her. 'Come on, we have to go!'

Deciding that Cam's gift would have to wait, Robyn snapped her bag shut, slung it over her shoulder and hurried back down to the courtyard. There would be time for it later. In that moment, all she wanted was to put Castello Fiore as far behind her as possible.

One week later

61

Greg Kirby closed the office door, shutting out the hubbub of the newsroom, and waved Robyn towards his desk.

'Just dump those on the floor,' he said, indicating a stack of newspapers piled on a chair. 'Can I get you something? Tea? Water?'

She shook her head, far too nervous to think about drinking anything. As she lifted the papers, she swept a quick glance around the office. It was chilly, the air conditioning cracked up slightly too high, and the room smelled faintly of coffee and aftershave. But it was the decor that interested her most. On the wall hung several front pages, all framed and blown up large. They were stories, she supposed, that Kirby was particularly proud of. He'd clearly been at this a while – one was getting on for ten years old. Although she could perhaps have guessed that just as easily from his receding hairline and the heavy bags under his eyes.

'OK . . .'

Kirby settled into his own seat, shoving aside a couple of empty mugs and a thick wad of folders so that he could prop his elbows on the desk. A large window occupied much of the wall behind him, through which Robyn could see a similarly anonymous London office building.

'What is this, then? I don't make a habit of taking unsolicited meetings, but when you said on the phone . . .'

Robyn nodded and took a deep breath. She imagined somehow telling her teenage self that she would one day be sitting across a desk from the editor of the *Guardian*. She would undoubtedly have been pleased, even if she would never have guessed the circumstances that would lead it to happen.

'You know what happened in Italy,' she said.

'Bits of it. Millie killed two people. Tried to kill one more.'

Robyn nodded again. 'Just before we left the island, I found this in my bag.' Moving slowly, she drew out a tape recorder and placed it on the desk.

Kirby frowned. 'What's—'

'Listen,' said Robyn. 'Just . . . listen. Trust me, you'll need to hear it to believe it.'

He sat back in his chair, intrigued, and she clicked on the little device. For a few seconds, there was only the sound of shuffling.

Kirby frowned. 'What's—'

'Just listen.'

A few more seconds of shuffling followed, then what sounded like the closing of a door.

'*Show me the picture,*' a male voice crackled.

'Who's that?' asked Kirby.

'Jeremy Lambourne,' said Robyn. 'They're inside the museum.'

'*Of course,*' came a reply. Cam. '*But first we're going to talk.*'

You're going to tell me about Owen Lock. About the roles Eva and Laurence played in his death, and what you did to cover it up.'

There was a long pause. Kirby was now leaning forward, jaw clenched.

'*I haven't the faintest idea what you're talking about,*' said Jeremy.

'*I think you do,*' Cam replied. '*I know you do. Eva was angry at Owen for what he'd written about her. For linking her to Rachel Carlisle. So Laurence had him beaten up. And when it went wrong – when Owen died – you made sure the police investigation went away.*'

'*This conversation is over.*'

There was another shuffling of feet as Jeremy seemed to leave. Then a new voice came through. It was slightly tinnier, causing Kirby to lean forward even further as he tried to make out what was being said.

'She had two tape recorders,' Robyn explained. 'This one –' she nodded towards the device on the desk '– must have been hidden in her camera bag when she and Jeremy went into the museum.'

'So what am I listening to now?'

'The other one. She's playing Jeremy the conversation she'd already recorded in the cove. With Eva.'

'*I didn't do anything,*' Eva snapped, her voice distant. '*It was Laurence who had the boys do it. And it was Jeremy who made the police investigation go away.*'

'*What boys?*' a crackling Cam demanded. '*What do you mean, made it go away?*'

'*He fucking deserved it.*' Eva's voice could be heard rising now. '*He told lies. Lies about me!*'

There was a click as Cam turned off the recording from the cove. Then a long pause.

'*Who are you?*' Jeremy asked. '*Lock's wife?*'

'*His widow.*'

'*And how did you get the dagger?*'

'*I didn't. This was all I wanted. The truth, in Eva's own words. Proof, at last, that she was the one who arranged Owen's death.*'

'*So you didn't kill her?*'

'*I had a boat, waiting to take me off the island once I had Eva's confession. But she grabbed the dagger — fetched it from behind a rock — and lunged for me. I tried to defend myself . . .*'

There was another pause.

'*I'm not a murderer, Mr Lambourne. All I want is justice for my husband.*'

'*The police won't see it that way. They'll see only the spurned widow who stabbed Eva Bianchi through the heart.*'

'*It doesn't matter. I have Eva's confession.*'

'*Worthless. When they learn you killed her to get it, they probably won't even listen to it.*'

'*That isn't what happened!*'

'*Perhaps not. But it's what they'll see. And when they find your fingerprints on the dagger, traces of Eva's blood on your clothes . . .*'

There was a fresh pause. A silence so hopeless that Robyn could almost hear Cam's heart breaking.

'*But that isn't how it needs to be,*' Jeremy said calmly. '*I want that recording. And any others you made down in the cove. You're an intelligent woman. I'm sure you have backups. Hand them over to me. Right now. And with one phone call I'll see that any evidence linking you to Eva's body disappears.*'

Kirby's eyes bulged.

'*Why would you do that?*' asked Cam.

'*My priority is to protect HCM. And that means protecting Laurence.*'

'*But you said . . .*'

'*I said the police won't care about the recording. Not once they've identified you as Eva's killer. Neither Laurence nor I would ever go to prison. But that doesn't mean it wouldn't cause some quite significant reputational damage if it ever saw the light of day.*'

'*And what about Eva?*'

'*Do you have any idea just how many murders go unsolved?*'

Robyn met Kirby's eye across the desk. He'd gone completely pale.

'*You would do that?*' asked Cam.

'*Let me tell you a secret. I don't care about Eva Bianchi. All I care about is protecting Laurence. Now give me your bag. Let me have all the copies you've made of that recording and I'll ensure you can't be linked in any way to Eva's death.*'

Inside the office, there came a knock, and Robyn turned to see a young man put his head around the door.

'Out!' Kirby ordered.

'But, Greg—'

'I said get out!'

The young man quickly retreated, shutting the door as he went.

A moment later, Cam spoke again. There was something different in her voice this time. Something defiant.

'*No. I don't care if I have to go to prison. Someone's finally going to pay for Owen's murder. I'm going to make sure this recording gets out. I'll make sure everyone in the world hears it, if I have to. You might be able to escape prison, but not – as you say – the "reputational damage".'*

There was a shuffling sound, as Cam presumably went to leave. It lasted only a couple of seconds.

'You aren't going anywhere with that recording.'

Jeremy's voice was as cold and level as always. Robyn must have heard him say this a dozen times now, but it still sent a chill rushing through her.

'Get out of my way.'

'Give me the recording.'

More shuffling, as Cam tried once again to escape.

'Move!' she shouted.

'Give. Me. The recording.'

More movement rustled from the recorder, louder this time. Cam must have been reaching for something inside her camera bag. Something that she was keeping next to the tape recorder.

'Move . . .' Her voice was suddenly smaller. She was frightened.

'Put that away,' said Jeremy. *'You've said it yourself. You aren't a murderer. The only way out of this is to give me the recording.'*

Kirby frowned slightly.

'The gun,' Robyn explained. 'I think she was keeping it inside her camera bag, next to the tape recorder.'

'And what if I don't?' Cam demanded.

'I've told you already.' For the first time, there was a flicker of emotion in Jeremy's voice. A hint of thinly veiled malice. *'My priority is to protect Laurence. To protect HCM. You are not leaving this room with that recording.'*

There was more movement, as Cam tried – presumably – to

get past Jeremy one last time. The shuffling rose, the sound of two bodies colliding.

'*Let go of me*,' she cried out. '*Let go!*'

Kirby looked down at his desk, his head in his hands. Then came a loud thump, and suddenly silence, save for the sound of Cam breathing heavily.

Robyn leaned across the desk and clicked off the tape recorder. 'She had a silencer on the gun. You can just about hear it if you really listen. But that's why there isn't a more obvious gunshot.'

'A silencer? How did she get hold of that? How did she even get a gun?'

'I don't know. But Owen did an investigation into the dark web, right? My best guess is that she learned a little about it from him. Used some of his sources, maybe.'

For a little while, Kirby didn't say anything at all. He stared at the desk, and when at last he spoke, his voice was quiet. Distant.

'Is there more?'

'She stops recording inside the museum a few seconds after that. But if you rewind to the beginning of the tape, you'll also find the entire conversation with Eva in the cove.'

'How did you know to bring it to me?'

'She tells me to. After the conversation with Jeremy, she leaves one more message. She gives me your name, tells me that you worked with her and Owen and that I should trust only you with the tape.'

'And then she slipped it into your bag.'

'Yes. She came and spoke to me just before she went after Laurence. We sat down together on the terrace and my bag was on the step between us. She must have done it then.'

'Why not give you both copies?'

'She was holding the other when the police arrived. I guess it must have been taken away as evidence.'

Kirby nodded. 'OK. And don't take this the wrong way, but . . . why did she give it to *you*?'

'I've thought about that a lot. Listening to Jeremy, I think she must have worried it might somehow disappear if the police took both copies. She knew I'd studied to be a journalist, so she must have thought I would know what to do with it. How to get it into the right hands.'

'That doesn't explain why she would trust you to actually do it, though. You'd known each other . . . what? A day or two?'

Robyn didn't answer. There was a cynical part of her that supposed Cam hadn't exactly been spoilt for candidates. But at the same time, there was a much smaller, slightly more hopeful voice that liked to think she had made her decision when they sat together on the terrace. During that curious moment when she had asked Robyn why she wanted to be a journalist.

I just wanted to help people, Robyn had said.

She remembered the way Cam had watched her, looking her straight in the eye. *And you don't still want to do that?*

Kirby sighed. 'It's a lot to take in. Oh, Millie . . .'

'Do you know her well?'

He gave a sad smile. 'I was best man at their wedding. Haven't seen her in a while, though. After what happened to Owen, she didn't want to stay here. She went freelance, picking up work for a few lifestyle mags. Safer work. Or so I thought.'

He was silent for a moment, apparently turning everything

over in his mind. 'How did she even get there? Onto the island. I guess it'll all come out when it goes to trial, but it can't have been a fluke. Do you have any idea?'

'I've been thinking about that,' said Robyn. 'I didn't notice it at the time. But, looking back, she slipped up. When I first met her – the day before the wedding, on a yacht Laurence had chartered – she said that she'd had to really push for *London Living* to cover the wedding. But when I spoke to her in the castle, about an hour after Eva had been found, she said that her editor had been desperate to cover it and was going to be gutted that they didn't have a feature any more.'

'Which do you think was true?'

'The first version, on the yacht. Her plan was still on track at that point. She was confident. She knew what she was doing. But when I spoke to her in the castle, she was a bit of a mess. I thought she was just upset by the sight of Eva's body, like everyone else. But in hindsight, she must have been terrified she was about to be caught. Her plan had backfired, Eva was dead and she was trying to work out how she was going to save herself. It seems much more likely to me that she would slip up then, rather than on the yacht.

'And it just makes more sense, doesn't it? As you say, she leaves her job here after Owen's killed and starts working freelance for a load of lifestyle magazines. She pieces together what she thinks must have happened, like I did, and reaches the conclusion that Eva and Laurence could have been involved. Then, while she's working for *London Living*, she gets wind of their wedding. It's going to be small, taking place on a private island and press are being invited to go cover it. Once she realised that it was her way in – saw the potential to get close to Eva and extract a confession – wouldn't it make all the sense in the world that she'd petition her editor to let her go?'

Kirby nodded slowly, considering her theory. 'You may well be right.'

A silence settled between them.

'You call her Millie . . .' Robyn said tentatively. 'That's the name I found for her online, too. When I googled her. But she told us all she was called Cam.'

Kirby nodded. 'Everyone here knew her as Millie. But she stopped going by that name after Owen died.'

'Why?'

'Because he was the first one to call her it. She was Cam before she and Owen met. And she decided to become Cam again after he died.' He suddenly looked pained. 'She really was heartbroken, you know. Imagine if even your own name reminded you of the person you'd lost.'

Not quite sure how to respond, Robyn instead motioned towards the tape recorder. 'Can you do something with this?' she asked. 'Can you save her from prison?'

Kirby shook his head. 'She knows she's going away. You heard her. She seems to be at peace with it.'

'But—'

'But we can do *something*. As Lambourne says, the reputational damage to HCM if this were to come out would be immense. Perhaps it'll affect Millie's sentence. Maybe it'll even mean Laurence Heywood has to answer for his involvement in Owen's death. I honestly have no idea. I'll need to consult our lawyers, come up with a strategy. But we have time before she stands trial. If you leave it with me, I'll make sure it's put to

362

good use.' He raised an eyebrow. 'I assume you were planning to leave it with me?'

Robyn nodded. 'She trusts you. It's all yours, on the condition that no one ever knows where you got it.'

'Can I ask why?'

Robyn hesitated, wondering if she should even be admitting the truth. 'After we left the island, I had to give a pretty detailed statement to the police. But I didn't tell them I had this.'

Kirby said nothing.

'I'm not trying to disrupt the investigation,' Robyn continued. 'If I wasn't sure that they'd already taken the other copy, I would have said something. But when I listened to it, and I heard how frightened she was . . . How desperate she was for me to get this to you . . . I want to help. I really do. But I'd prefer not to be arrested myself in the process. If you can promise me you won't tell anyone where you got this, it's all yours.'

'Done.'

Robyn blinked at him. She'd expected some resistance. That he'd say she had to go on the record, or something to that effect. She didn't protest, though. Instead, she thanked him, rose to her feet and shook his hand.

'Hey,' he said, as she was turning to leave. 'You studied to be a journalist . . . So have you just not managed to pin down a job?'

Robyn paused, caught off guard. 'No, I . . . It sounds a bit pathetic, but I guess I just haven't really tried.'

He gave a little shrug. 'Well, maybe you should.'

62

As she left Kirby's office, Robyn felt an intense sense of relief.

She'd been required to stay in Italy for two more days after leaving Castello Fiore, sitting with a translator as she gave her statement to the police. And since returning to the UK, she'd been called twice more to expand on some of the details she'd provided. She hadn't lied, as such. She told herself that repeatedly. But she knew she'd been rolling the dice by not divulging that she had the tape recorder.

There was something else behind her relief, though. A sense of satisfaction, knowing that, in some way, she had helped Cam. She had no idea if it would be enough to ease her sentence. Or, for that matter, to ensure Laurence eventually served prison time. But with the recording now in Kirby's hands, she was confident that she had given Cam the best chance she could at finally seeing justice for Owen.

On her way back to the lift, she passed again through the newsroom. All around her, phones rang and reporters typed furiously at keyboards. She tried to imagine what her younger self would have made of it all, Kirby's parting words echoing in her mind.

Well maybe you should.

As the lift carried her back to ground level, she thought of the others who had been on the island. In the days since their return to London, Toby and Margot had spoken once on the phone, but it had been a brief, strained conversation. Not a word had been said between him and Laurence.

'He's still your brother,' Robyn had said. 'And however much you hated Eva, he's lost his fiancée. It wouldn't hurt to check in on him.'

Toby had said nothing, and Robyn had decided it best not to press. He was pouring all of his energy into laying the groundwork for the bar, while Laurence and Margot were furiously preparing for the trial against Cam. Both seemed to be terrified. Not just of Cam, though. From what Toby could glean from his brief conversation with Margot, it seemed to be Stephen who had them running scared. He had apparently gone completely dark since returning from Italy, rejecting any attempt at communication and showing no interest whatsoever in helping with the trial. Robyn's first thought was that he'd fled. Toby, however, theorised that he might be planning to make a plea; his own freedom in exchange for a confession as to how Owen Lock died.

'Mum and Laurence are scared,' he had insisted. 'Properly scared. They wouldn't be freaking out like this if they just thought he'd done a runner. The only explanation I can think of is that they're expecting him to make some kind of move against them.'

'Do you really think he'd have the nerve?' Robyn had asked.

'Wouldn't *you*? He has a kid on the way and it sounds like Abigail is seconds away from moving out. If he has a choice between potentially joining them in prison or throwing them under the bus and saving his own skin, I know which I'd choose.'

Robyn had said nothing more on the subject. If Abigail had been telling the truth when she cornered her in the casermetta – if, on the night Owen was attacked, Stephen really had been trying to *stop* Chadwick and Miles – then a small part of her wanted Toby to be right. And she wanted even more for the agreement she'd reached with Greg Kirby to help ensure the right people faced justice.

As for the Heywoods, she hoped there might somehow be a reunion. That, for Toby's sake, the bridges burned could eventually be rebuilt. But it seemed now wasn't the time.

She hadn't heard much of Vito, Paola and Dina, although she gathered from her conversations with the Italian police that they had been whisked straight into a witness protection programme, overseen by a specialist mafia task force. Sofia had apparently been taken in too, along with her son, although she would undoubtedly be facing charges of some kind for her role in attempting to steal the dagger. Robyn doubted she would ever see any of them again, but she hoped they would all be OK. Even Vito. None of the others would have been mixed up in this if not for him. But he didn't deserve what had happened.

Stepping out onto the street, she looked at her phone and checked the time. Toby's meeting with the bank wasn't due to finish for another twenty minutes, but she sent him a message all the same, reminding him to tell her how it had gone.

Toby . . .

During their remaining time in Italy, once the relief of

leaving the island had passed and they had begun the process of giving their statements to the police, their relationship for the first time had felt uncomfortable. They tiptoed around each other, Robyn's resentment returning at being kept so firmly in the dark while Toby's disbelief that she could have considered him a suspect seemed to grow by the minute.

The atmosphere between them became so tense that on the journey home they barely said a word, causing Robyn to wonder as their plane touched down at Gatwick if they would be parting ways in arrivals.

Instead, they had gone together to Robyn's flat, Toby had fixed them each a drink and they had finally talked. They'd stayed up well into the night. Both of them cried. But somewhere around three o'clock, a breakthrough had been reached. An agreement that they needed each other – wanted each other – and that while there was work to be done, neither of them was truly willing to let the mistakes made in Castello Fiore be the end of them.

Still standing outside the *Guardian*'s offices, listening to the distant rumble of King's Cross as she deliberated between finding a coffee shop or heading straight to the Tube, Robyn's mind strayed to Jess. That morning, just an hour before she had set off for her meeting with Kirby, her old friend had sent another message. She fished it out now, reading it for what must easily have been the tenth time.

Hey Rob! Applications for this junior role are closing in a couple of days. Are you going for it? My editor's had a ton of CVs, but I'll still put in that word if you like. I reckon she'd love you. Xx

Robyn looked back at the building she'd just left, the *Guardian*'s name emblazoned on the glass. To write for *Cosmopolitan* wouldn't quite be the hard-hitting investigative role she'd pictured for herself, all those years ago. But it would certainly be a start.

She felt her phone buzz in her hand, alerting her to a new message. Not from Jess, though. This time it was her manager at the Willows, asking if she could come in to help out with a stag party.

Robyn stared at the screen, considering the two requests.

Cosmo. Or the Willows.

A smile touching the corners of her mouth, she took a deep breath, made her choice and dialled.

Acknowledgements

As ever, there are several people I need to thank for helping me get this book over the line.

First up are two people who I've never actually met, and who, quite honestly, I don't suppose I ever will. But without them, there is no way this story would have come into being.

In May 2022, my wife and I visited Lake Garda, stopping for an hour one morning to explore the stunning castle in Malcesine. While inside, we saw a wedding taking place. With the incredible Italian architecture, the lake in the background and the glamour of the occasion itself, it was an image that immediately had me hooked, and with it came the idea of Eva and Laurence's wedding. So thank you to that happy couple, who I'm certain are considerably better human beings than those marrying in this particular story. If you ever happen to read this, I hope you had a spectacular day, and that you'll have a long and happy life together.

Thank you to Harry Illingworth, the best agent an author could wish for, for all of your guidance and support these past few years. It's been quite a ride, and I can't wait to see where it takes us next.

ACKNOWLEDGEMENTS

To my editor, Emily Griffin, thank you for your continued brilliance. I'm endlessly grateful for your keen eye and the incomparable wisdom you bring to these books.

Thank you to Laura O'Donnell and Sam Rees-Williams for doing so much to publicise these stories. Thank you as well to Joanna Taylor, for your editorial support, and to all at Century who work so hard behind the scenes to make these books a success.

Thank you to my brother, Harry, for lending some much-needed medical expertise to the case of Rachel Carlisle. A big thank you as well to Marta Napodano, for your invaluable help with the Italian phrases that appear in this book. Needless to say, any errors that might have slipped through, whether medical or Italian, are entirely my own.

Thank you to Merl for your day-to-day support. And finally, as always, the biggest thank you goes to my wife, Hayley. I don't imagine I'll ever stop hearing about how suspicious it is that I had the idea for this book just a few months before we ourselves got married. I suppose that's fair enough. But suspicious novels aside, I'm so grateful to have you by my side. Turns out writing a book can be pretty tough, and from sharing in the good days to keeping me going in the bad, there's no one else I'd rather be doing this with.